Annie Laura's Gift

Annie Laura's Gift is an elegantly written, immersively moving novel. And it is a deeply resonant one in this politically parlous age, as it forcefully reminds us of the trials and triumphs of the immigrants who have created our country.

—Robert Olen Butler, Pulitzer Prize winning
author of *A Good Scent from a Strange Mountain*

In *Annie Laura's Gift*, Milinda Jay delivers a gripping, emotional tale with a main character worth rooting for. Annie Laura is stubborn, feisty, and heartbreakingly brave as she fights for her family. An unforgettable story in a unique and captivating setting.

—Stephanie Dees, award-winning author
of the Sweet Southern Romance series

Annie Laura's Gift is a novel that is timely as it is beautiful. Milinda Jay brings to life the grit and determination of her immigrant great-grandmother. Overcoming hardship and a haunting crime, Annie Laura forges a new life in nineteenth-century hardscrabble Florida. *Annie Laura's Gift* is an inspiring, page-turning work of historical fiction. You'll read this book and cheer.

—Michael Morris, author of
Man in the Blue Moon

Drawing from her own family folklore, Milinda Jay spins a survival saga of a first-generation German American in the hardscrabble South that is both warm, relatable, and hard to put down. A native of West Florida, Jay writes with deep insight into women's lives in rural, turn-of-the-century Southern culture—their challenges, allies, and hard-fought victories. *Annie Laura's Gift* is a book to share with friends.

—Janis Owens, author of *The Cracker Kitchen*
and *American Ghost*

MERCER UNIVERSITY PRESS

Endowed by

TOM WATSON BROWN
and
THE WATSON-BROWN FOUNDATION, INC.

Annie Laura's Gift

MILINDA JAY

MERCER UNIVERSITY PRESS
Macon, Georgia
2021

MUP/ P618

© 2021 by Mercer University Press
Published by Mercer University Press
1501 Mercer University Drive
Macon, Georgia 31207
All rights reserved

25 24 23 22 21   5 4 3 2 1

Books published by Mercer University Press are printed on acid-
free paper that meets the requirements of the American National
Standard for Information Sciences—Permanence of Paper for
Printed Library Materials.

Printed and bound in the United States.

This book is set in Adobe Caslon Pro.

Cover/jacket design by Burt&Burt.

ISBN   978-0-88146-778-9
Cataloging-in-Publication Data is available from the Library of
Congress

In 1882 more than a million German immigrants came to the United States. They came seeking a new life, with hope in their hearts and stars in their eyes. They came to America, the land of the free.

If I take the wings of the morning and settle at the farthest limits of the sea,
even there your hand shall lead me, and your right hand shall hold me fast.
Psalm 139:9-10

For Ellie

so that you may know the heroic women who came before you

Preface

Much of the story you are about to read is based on family history. Most of this story is fiction.

What is true is that Annie Laura is based on my great-grandmother—a truly heroic woman, an immigrant who overcame tragedy and not only survived but thrived. She believed in God, family, and the land, and because of her courage, my family exists. This book is a thank-you note to her for a life of integrity and grace, and for my grandmother, the beautiful gift she gave.

I could never have written this book without the truths uncovered by my cousin Sandy Moore's painstaking research and her incredible generosity in sharing everything she found. She took the time to make timelines, copy pictures, hire a translator for our great-great-grandfather's diaries, organize family meetings, and lead family hikes around the Chipley, Florida, homestead. She relentlessly pursued any leads she could find that might give me more insight, and together we pored over nineteenth century county records and land grants, and we badgered cousins for family stories. Without her, the story of our wonderful great-grandmother would be lost.

My friends in the Cheshires writing group—Mark, Tony, Marty, Carole, Ruth, and Rich—continue to polish my prose.

Jill B., Tanya B., Kathy H., Robert C., and Billy B. were kind enough to read the complete manuscript in draft form and offer me invaluable insight.

Thank you to Becky K., Kathie B., Erin C., and Erica M. for their generous advice and help with publicity.

Many thanks to the wonderful staff at Mercer University Press. Their diligence and utter dedication to the written word allows writers to continue writing. And to their anonymous editor, you are fabulous.

Thank you to my children, Jenny, Megan, Richard Ross, Robbie, and Morgan, whose patience for my obsession with the past allows me the freedom to create.

And most of all, thank you to my husband, Hal Stephenson—my partner, my love, and my friend.

Annie Laura's Gift

Cairo, Georgia

1885

Prologue

"You and me, we have a child, Elijah. Made when the mockingbirds called." Miss Harriet's voice was soft and low.

I stopped so quick, the bucket of spring water I was fetching for Mama sloshed down my wool skirt. I leaned against the side of the house, my shawl catching on the splintery wood. I gathered my sagging skirt in one hand and steadied my bucket in the other. Water was too hard to come by to waste, but Miss Harriet's words would have shattered a river rock.

I eased around the corner so I could see this man pretending to be Miss Harriet's husband. Her real husband was going to be mighty angry. He'd already put her out of his house and set her in this lonely cabin by the sweet-smelling spring. I guess he'd got tired of her. Her young'uns came to visit her, at least two of them did—the youngest, Mary Scarlet, and the oldest, Morris, the doctor man.

"You've been gone for twenty-six years, and not a word, not a single word until you show up on my front steps..." Miss Harriet's voice broke. "I thought you were dead, Elijah. Dead and gone. Everyone thought so, and my daddy was worried, wanted me to be taken care of, told me John Calvin Blakely was a good man and I ought to marry him."

I didn't like to hear Miss Harriet cry. In the two weeks since she'd taken my family in, letting us camp in her back pasture to wait on Mama's baby, she'd become my friend. When I shared my dream with her about wanting to own a big piece of land, with cotton as far as you could see, she'd said, "Be careful what you dream on, Annie

Laura. You just may get it." I think she was trying to give me a warning. What she gave me was hope.

It was high noon. The birds had hushed their morning song, and into the silence, the man, Elijah, spoke. "A girl or boy?" His words were gentle, like a caress.

I couldn't help myself. I had to see the man, even if it meant I might be seen and thought to be eavesdropping. Which I was.

I peeked around the corner. This Elijah man was tall, a head taller than Miss Harriet. He wore a rumpled linen suit, and he was so skinny he looked like a line drawn right down the middle of Miss Harriet's voluminous skirts. He had his arms around her, and she clung to him, like he was a vine hanging over rushing rapids, and if she let go she would surely drown.

I couldn't see Miss Harriet's face. It was buried in Elijah's skinny chest.

Suddenly, she jerked away like it pained her to touch him. She opened her mouth to speak, and I listened close. But just then, something caught my eye in the big old magnolia tree directly behind Miss Harriet. Perched up on one of the highest branches sat Benjamin, Miss Harriet's eleven-year-old middle son. He was holding something in his hands. I couldn't see what it was, but I reckoned it to be his slingshot. He was a deadeye and could kill a rabbit scampering across the pasture faster than I could blink.

"You need to git on back to where you been hiding all these years." Miss Harriet's voice cut clear as a church bell through the quiet and jerked my attention away from Benjamin. "If John Calvin were to see you here, he'd shoot you. Or worse."

Miss Harriet's husband, Mr. Blakely, was a mean-looking man about the same height as Miss Harriet. But where she was soft, he was muscled all over, and his muscles weren't the smooth type. They were knotty, riding on him like sores.

I looked back up at Benjamin sitting in the tree like an old bobcat ready to pounce on a baby deer. He hadn't seen me yet.

"I'm sorry. So sorry. But I've got something here for you. Something that could give us hope." The man held out a packet and tried to give it to Miss Harriet, but she wouldn't take it.

I certainly would have. If it had been me, I would have ripped that packet open quick as lightning to see what was inside. Maybe it was money enough to buy the land I longed for.

He tried to give it to her again, and she slapped it away. "Don't you see?" She clutched his ragged linen lapels, like she was begging. "I'm all out of hope. And whatever that is," she said, releasing him and pointing to the packet on the ground, "it's not enough. I been pushed aside so often that hope is nothing but a sour taste in my mouth."

"But he must have loved you once," Elijah said, like the words were painful to speak.

She laughed bitterly. "I reckon all John Calvin wanted out of me was my land and a couple of babies. After Mary Scarlet, my least one, was born, he sent me away, here to this cabin. Said I wasn't fit to be a mother. Hired his daughter by his first wife to care for my little ones."

"My God, Harriet. What kind of monster would take a mother away from her babies?"

The hair rose on the back of my neck. Benjamin up in the tree didn't like anybody talking bad about his daddy.

"I don't regret the leaving of him," Miss Harriet said. "I regret being forced away from my children. But my little Mary Scarlet comes to visit. She sneaks in when she can. Her Aunt Tabitha helps her." She smiled at this.

Elijah took her hands in his, gentle-like.

But she looked him dead in the eye. "Where have you been? What took you so long to come back home?"

"I got hit, way up north at a place called Gettysburg," Elijah said, his voice so quiet I had to strain to hear it.

"And it took you twenty-seven years to get home?"

"I was out of my mind for a time wandering around God knows where. Until a family took me in, helped me out."

"Twenty-seven years is a lifetime."

"But you up and married. Why? What happened? Didn't you know I'd come back for you?"

Miss Harriet grasped her head between both her hands, like she had a bad headache. "They told me you were dead."

"Who told you I was dead?" His jaw tightened, and his fists clenched.

"I don't remember. Daddy. I think."

"He never did like me much, did he?" He blew out of his nose like half a laugh, but he wasn't smiling.

"I waited. And waited. And Mama and Daddy, they made it clear I needed to be out of their house. I moved back into our little cabin. But, God, Elijah, it was so lonely. So very lonely." Miss Harriet looked out over the pasture. Surely, she would see Benjamin in that big magnolia tree.

Elijah flinched. "I'm so sorry, girl. It's not your fault. My head wasn't right, my own mind wouldn't let me do right. But I've been working for us, Harriet. I've got this, and it's enough." He held the packet up again.

Miss Harriet didn't even hear him. She was off in a world of her own. "I married John Calvin because of the love I shared with you."

Elijah looked at her, his eyes squinting like he was trying to understand words that didn't make much sense.

"I thought he loved me." She stepped away and looked out over the spring, sparkling in the noon sun. Then she whirled around and clutched him, shook his arms like she was trying to shake the life out of him. Or into him.

"I was hungry for the love I remembered from you," she said. A single tear caught the sunlight and sparkled as it trickled down her face. Elijah brushed it away. Even from where I stood, I could see that his hand trembled as he placed it on her cheek, his thumb pausing on her chin. The moment felt so private I was embarrassed to be there.

Benjamin loaded his slingshot.

"We had some good times, didn't we?" Elijah said, like he was trying to cheer her out of her tears. When he laughed, the morning air seemed lighter, and she smiled, and I forgot about Benjamin and his tree-hiding place. "I dreamed of the babies we would have together," he said, real serious.

I felt my face get all hot. And then I saw Benjamin lift, aim, and hold.

"Our son's name is Morris," Miss Harriet said. "He's a good man. You'll be proud…"

I wanted to warn them about what Benjamin was about to do, but my voice was stuck in my throat, and I couldn't move.

Elijah pulled Miss Harriet into his arms and said in a voice gruff with emotion, "Where is he?"

Miss Harriet hugged him hard. And then Elijah kissed her full on the lips. Miss Harriet melted into him and kissed him back like she was hungry, and he was food.

I heard the tree branch creak. Benjamin pulled back his slingshot and took aim. I dropped my bucket and moved forward to pull them apart, to warn them.

"No!" My mouth might as well have been full of molasses.

They clung to each other. And then a sound like a hickory nut hitting an oak tree took them both to the ground. I couldn't tell which one had been hit.

I looked up in the tree and Benjamin grinned. Fury rose in me. I darted from my hiding place and knelt beside Miss Harriet. Elijah was hit, and he was knocked out cold.

We pulled him into her cabin. He was not very heavy, though his long legs got stuck in the door. I helped her untangle them and drag him across the pine floor. His heels caught the blue and white rag rug, and it came with us to the bed.

I ran back for my bucket to bring in some cool spring water for Elijah. Hiding beneath my bucket was a packet, so gray and dusty that it blended in with the dirt yard, and I nearly missed it. The packet must have fallen when Mr. Elijah got hurt. I picked it up—it felt like it was filled with papers and something hard like a rock in the bottom. I stuffed in in my apron pocket to give to Miss Harriet.

When I returned, Miss Harriet dipped her clean white handkerchief into my bucket. Rivulets of water dripped from the lace. She swiped gently at Elijah's wound. Blood and water trickled down his forehead, and Miss Harriet said the blood was good. "It means there won't be much swelling on the inside."

I wondered if Benjamin was going to come in and finish his business. I was sure he was trying to kill Elijah. Before I could say anything, Miss Harriet spoke.

"Go get Morris. Run as fast as you can."

I did what she said, but I was scared when I walked outside again. I looked around for Benjamin, frightened he would get me next.

I fled to the safety of town just a half-mile away. Mama would have to wait on our drinking water. When I got to his doctoring office, Morris, Elijah's son whom he'd never laid eyes on, was gone. But old Mr. Everidge was there like always. He sat in his rocking chair whittling away. He looked up when he saw me all panicked. "You lookin' for the doctor?" he asked.

"Yes, sir," I answered.

"Why, he's gone. Left a while ago. Gone to deliver your mama's baby. Humph," he groaned, adjusted his bad hip, and went back to his whittling.

I ran as fast as I could to our camp. The blood rose in my ears, and my heart tried to pound it back down. Mama. How could it have happened so fast? I remembered her rubbing her back this morning, but she told me it was because she had lifted too much firewood the day before.

First thing I saw when I reached our camp was the flowers embroidered on Mama's best quilt drowning in a pool of red. When I saw the blood, I forgot why I was there.

The hands that held Mama were big. In those hands, Mama looked like a child. It was Morris holding her, bathing her forehead with a cool cloth. He spoke to her, his voice quiet, like he was talking to a frightened child.

"It's going to be all right," he said. "We're going to get this baby out, and next thing you know, you'll be holding her, and everything will be fine. I just need you to help me a little bit. We've got to turn this baby."

Mama shook her head, and then squeezed her eyes shut and moaned like she was being ripped open.

The midwife, Morris's Aunt Tabitha, dropped white cloths, one right after the other, into the iron kettle of boiling water pitched over the fire. She used her stick to fish them out and hang them on Mama's wash line.

When the cloth cooled, Morris pulled it from the line. He used it to help staunch the flow of blood that was dripping out of my Mama. Morris smelled of something strong and pungent.

"It's disinfectant," he said when he saw my nose all squinched up. "It keeps people from getting real sick birthing babies." His blue eyes crinkled into a smile. "Your mama is going to be fine," he said. "The baby is just turned the wrong way. It happens sometimes, but we can fix that. Now, I might need your help."

He took my hands in his. My stomach did a flip-flop and my face got hot. How could I feel this way with Mama bleeding right in front of me? I forgot I was supposed to be bringing him to help his own mama and his real daddy. When Morris touched me, I couldn't think.

"Your hands are small," he said. "Just right. If Tabitha can't do it, you'll need to turn the baby." He put my hands down and said, "Go wash. Tabitha will show you how."

I felt ashamed, then, like I'd disappointed him on account of my dirty hands.

Tabitha scrubbed my hands with the boiled water, now cool, and some lye soap.

I returned, my hands held high for Morris to inspect.

He smiled again, bringing out a single dimple. I wanted to touch that dimple, feel the warmth of his face in my hands.

Mama moaned.

"Come on, Aunt Tabitha," Morris said. "We need to turn the baby now."

Tabitha moved me aside, and Morris began massaging Mama's belly. Mama screamed. Tabitha inserted her hand inside my mama, and Mama screamed again.

"Hold steady," Morris said. "We've got it. She's turning."

"Yes, she is," Tabitha said. "I've got her head."

"Push, Mrs. Brock," Morris said. "Push with all your might. I know you can do it."

Mama made a feeble effort to push but moaned instead.

I saw the look pass between Morris and Aunt Tabitha, and I knew my mama's time was growing short. I'd heard of babies dying inside their mama's bellies, and the mamas dying, too. I needed Mama. I couldn't let her die. Papa might start up his drinking all over again.

"Come on, Mrs. Brock," Aunt Tabitha said, but Mama just shuddered like the mule I'd seen die right in the middle of the road, too worn out to carry a family any farther.

Morris took Mama's wrist. He shook his head again.

"No!" I screamed. My mama was not going to die. Not here, not with me this close.

I held Mama's face between my clean hands. I made her open her eyes. "Look at me, Mama. Look at me." Her eyes fluttered. "Come on, Mama, you can do this," I said. "Push hard, or our baby is going to die. Do you hear me? Push!"

Mama whimpered, but she opened her eyes again, looked hard at me, clenched her jaw and pushed, the cords standing out on her neck and her face turning beet red. Out gushed more blood than I've ever seen, and along with the blood, my baby sister, Eva.

Tears streamed down my face, "You did good, Mama," I said. "You did good."

Mama smiled wanly.

Tabitha took Eva, wiped her off, massaged her, and laid her on Mama's belly. Tabitha smiled at me. "You saved them," she said.

Her words made my stomach fill up with something that felt sweet.

"You make sure she doesn't roll off," Morris said to me, and placed my hand on the baby.

I would have done anything for Morris, and for my mama. I held the warm, wet baby with one hand and touched Mama's cheek with the other. Mama's weak smile was beautiful. She gazed down on my new baby sister and pulled her to her breast.

Suddenly, Mama jerked and moaned. Tabitha put one hand on the baby, and Morris held a cloth to Mama where what looked like a river of blood gushed out.

I'm ashamed to admit that I fainted dead away.

In the chaos of those days, what with keeping Mama alive and the baby with her, I forgot all about Miss Harriet and Elijah. I didn't tell Morris. By the time I remembered, the packet of letters was still in my apron pocket, and Elijah and Miss Harriet were both dead.

Chapter 1

Falling Waters, Florida, 1898

"I've got some yeast rolls and ham if you boys are hungry," I say.

My tenant-farmer, Tom Green, looks up from the swishing grunt of the saw, and his two sons, Seth and Isaac, grow still. The giant blade is caught halfway in the ancient pine. Its sweet, pungent scent fills the air, thrilling me. Soon the land will be cleared, and we can plant cotton and peanuts. The land will repay us for our back-breaking labor.

The dream I shared with Miss Harriet those many years ago is about to come true. I only wish she were here to see it. She would have been proud of me. And I desperately need someone to be proud of me. My father certainly isn't. *"You've rained down shame upon me and my house. Farming like a peasant. I thought I'd done better for you."*

But I refuse to think about that today, and I hold my basket out to Tom and his boys. The boys are sixteen, growing, and hungry, but Tom says, "I thank you ma'am, but we ain't hungry just yet." The boys look down and shuffle their feet, hitch up the pants that are too big for their skinny bodies. "I reckon my missus will be happy for supper vittles, and we thank you."

I lower the basket to my side, confused. "I'll take them to her," I say.

He hears the doubt in my voice and looks away.

Why won't he let me feed his boys?

Something flits across Tom's face, like he wants to stop me going to his house. I stand there for a moment, awkward. I wonder, is his missus ill? I want to ask him questions, but his face shuts down.

"All right, then," I say. "I thank you for all your hard work." But they've already bent their backs to the ancient pine.

I head up the deer path through the thick woods. Maybe his wife is carrying and needs doctoring. The Lord knows childbearing is a risky business. But then again, she might not take to a foreigner helping her out. Even though I've been here for many years, I'm still a foreigner—the German come to rob upstanding Americans of their land and jobs. I thought it would go away.

The trees are winter bare. Heavily mossed squirrel nests sit high up in the mistletoe-dotted oaks. The green of spring is a promise rather than a gift, but buds on the wild blueberry bushes work to lighten the burden laid on my heart.

When I emerge from the woods and into the clearing, a snug cabin comes into view. I smell moonshine and hear a man's voice.

Tom's sons are with Tom, out in the field. What man is with his wife?

A woman giggles. A hound dog puppy, tied to the rickety front porch stair rails, bellows, alerting all to my presence. She bounds toward me. There is a yelp of pain. The pup has wound itself up in the frayed rope and created a noose around its neck. I reach down and untangle the rope. The boney pup, a girl dog, licks my hands and wriggles her thanks. She jumps up when she smells the food in my basket and tries to thrust her all-a-quiver nose inside. I hold the basket high to keep her from eating the family's supper. Tom and the boys need food.

A woman who appears to be Tom's wife, comes to the front door, buttoning her bodice, her white-blonde hair partially loose from its bun. She doesn't look ill to me.

"What do you want?" she yells, her shrill voice startling me so badly that I drop the basket. The puppy gobbles three tumbling ham-filled rolls.

"I was bringing your family some supper."

"Well, it's about time you extended some hospitality. Last house we stayed in, the woman brought us food on the first day. It took you nearly three weeks. Y'all running short on vittles at the big house, or is that the way Germans do things?" The woman sways against the solid doorframe and twirls a piece of loose hair.

I'm stopped by her rudeness. I've never been berated for bringing a gift.

I hear a familiar chuckle from inside the cabin. The woman sweeps up her tangled blonde tresses, secures them with her hairpin, glances back and laughs a raucous, jarring laugh.

Anger swirls thickly in my throat, making my ears ring and my nose tingle.

The voice in the cabin belongs to a man who is not her husband, a man who will bring grief to Tom, his wife, and their boys. I lean forward, ready to warn her, *he is not what he seems*. Before the words form in my mouth, something moves behind me.

"Mama?" a tiny voice hums, and a little girl with tangled hair, a dirty smock, and no shoes appears from the woods. In her small, bruised hands is a bunch of green leaves. "Flowers for you, Mama," she thrusts them at her mama, her smile beseeching. She can't be more than three years old.

I feel the anger wash right out of me when I realize the child clutches poison ivy. I watch in horror as she rubs her eyes, scratches her arm and then her neck.

I kneel, eye level. She looks at me curiously, reaches out to touch my hair, but the ivy she clutches stops her. She looks at it.

"You could lay it all down on the ground here, and then your mama could see the pretty leaves."

She looks up at her mama, who laughs and goes inside.

The child turns back to me. She wants me to bring her mama back outside—I can see as much in her eyes.

"She'll be back. Look here. I have a roll you might want to take a bite out of. It's good!" I reach in my basket for a roll, take a bite, chew it, and hold it out for her. It works.

She drops the poison ivy and snatches the roll, wolfs it down with the same energy as the puppy, and smiles shyly up at me. The red welts rise around her eyes, arms, and hands. How long has she been alone in the woods playing in the poison ivy?

"Can you come with me over here?" I ask and point to the clearing beyond. I walk ahead holding the basket, enticing her to follow. "Let's get you all washed up, and I'll give you some more of these good rolls."

She follows me, and I lead her quickly to the small spring-fed lake that runs behind the property, separating my land from that of the man inside the house.

Does Tom suspect his wife of entertaining men while he and the boys are out working the fields? Is that why he didn't want me to come?

I douse the little girl with the creek water, knowing she would be better off if she would jump completely in. Without warning, the little girl does just that, shedding her clothes and kicking and splashing like a puppy despite the chilly water. It's a God's wonder that she hasn't already drowned, what with the mother not paying a bit of attention to her. I grab her to keep her from veering too far, and rinse off the poison as best I can. It would be better to use soap, but I figure that the woman has no lye soap made, and water is better than nothing.

I scan the banks for some jewelweed. Along the edge, away from direct sunlight, is a plant three feet high with a fan of leaves. I reach out, break off half the plant, crush the stem in my hands, and rub my hands together vigorously, milking the plant for the paste that will soothe the little girl's pain. The jewelweed flowers are a pretty orange in the late summer, but for now, it is just a green plant that will relieve the little girl's painful itching. It will need to be rubbed on the welts several times a day until the poison ivy-induced swelling is gone. I doubt her mama will care.

I rub the little girl down with the milky substance. She doesn't want to put her clothes back on. They are dirty and probably filled with poison ivy. I strip off one of my white petticoats and wrap the child like a baby.

She giggles and says, "I love you," then hugs me with her thin arms. "What's your name?"

"Annie Laura," I say, and kiss her cheek. "And I love you, too!"

She smiles and clings to me like a little monkey.

I carry her back to the house and see that her mother has taken the basket of rolls inside. I suspect she plans to feed her visitor. I carry the child up the cabin stairs. The door opens.

"Did you run off a'cause of being jealous?" the woman asks, an ugly sneer making her young face old.

"Jealous?" I ask, confused.

"This handsome man in here says you've had the hots for him since you were kids. Says he can't keep you off him. Says the reason you've shown up here at the cabin is mostly because you come looking for him 'cause you heard he was courting me. Says you're a regular German whore." The woman snickers. "I tell you what. I'll trade you. You take the brat, and I'll take Handsome, here." She slaps her leg and chortles.

I shudder at the sight of Benjamin Blakely, our paths have been forever crossed since his family moved here the same year mine did. I'm taken back nine years to the day I met the friends that keep me safe from him.

Falling Waters, Florida, 1889

"I ain't writing on it," Benjamin Blakely said, shoving the slate to the floor, his fists clenched.

Morris Blakely, our doctor-turned-teacher at least until a proper replacement could be found, held the offending slate. "May I ask why not?"

It was clear that our picture-book-handsome teacher was not going to give his brother any special treatment.

Benjamin spat on the wooden floor. "I ain't touching nothing a nasty foreigner touched." He shot me a look of pure, unmitigated hatred.

"I don't know what you're complaining about," a muffled voice behind him said, "I heard your daddy put your mama out of the house when you were just a young'un."

Benjamin uncoiled like a rattlesnake. His fist slammed into the boy, who toppled over the desk behind him. Books and children scattered. The boy lay on his side, hands cradling his nose.

The trembling started in my chest, traveled down my arms and legs until my entire body shook. If this boy knew about Miss Harriet's secret, did he know his mama's death was my fault? Did he

14

know about the doctor-turned-teacher Morris delivering Mama's baby while his own parents screamed in agony? The day hurtled back, and suddenly I was drenched in sweat, smelling the flames that licked a small wooden house. Miss Harriet's house.

I was thankful the eyes of the entire classroom—all except the girl sitting next to me—were on Morris, waiting to see what he would do next. They expected fiery, hot anger. They were talking about his mama, too. Instead, his voice was calm, almost conversational, but his clutched fists told a different story.

"Ok, boys and girls," Morris said, his teacher-voice strong. "The weather is going to get cold very soon, and I need you all to go outside and gather sticks for the woodstove. Put them in the bin as neatly as possible. Maggie, would you be responsible for making certain they're stacked neatly?"

The girl sitting next to me blushed furiously. "Yes, sir," she said. Maggie was plump and blonde, and her kind eyes and gentle ways made me want to know her better. But, I didn't expect her to want to know me. I was a foreigner. And, for the moment, I was thankful her attention had been snatched away from me. I needed to pull myself together. I needed to stop shaking. I touched the place on my forehead where Benjamin had hit me with a rock a few days earlier. It was still tender.

As Morris intended, the class forgot Benjamin and exploded in a mad, eager dash for the field and woods beyond. I forced myself to stand. Morris might want to know why I was shaking. I stood on trembling legs and walked out alone, clutching my snow-white apron and feeling every bit the dirty immigrant whose hands made a writing slate untouchable.

"I wonder what Mr. Blakely is going to do to his brother? I bet he gets a lickin' from his daddy when he gets home," Maggie said, walking up beside me so quietly that I jumped. "By the way, I'm Maggie." She held her hand out in a friendly greeting. "Don't mind him," she said noting my trembling and pointing to Benjamin's slouched back as he ambled out. He clearly had no intention of doing anything his brother requested. "He goes after the easy target. He prefers them to be alone. Don't be afraid. You've got friends here."

I smiled so big my cheeks hurt. "How does John Sebring Corley know all that about Benjamin's mama?" My words spilled out before I could stop them, but I had to know. Because if he knew the whole story, did he know it was all my fault?

"Well, I don't know the whole story, nor does John Sebring, but I think Benjamin's ma passed, and I don't think it was of natural causes.

"But how does John *know*?" I fell into step beside her.

Maggie shrugged. "Mr. Morris Blakely and Benjamin, they're brothers, but they don't have the same daddy. John Sebring's aunt lives in Cairo. He stays with her a lot. I think that Morris and John are somehow related. I'm pretty sure everybody here is related to everybody else." She laughed, but it was the laughter of kindness, not judgement.

That meant John Sebring knew something.

Maggie looked at me. "Are you okay?"

"I thought I saw a snake," I lied. More than anything in the world, I needed a friend. What Maggie didn't know about me wouldn't hurt her.

Maggie nodded. "There are plenty of them around here."

I breathed a sigh of relief, quiet-like, even while I felt guilty for lying to my new friend. I followed Maggie to the edge of the woods behind the schoolhouse. I was still worried about what else John Sebring Corley might know. But I tried to get my mind off it. "By the way, I'm Annie Laura," I said, though I guessed she knew my name like I knew hers. Still, it seemed the polite thing to say.

"You're from Germany?" Maggie asked.

"Yes." I blushed and my fists curled. "But, I'm American." I tried not to sound defensive, but I couldn't help it.

Maggie nodded. "Of course, you are," she said matter-of-factly, as if I had stated the most obvious thing in the world. I loved her for it. "My Oma was from Germany, and she talked just like you."

I felt my face get hot like it does when I'm excited. "She is here now?" I asked. Maybe my Mama and Papa would have someone from home to talk to.

"No," Maggie said, "she died of the cough a year ago."

"Oh," I said, disappointed for myself and sad for Maggie. "I'm sorry."

We walked through the piney woods to a saw-grass clearing, then ducked beneath the shelter of a giant oak tree. The limbs of the tree spread out for twenty feet all the way around, and Spanish moss clung to the branches, making lacy curtains that reached nearly to the ground. Beyond the reach of the sheltering branches, the earth was scattered with pine straw and thick with magnolia leaves. It was quiet in here, a place you could share secrets and be sure no one heard. Gray sticks littered the clearing, broken off from thick dead vines encircling the nearby magnolia. I knew soon enough we would be interrupted by the other children. This was a treasure trove of the dried sticks Morris asked us to gather.

"My Pa is sad, real sad," Maggie said, reaching down to pick up the sticks. She had tied her apron into a makeshift bag, and she tucked in the sticks. "My Oma took care of the youngers. Now it's just me and him in charge of my little brothers and sisters."

I copied Maggie, tying up my own apron and filling the makeshift pocket with the gray sticks. I didn't want to ask the obvious question. Where was Maggie's mama? I didn't have to.

"My mama passed when she birthed the last baby, a little girl. The baby passed, too."

Her words were emotionless, but I could see the pain in her eyes.

"Pa insists I go to school, even though it means he has to take care of the children while I'm gone. And, I like school fine. Mr. Morris Blakely, he's real nice. He's leaving soon as we find a real teacher, though. He's going to go back to doctoring, maybe way back in Cairo, Georgia, even though my daddy says ain't no money in doctoring, and he would be better off just to set here and teach school and run his farm."

The news made my heart hurt. I liked seeing Morris every day. Cairo, Georgia, was a place I had no intentions of returning to.

Our aprons were full of sticks, and Maggie held up the curtain of Spanish moss so I could pass through without getting moss and redbugs tangled in my hair.

"My daddy likes studying up on medicine, too," I said. And it was true. Papa had been a medic in the Prussian army in the Franco-Prussian War. He loved curing ills, almost as much as he loved creating his beautiful cast-iron stoves. "Who helps your daddy out while you're in school?"

"I run home quick as I can after school, so I can help Pa."

I imagined what life would be like at my own house with no mama. My heart hurt for my new friend, and I wanted to help her out.

"I think my mama could help your pa," I volunteered. "Maybe you could bring your brothers and sisters to our house some mornings, and she could watch them. How many do you have?"

A look of fear crossed Maggie's face.

"Only three," Maggie said. "Lost Owen to the cough this time last year. He was the youngest. Like to broke my daddy's heart. Thank you kindly, but I don't think Pa would stand for it."

Maybe that look of fear just meant that Maggie was afraid her brothers and sister would be too much trouble. "How old are they?" I asked.

"Five, four, and three," Maggie said. "My mama had a baby every year for a while there. Did yours?"

"No," I said, getting the impression that Maggie was trying to change the subject. "There's only me and my little sister, Eva. We had a brother that I don't remember. He died on our way over here."

"You lived in Germany?" Maggie asked, relieved, it seemed, to move on to a new subject.

"Yes, until I was nine."

"What do you remember?"

"The bitter cold!" I said, "And, my Oma. But that's about all."

"Is your Oma still alive?" Maggie asked.

"Yes, she is. She might come to visit us very soon, all the way from Germany. I hope she comes to stay!"

"This country is hard on the old ones," Maggie said wisely. "My Oma caught the fever and died only a year after she got here. I'm thirsty." She looked back, and I followed her gaze. We were about to be invaded. "Let's leave before all these young'uns get here and make so much racket we can't hear ourselves think. You want some water from the spring?"

"Yes!" I said, maybe a little too cheerfully. I didn't want to scare her, but I couldn't keep the excitement out of my voice—to find someone who might want to be my friend was what I'd hoped for.

Maggie led me past the clearing and we trekked through the woods for the spring. The voices of the other children disappeared in the distance, swallowed by the leaves and solid oak tree trunks that now surrounded us. Maggie stopped beside a collapsed tree whose brittle branches were there for the taking.

"I'm surprised no one came here for sticks," Maggie said.

I stopped. Something moved in the bushes. It wasn't the wind. I put a finger to my lips. "It sounds like someone did," I whispered.

Maggie looked around, fear in her eyes.

She didn't strike me as the sort to panic easily, so I listened carefully. Birds chirped, and it felt cooler here than it had under the oak tree. Whatever I thought I'd heard seemed to be gone. "I don't see anything, so I guess whatever it was didn't think we were worth the time." I said this loudly. I wanted whoever was spying on us to know we knew he was there. The tender spot on my forehead throbbed. I didn't want to give Benjamin Blakely a chance for a repeat.

As soon as we reached the crystal-clear spring, I leaned down and cooled my throbbing forehead in the icy waters.

"What happened to your face?" Maggie asked.

"Benjamin Blakely," I said, tugging up my petticoat to dry off my face.

Maggie nodded. "You, too?" And she held her hair up so that I could see an ugly red mark on the side of her neck. It looked like handprints.

"Did he choke you?" I asked, horrified.

Maggie nodded again and rearranged her blonde curls to hide the mark. "It's my own fault. I know better than to traipse around in the woods alone." She looked past the spring to a graceful oak tree, majestic with gold-dappled, sun-kissed leaves.

"Did you tell anyone?" I asked.

"No," she said. "My daddy would kill him." Crows cawed in the silence.

Our shared pain gave me a strange hope. Maybe I had found a real friend, the kind Mama and Oma talked about. "A good friend is worth more than gold," Oma said. "She shares your joy and helps carry you through your pain. A husband is a good thing, but a friend, ah! That is what makes life livable."

There was a rustling in the bushes. I grabbed Maggie's hand. Maggie held a finger to her lips. We sat, silent, holding hands. Maybe it was just a rabbit in the brush. But the footsteps were way too heavy for a rabbit. What if it was Benjamin Blakely come to get both of us? My scalp prickled.

Through the trees emerged a boy headed for the spring, nursing his bloody nose. It was John Sebring. I breathed a very quiet sigh of relief. I didn't want to embarrass him if he hadn't seen us, and I imagined Maggie felt the same.

But when he had soothed his nose in the icy water, he looked up through a maze of dripping blonde curls and said, "Hiya!" His eyes danced with mischievous good humor. "How do I look?" he asked.

"Like you been kicked in the face by a freshly shoed horse," Maggie said.

"That was what happened, right?" he said, one eyebrow cocked high.

I felt like he was making a joke, but I couldn't be certain. My English was perfect, but there were still some things that were hard to understand, especially jokes.

"He is going to kill you one day if you aren't careful," Maggie said.

John Sebring's nose looked broken to me. I wasn't sure how he was carrying on a conversation. It had to hurt.

"I'm not worried," he said. "By the way," he said turning his charm fully on me, "I'm John Sebring Corley. I got kin in Cairo, Georgia. It's how come I know so much about Benjamin Blakely."

"It is a pleasure to meet you," I said. But my face flushed.

"And you," he said, taking an exaggerated bow and kissing my hand. There was nothing but friendliness and good humor in his eyes.

I couldn't help but be pleased and surprised. His silly gallantry took my mind away from Cairo. While I knew John Sebring was teasing with me, it was lighthearted—he meant me no harm.

It felt like it was the three of us against Benjamin Blakely.

"You are a rogue," Maggie said.

"And you," John said, bending at Maggie's feet, "are a true lady. One day, I will win your favor, and you will be mine forever!"

Maggie laughed delightedly, and I laughed with them. It looked to me like John was sweet on Maggie. And Maggie blushed when he spoke to her again, so I guessed the feeling was mutual.

We gathered up our sticks and shared them with John.

As we headed back to the schoolhouse, Maggie surprised me with her question to John. "What do you know about Benjamin Blakely's parents?" she asked.

Instead of answering, John looked nervously into the woods, then motioned us forward, "Wanna race?" he asked.

Maggie studied him and then shrugged. "Give us a second to tie our sticks up and we will."

I followed Maggie's lead. I lifted my apron and retied the branches, knotting them securely.

"Ok," John said. "ready, set, GO!"

21

Maggie fell behind quickly, but John and I were neck and neck. How was he running with the pain in his nose? It had to smart with each pounding step. I glanced over at the blood trickling over his lip. He ignored it like it was nothing. When we reached the meadow behind the schoolhouse, I looked back at John, who was a foot behind me. I didn't want him to suffer further humiliation.

A broken nose might be a badge of honor. But losing a footrace to a girl, that would be humiliating.

I needn't have worried. John Sebring poured it on in the last few seconds and beat me soundly.

Maggie caught up to us as we stood panting. She gave me an admiring look, then directed us to stack our sticks in the bin. John stood in line behind me.

"You run really fast," he whispered.

I shrugged my shoulders and, alongside my new friends, stacked my sticks in the wooden bin, insurance against the coming cold winter.

Chapter 2

Falling Waters, Florida, 1898

I prefer not to see Benjamin Blakely stroll out onto my tenant's front porch. I want to turn and run. But the little girl shivering against me gives me courage. "I'm going to take her on home with me if you don't mind," I say to her mama. "She's gotten into some poison ivy, and I've got some liniment that can help."

"I ain't got time to mess with her."

I carry the little girl back down the steps. "Mama!" she calls, panicked. "Mama!" She screams and kicks at me, wriggles down, clutches my makeshift petticoat blanket around her shoulders, and buries her head in her mama's skimpy skirt.

"You're messing up my dress," her mama says, shoving the child. The little girl sprawls on the wood porch. She scrambles up, struggling to keep herself covered, and relaunches herself at her mama.

"Mama!" she screams.

"Get your dirty hands off my silk!" the woman says and thrusts the child at me.

I cradle the sobbing child in my arms and flee.

Benjamin Blakely's laughter echoes within the house.

My skirts tangle around my legs, and I cascade down the stairs. I cushion the little girl and land on my back. Benjamin Blakely moves beside the woman, not bothering to button his pants. They laugh like they're watching a street show.

I stand, holding the miserable child tight, and walk away.

I'm almost to the safety of the woods when the woman calls out, "Handsome says this here is his land. He says it won't be long before you are gone and he is the king of the hill. Then we might let you sharecrop. If you're nice."

I'm shaking with anger before the thick woods hide us. What a ridiculous assertion to make. The land is mine, free and clear. What does Benjamin Blakely have to do with my land? If it weren't for the little girl in my arms, and the three hard-working men beyond, this woman would be off my land before sunset.

Benjamin Blakely's mouth is full of lies. But I shiver. There is a certainty in the woman's tone that frightens me.

The only thing that stands between my family and starvation is my land, the land I've fought to keep for seven long years. And this year, the land has finally prospered enough for me to add acres and hire a tenant farmer. My family—me; my little sisters, Eva, who is thirteen, and Maisie, who is five; Mama and Daddy—is healthy. The land feeds and clothes us. It gives us assurance against hunger and fear. It makes us Americans.

I can handle the earth swallowing us up in the blink of an eye better than I can handle having my land taken away.

Silly thoughts. No one is going to take away my land. Least of all Benjamin Blakely.

The little girl whimpers in my arms.

Chapter 3

I try not to think about the woman's words. I don't have to worry about the likes of Benjamin Blakely taking my land. It's ridiculous; I've paid for it with over a decade of sacrifice. While Papa hasn't sold a stove in years, my farm thrives.

Besides, I have other things to think about. For one thing, after three weeks, Maisie is growing increasingly attached to the little girl I brought home. Emma is older than I imagined, closer to Maisie's five years than the three I originally guessed. When I first brought her here, she was severely malnourished and acted like a baby, but Maisie adores her, loves having someone to baby rather than being babied. And now the two are inseparable.

However, since the redness and swelling from the poison ivy have finally disappeared, must I take her back to her own family? I find myself stalling, and not just for Maisie's sake. I don't want to face the horror of that cabin again. And why hasn't Emma's mother come to get her? What kind of mother leaves her daughter with strangers and doesn't even check on her for three weeks?

But I can't keep the child away from her daddy. Tom is a good man. I decide to take her to him.

I set out early in the morning when I know Tom will be working in the field. I hold Emma's sweet, soft little hand, and we walk through the glorious spring woods. The dogwoods offer up their delicate white flowers, and the live oaks spread shimmering spring-green fans. The pines and magnolias, which looked so lush and refreshingly green during the brown winter months, now look old and tired in contrast to the newly sprouted leaves around them.

"Where's Maisie?" Emma asks, looking back for her friend.

"That sleepyhead couldn't wake up," I say, and pray for forgiveness for the white lie.

Emma giggles, and the sparkleberry trees brighten our way, their tiny white bell-like flowers waving gently in the early-morning breeze. "It looks like fairies," Emma says, pointing up to where the sparkleberries dance, and I agree, thankful that the beautiful tree has taken her focus for the moment.

I love them, too. "My mama says they put on a glorious new outfit every spring and shine brighter than any tree in the woods. Though they are little, they are mighty, she says."

Emma thinks on this for a moment. "What's mighty?"

"Well, that means strong."

"I'm not mighty, then," she says, kicking the fallen flowers. "My mama says I'm nothing but a scrawny piece of bacon left out too long in the heat. Spoiled, weak, and worthless." She repeats these words like she's heard them so many times that she's memorized them, with no idea of what they actually mean.

I feel my jaw tighten, and I want to lash out. But she looks up at me, the hope in her eyes shadowed by fear.

"Well," I say, "you don't look like bacon to me!" I force myself to smile like it's all a big joke.

A moment passes while she thinks. "No," she says, giggling. "I don't look like bacon! I'm a little girl! I'm not bacon!"

"Yes," I say. "And you are very, very kind, and you helped me pick up that heavy, wet laundry basket."

Her eyes shine. "I did. And it was heavy!"

"And, besides that, we love having you with us."

"Why are you taking me home?" she asks.

I swallow. "Your daddy just has to see you!"

She smiles. "And my brothers. They like me," she says matter-of-factly.

In the distance, we can see Tom along with Emma's big brothers working to clear the land. Tom ties a rope around a burnt-out oak stump and fastens it to the new mule. We watch as the stump stubbornly refuses to budge.

"Come on, girl, you can do it," he says and pats the mule's rump.

When he looks up and sees Emma, his face brightens. She runs to him. He drops the mule's bridle and picks up his baby girl, swinging her in a happy circle. She jumps down from his arms and runs to her brothers. They bend down and hug her, and she gives them each a kiss on the cheek. Then, she looks back up at me as if to say, "I told you!"

"Miss Annie Laura says I'm not like bacon and that I'm strong, so I think Mama is going to like me now."

The boys' faces fall, and Tom nods at them. "Take Emma to see…" he falters.

His sons look up at him, and silent understanding passes between them. They lead Emma away; she chatters cheerfully about Maisie and helping me with the wash.

"I'd be pleased if you could take care of her, ma'am," Tom Green says as soon as the trio is no longer in hearing range. He ducks his head and swipes at his eyes.

I try to hide my surprise, thinking he must just mean for today.

But he sees my expression and clarifies. "I mean for good," he says and sets his jaw. He picks up the dangling bridle and pulls the mule forward. "Come on, girl," he croaks to the mule. "Let's get this thing out."

I feel unsteady on my feet for a moment. "Of course I can, Tom. She's a little angel." Is his wife gone? I can't ask that question out loud.

"I'll bring her out to see you," I assure him.

His face reddens, and his eyes fill. He swats at his cheek with a surprisingly clean blue bandanna. I wonder who does his wash.

"I'd like that, ma'am. I'd like that a lot. I'd be pleased if you could just bring her out here every now and again so we can see the little mite. You don't need to traipse all the way back to our homeplace with her."

I nod.

Tom turns to the stump and tightens the loop and rope. The boys have returned with Emma, and he motions for them to get on either side of the mule. She strains, and the stump moves ever so slowly. The boys hold her steady, gentling her, moving her forward inch by inch. Roots crackle and pop, and finally, with a great heave, the stump falls on its side.

"Yay!" Emma hoots, and claps her little hands. Her brothers smile, and her father looks away.

I take her hand. "See y'all in a little bit," she says, and skips alongside me. "Are we going to see Mama now?" she asks.

"Not right now."

"But I think she'll like me now. Let's try, okay?"

My lips feel dry. I lick them and pray for inspiration. And like an answered prayer, Maisie comes running out of the woods.

"You left me!" she says accusingly.

"But you're here now," I say, so relieved I can barely breathe.

"Can we play?" Maisie asks.

"Goody!" Emma says. "I was scared."

"Of what?" I ask.

But she ignores my question. "Play with Maisie, play with Maisie, play with Maisie," she sings, wrestling her hand away from mine and grabbing Maisie's. They run together for home.

I puzzle over Tom. Does he want me to take Emma for good? Does he distrust his wife so much? Tom and the boys look skinny. Too skinny. We have plenty to eat at our house, so maybe that's it. Maybe he doesn't want his little girl to go hungry like her brothers.

I need to talk to Morris. He recommended Tom and his family to be my tenants. He said nobody worked as hard as Tom and his boys.

Does Morris know anything about Tom's wife?

Chapter 4

The next day, I'm planning how I can quiz Morris about Tom's wife when I hear the dog bark. I look out the window and a welcome sight greets me. John Sebring and Maggie, my old childhood friends, have come to call. Maggie, heavy in the last months of pregnancy, balances a cloth-covered plate on her belly. John ties his horse to the hitching post while his wife walks up the wooden stairs and onto the wide front porch. I lay aside my straw hat and work gloves and hurry out to greet them.

When John glances up and sees me, he gives me his snaggle-toothed welcoming smile, a reminder of a long-ago fight with Benjamin Blakely that left a gaping hole where John's front tooth had once lodged. Benjamin hadn't been able to walk away. When he woke the next morning from his drunken stupor, Benjamin didn't remember pulling John Sebring out of the feed store by his wiry blonde hair, nor did he remember John's fierce punch that laid him out and lost him the fight. I laugh every time I see that snaggle-toothed smile. John Sebring carries it with élan.

"What brings you here this lovely morning?" I ask.

"Maggie brought some soda crackers over to settle your mama's stomach. She said it worked so good for her, she wanted to share the wealth."

Mama's stomach?

John reads my puzzled look. He blushes to the roots of his wiry blond hair. There is a long pause. "She's in the family way, Annie Laura."

My stomach tightens, and anger fills my head until my ears whir with it.

"That's very kind of Maggie," I say snapping off my shawl and hurtling through the door John Sebring holds open for me.

Maggie engulfs me in a hard-bellied hug. I go stiff in her embrace. She pulls away and studies my face.

"It was bad enough with Eva," I whisper. "But when Maisie was born, Morris warned Papa that another pregnancy would kill her." My words are fierce, my soul a ball of smoldering fire.

"What is done is done," Maggie answers quietly. "All we can do is help her to be as comfortable as possible through it."

I look up into Maggie's tear-filled eyes. I nod and acquiesce.

Mama appears beside us. "Mama!" I say, hugging her gently, "When were you going to tell me?"

"I didn't want to upset you," Mama says, looking down at her hands. "You've got enough on your shoulders."

"Ahh, Annie Laura," Papa effuses from his chair beside the woodstove.

I lunge in Papa's direction, but Maggie holds me back.

"We need our little boy, don't you know?" Papa says, stroking his white beard.

"Think of your mama," Maggie whispers to me.

"Of course, you do, Papa," I say, biting the inside of my mouth.

"Bring me a drink, Annie Laura. I think this is cause for celebration," Papa says, bleary eyed from his previous night's revelry.

Mama squeezes my hand in supplication, and for her I comply. But I can't control my anger.

I pull down Papa's stein, slam it on the side board, and pour the homemade brew out of the bowl Mama has covered with cloth.

I clutch the stein in my hands, planning what to say to Papa.

I look at him and I see a drunken murderer. Morris's warning, *Another pregnancy will kill her,* forms a sick singsong in my head.

There must be murder in my eyes because John Sebring reaches for the stein. He lays a warm hand on mine and says, "I'll take it, Annie Laura. Why don't you and Maggie go out for a walk. Go, now." He gives me a gentle but forceful push.

I move forward like a wind-up toy. Maggie takes my arm.

"My Annie Laura girl thinks I drink too much," Papa says.

I stiffen and whirl around, but John steps between Papa and me. Maggie pulls me to the door.

30

"I don't," my lying papa says. "A little brew warms the belly and calms the spirit."

The room is silent. But he continues. "No harm in a little cheering, is there now?"

I slam the door shut, but not before I register the awkwardly silent response to Papa's foolish words. It's a small victory. The door bangs the wooden frame, shaking the house, only to spring open again as if compelling me to go back inside and throttle Papa. Maggie closes it so that it stays. I thrust my entire weight against it, wishing I could keep everything I've just learned trapped inside. "I wish he was dead," I say.

Maggie takes my hand, but I jerk it away. "I mean it," I say.

Maggie says nothing. There's nothing to say.

I trip down the first stair.

"Slow down," Maggie says, helping me up. "I can't pick you up again unless you want me to have my own baby right here and now."

She takes my face between her soft hands and forces me to look into her eyes. "You can't change him, Annie Laura. All you can do is help make things easier for your mama, like you've always done. Okay?"

I nod, and we walk towards the creek bank where the grass grows soft, the land is level, and walking is like skimming over the Gulf on a calm winter day.

Chapter 5

The distant sound of hoofbeats drums the clay road.

"Who's that?" Emma asks, pausing her clapping game with Maisie, a troubled look on her face.

"We'll see," I say. A moment later, Morris appears, a document bag hanging from his saddle.

"What in the world has brought you here in such an all-fired hurry?" I ask, though my heart sings at the sight of him.

"Fear," he says.

I think he might be joking with me. He isn't.

"I need to talk with your papa."

"He's still asleep. He was up until dawn. He won't awaken until near sunset."

Morris's lips are set in a straight, grim line. Does he know about the stench of alcohol escaping in Papa's sweat while he sleeps, filling the house?

"Then I'll come back," Morris says, and puts a foot in his stirrup. But his horse is lathered, so he pauses, removes his foot, and pats the exhausted creature's neck. "He needs to rest," he says. "Do you mind if we stay until he's watered?"

"Of course," I say, pleased. "Can I bring you some water?" I want him to stay long enough to tell me what he's afraid of.

"I'll just see to the horse," he says.

He removes the horse's tack and leads him over to the watering trough. As the animal drinks, Morris uses a cup he pulls from his saddle to douse the horse's legs and hindquarters with water, then patiently scrapes the water off with quick but patient motions.

He glances up at the porch. "I see you've still got Emma," he says.

"Tom wants me to keep her," I say.

"I'm not surprised."

"Any idea why he might want me to do that?"

The look on Morris's face tells me he does.

"Tom's boys and Emma are the only children that survived with this crazy woman," Morris says, his voice flat. "All three of her other children died as toddlers. One was lost in the woods the last place they lived. A second caught herself on fire playing near the fireplace."

Horrified, I glance at the porch to make certain Emma hasn't heard. But the girls aren't there.

I search the window and see that they've moved inside and are sitting with Mama at the kitchen table. Emma's head bounces up and down, giggling. Mama laughs, too.

"Tom's wife was sleeping off the previous day's alcohol, apparently." Morris pauses in his dousing and scraping long enough to cast a reproving glance at Papa's bedroom window. "She gets them through infancy and then ignores them." He punctuates the sentence by slamming the cup into the trough.

"The third child, another girl, died of typhus," he continues. "The woman has had a string of men. The family has been kicked out of every sharecropping job they've had because a husband or son finds the way to her bed. But Tom loves her. Go figure that one out."

But I have some idea. Mama loves Papa, in spite of his drunken self.

"How did you find out?" I ask.

Once his ministrations have cooled his horse, Morris leads him away from the trough and into the shade of the old oak tree. He walks him around a bit before releasing him to munch on grass stubbles.

He is avoiding my question.

I wait.

"Tom told me," he says.

"Today?"

He shakes his head.

"I'm wondering why you didn't tell me this before you let me hire them."

"I knew you probably wouldn't hire him if I did. And I also knew that while the woman is trouble to most families, she would be harmless to yours. You have no men in your family other than your papa, and he is still infatuated with your mama."

I swallow hard and nod. It's true enough. The way Papa looks at Mama is embarrassing.

"And no one works as hard as Tom Green and his boys. It's like they are trying to make up for the mama."

"And you knew we would find Emma and take her in?"

Morris almost smiles at that. "I took care of two of the babies they lost. I couldn't stand watching Tom lose another one. I was afraid it would kill him. I knew she would be in good hands with you."

"You're mighty sure of yourself, Morris Blakely."

He looks at me, trying to read my expression.

I smile and shake my head. "I'm only sorry it took me so long to get to her."

Morris's initial relief is replaced with a faraway look. Whatever it is that made him ride like a man running from his own shadow is with him still, and it has nothing to do with Emma or with Tom's wife.

"Now are you going to tell me what's bothering you?"

Morris rubs his fists over his head and clenches his wiry curls.

Just then, Maisie and Emma come running down the porch stairs. They stop in front of Morris. Emma stands behind Maisie, three fingers in her mouth, while Maisie pulls on Morris's pant leg. "Can we keep her?"

Morris focuses his complete attention on Maisie's question. He leans down so that he is eye level with both little girls. I have to smile.

"For now," Morris says.

"Hooray!" Maisie says. She hugs Morris tight, takes Emma by the hand, and leads her to the top of the porch stairs where she's set the travel chest filled with her most precious possessions—two ragged cloth dolls, a play stove Papa cast for her, a ball, some stones from the creek, and a few pieces of tattered ribbon. She divides all of it into two neat piles.

"You choose the ones you like best," Maisie says. Emma seems paralyzed by the treasures spread before her. Maisie takes her friend's hand and guides it to the bigger pile. "These are all yours. For keeps."

Emma, wide eyed, clutches a tattered ribbon and a handkerchief doll and whispers, "Thank you."

"It's a good thing Emma learned her manners from her daddy," I say soft enough for only Morris to hear.

Morris smiles, but I know he isn't really hearing me. "Can you take a little walk?" he asks. "I want to give him a good rest." He motions to his horse. "I've got a long way to go."

Oh, Lord. Please tell me Morris isn't leaving.

"Yes." I try to keep my voice steady. I glance over at Maisie and Emma. The girls will be fine on the steps for a few minutes playing with their treasures.

"We won't go far," he says, noting my gaze.

We walk until we come upon an old lightning-struck oak, felled in a brutal storm. It's our place for talking.

Morris's horse follows us and grazes close by. "He's a loyal companion, that one," I say.

But Morris doesn't hear. He stares out beyond my field of cotton, and over to the woods being cleared by Tom, encompassing all the land that Papa refuses to acknowledge, the farm that shames him. When will Papa come to terms with the truth that the money from my crops is supporting us?

Morris turns abruptly and looks over the adjoining field, his own family land, the crops growing waist high in the bright noonday sun.

What is he looking for?

As if hearing my unspoken question, he looks down at me and brushes a stray hair from my face.

He clears his throat. He tries to speak, but coughs as if the words gag him.

"Are you okay?" I ask.

He nods and takes a deep breath. He swallows, lets out his breath. "John Calvin, the man I called Daddy, died six months ago.

35

For the past ten years, I've worked like a dog to help make the family land profitable."

I nod. "You've worked hard, Morris. No one could have worked harder."

"Except you."

I let his words fade without responding. I appreciate the compliment, but I'm eager to hear what he's having such a difficult time sharing.

"Sure, I've worked hard. Aside from the three years I took off for more medical training at Johns Hopkins." He squints into the distance beyond his land, as if trying to piece something together.

He studies his hands and then takes mine in his. Is he telling me he's going way up north, back to Johns Hopkins? Maybe to teach? My heart drops down into my stomach. I don't think I can make it here without Morris. I depend on him for my sanity.

Suddenly, his face reddens. He drops my hands, and his turn into fists. "Daddy made Benjamin the executor of the estate."

He stands, picks up a solid clay rock and hurls it. It explodes in a shower of orange against the trunk of a nearby oak.

He picks up another and aims it at a faraway oak. He hurls another, and another. Each explodes until the sky seems as orange as the clay beneath us. He throws until there is nothing more to throw. When he sits back down beside me, his shirt is soaked with sweat. His breath comes in short gasps.

"What does that mean?" I ask when his breathing returns to normal.

"It means that Benjamin makes all the decisions about land use."

"He'll mortgage it all away to pay off his jail fines and gambling debts," I say.

Morris closes his eyes and nods. "Already, he's put up the best section for sale."

"What will you do?" I fear his answer. If the land is gone, Morris may well be leaving Falling Waters, perhaps returning to Cairo in

Georgia and starting over there where his mama left him her land. Or, returning north. The thought fills me with despair.

"Why do you need to speak with Papa?" I ask. What could Benjamin being the executor of the estate have to do with us?

"I have an idea that I need to talk to him about before I can say anything to you. I'll come back and talk to him another day. Please. Trust me."

Is that closely guarded hope I see glimmering in his eyes?

Chapter 6

A few days later, Morris returns. When he ties his horse at our hitching post, he looks relaxed, even happy. Has Benjamin signed some portion of land over to Morris? I can hardly keep myself from begging him to tell me what he needs to talk with Papa about.

"I've been visiting with Dr. Davidson from Quincy. You remember me talking about his herb garden?" Morris answers my question before I even ask. "He was kind enough to ride over to help me get started. He's still here. I want you to meet him."

"Get started with what?" I ask. But hope rises in me like iridescent soap bubbles. Maybe Morris will be staying! Not moving to Cairo after all. I can't keep the excitement out of my voice. "How can I help?"

"A few weeks ago, Dr. Davidson showed me around his herb garden and dispensary. It's a sight to behold. He grows all the expensive herbs and potions I import from Pensacola. So expensive that there's no profit in practicing medicine. But, if I could grow my own...and if you could help me..."

"Is that what you wanted to talk with Papa about?"

His smile crinkles his eyes and deepens his dimple.

"Here? We could grow the medicine right here?" This year's crop of cotton looks to be the best I've ever grown and will be ready for the picking in a few short weeks. But rotating my crops and planting something else could help nourish the depleted soil. More importantly, a joint venture might keep Morris here. But only if Benjamin doesn't do something stupid and jeopardize Morris's portion of the land.

"I'm planning an herb and medicinal crop on my land. Benjamin has promised to let me keep a small portion. It'll be just enough to grow herbs on."

"That might be a good idea for my land as well."

"And we need more cows." Morris says.

"Why more cows? Isn't my Moses enough?"

"Milk is an essential ingredient in many of Dr. Davidson's remedies. Maybe we can even build you a barn closer to the house for Moses so that you and the girls don't have to hike so far. Annie Laura, you should see his henhouse. It is pristine. Eggs are another necessity for his remedies. But he insists on very clean hens. He has built his henhouse to keep the hens nesting up off the ground. They have to walk up a ladder to roost!"

"A henhouse like that would take me an entire summer to build."

"Maybe," Morris says. "But it would be worth your labor to have more hens laying more eggs."

"What about Papa?" I ask.

"You let me take care of him," Morris says. He waves at our front window where Papa sits at the table, calmly sipping from his favorite porcelain mug.

Morris climbs the stairs two at a time, and I'm right behind him. We're greeted by the sweet smell of hot cocoa and the warm scent of baking bread.

"Why, look who's here to see you this morning, Otto. It's our friend, Morris," Mama says, her voice oddly placating. The room crackles with tension.

"Why are you speaking to me in that voice, as if I am old and feeble and would not recognize a family friend?" Papa asks.

Mama smiles, but her lips tremble.

I put a hand on Morris's arm to stop him from sharing our plan. The timing is not good. Morris nods. He understands.

He sticks out his large, capable hand and envelops Papa's small artisan's hand.

"Good morning, sir," Morris says.

"Do sit down, young man," Papa says. He sits up a bit straighter in his chair and straightens his rumpled vest. "Bertha will bring you some cocoa."

Morris turns to Mama. "Thank you, ma'am. You make the best cocoa I ever tasted. How in the world do you create such a divine delight?"

If those words had formed in the mouth of any other man, I would have thought him effeminate, but out of Morris's mouth, they sound just right. Is it the way he holds his head? His utter lack of pretense? His broad smile, big enough to include whoever is in the room?

"You are very kind."

Morris hugs Mama. "How are you feeling?' he asks.

Mama holds her belly, blushes and laughs. "Good," she says. Then she raises her chin, her mouth firm. "Otto," she says, "make room for our guest."

Papa clears his messy newspapers.

Morris has worked his magic. Mama feels it.

Morris turns his attention to Papa. He knows the tension has eased and he can say what he came to say. "I've been talking to Dr. Davidson. He has some news you might well be interested in."

"Oh?" Papa asks. His army medic days make him interested in anything a renowned doctor like Davidson might want to share. He struggles to straighten his wrinkled shirt, his hands shaking.

"He knows how we can grow our own medicines," Morris says.

"Pah," Papa says, pushing away his cocoa. "Only peasants grow things. And my daughter here, who has shamed me before the entire community. She thinks she can grow cotton. She thinks I don't know about it." Papa slams the table. His hot cocoa wobbles, and Mama catches it before it stains Papa's rumpled white shirt.

"See what you've made me do?" He points an accusing finger at me. "You're ruining our lives. I'll get no respect in town. Who will buy from an artisan who does peasant work?" Papa's angry words force spittle from his lips. It sprinkles the table and Mama's hair.

The unfairness of his words wounds my soul. It is my hard labor that feeds us and keeps us in this house, my excess crops that pay the mortgage, and Mama's sewing that buys shoes. How dare he pretend that he is in any way responsible for our ability to hold our heads up in town? My anger grows until it is a raging fire inside of me.

Morris grips my hand in warning. "No," he says calmly as if Papa has not made a scene. "Peasants aren't allowed to grow such medicines. You need a special license."

"Is there a guild?" Papa asks.

"Well," Morris says, improvising on the spot, "there certainly might be a guild. I'm getting ready to take Annie Laura over to the house to meet Dr. Davidson himself. Would you like to join us?"

"Not today," Papa says, sinking into his chair, his eyes suddenly weary. "I will leave that to young people."

And your peasant daughter, I think bitterly.

I want to throttle Papa. But I also want him to shake away whatever it is that makes him melancholy, that robs him of his boyish enthusiasm, that makes him suck hope from a bottle like a baby nursing a dry breast. Papa's heart is sick.

But Morris nods compliance with Papa, and Papa, believing himself to be understood, chats with Morris about the weather and the raising of the American flag over Puerto Rico.

"For greed or to protect the people, that is my question," Papa asks. His words are a bitter accusation, an indictment against his new home.

Morris studies Papa. "I hope the latter," he says evenly.

When Morris finishes his cocoa, he turns a bright smile to Mama. "Thank you, ma'am," he says, and kisses the top of her head.

"You are most welcome." She nods as if all is well.

My heart hurts for my mama.

Morris stands and addresses Papa. "I'll be sure to let you know what he says. You rest and take care of yourself, and when we return, we will open a whole new world!"

Papa seems to wilt around his mug of cocoa. "If there really is a guild," he grunts.

"I'll research everything I can find and report back to you."

Papa appraises Morris through narrowed eyes, his hands gripping the mug.

I kiss Mama's cheek and turn away before Papa can say anything more.

"Race you!" I whisper when Morris and I make it out the door. I can't wait to get away from Papa. He has a way of turning Mama's pleasant kitchen into a field of briars. Morris feels it, too, and we bolt down the stairs and across the neatly swept front yard like two kids.

I can feel Papa's calculating eyes upon us even through the front window. But I don't care. Morris Blakely makes me feel safe and full of hope.

"Let's take the field," Morris says, struggling to keep up with me.

"That's the long way," I call over my shoulder, laughing.

"That's the fun way," he says. "More challenges."

It's a full-out race, and I'm winning. I glide through the fields, careful to avoid stepping on my precious cotton, and sprint for the creek bank. I look for a place to cross the rushing water. I'm fast, but Morris has the advantage of longer legs—he can leap across the creek wherever he wishes.

His footsteps pound behind me, and he takes a giant leap, crossing the gently flowing stream.

If he can do it, so can I. I leap, but I miss the bank and land in the water, soaking my shoes. I slog through to the creek bank, my black lace-up boots making a sucking sound in the wet, sandy clay.

Ahead of me, Morris's hat slips off his head, dangles on its leather strap, and with every running step it flaps against his back. I giggle at him, at our unencumbered joy. Morris sprints across a small clearing that divides our land from the Blakelys'. It's not the way. Why is he running that way? I take a deep breath to call out, but then I see.

He's headed for a stumbling figure that looks like Papa. He must have taken the road and beat us here.

"Otto!" Mama screams, clutching her belly and running close behind my Papa. "Otto, stop!"

I hoist my skirts and run towards them. The last thing Mama needs right now is to be running.

The unimaginable happens. Morris reaches forward and pushes my papa with all his might. Papa tumbles to the ground. Morris falls backwards, felled by something I can't see.

Mama kneels beside Papa.

"Papa!" I scream.

I drop down at his other side. I touch his forehead. He reeks of alcohol.

"Your papa is fine," Mama says, her breath coming quickly. I imagine Mama pushing away from the table and chasing Papa down the stairs and down the dirt road. I see in her face years of such tending, and the furrows Papa has created. Deep worry lines on her forehead, wrinkles around her mouth. Mama has grown old. It hurts my heart. Is this love?

"Tend to Morris," Mama says. She eases Papa up gently and leads him stumbling away, moaning his peevish complaints.

Fury blazes in me. "What were you thinking?" I bellow. I stand, prepared to kick Morris where he lies, but his long arm reaches out, hooks my ankles, and pulls me to the ground.

Infuriated, I pound the dirt. "What is wrong with you?"

"Annie Laura!" Mama calls, her voice tight with anger. "Open your eyes." She points to the obvious, except that I nearly missed it.

A rusty barbed-wire fence line. Newly posted. Benjamin's handiwork, I realize immediately from the shoddiness of the job. "Your papa is fine," Mama says again. "But look to Morris."

There's blood pouring from Morris's face.

He was saving Papa and me from the same fate.

"Oh, my Lord, Morris. I'm so sorry!"

His smile is weak.

"You're like a raging bull when a member of your family is threatened," he says, and closes his eyes, his head cradled by the soft ground. He's taken the full impact of the wire while keeping both Papa and myself safe.

I rip off my shawl and wrap it securely around his head. The blood continues to pour, more blood than seems possible. The gash is long and deep, too deep to heal on its own. He needs help before he loses all the blood pumping through his precious body. I have to get him to his house, where Dr. Davidson is waiting.

"Come on, my friend," I say, pulling him to his feet. He stands up, wobbles, kneels. I hoist him up again. "Here, you stubborn fool. Lean on me."

Reluctantly he grips my shoulders, and I wrap my arm around his waist. "Let's get you home before you expire right here in the scrub."

"Dr. Davidson," Morris croaks.

Chapter 7

I'm glad Dr. Davidson is there. He'll be handy with the cleaning up and the medicine. But it's Mary Scarlet I hope to see. I trust her with the sewing up of Morris's face more than I would trust any man.

Blood soaks the makeshift bandage, trickles down his face, drips onto my dress. The Blakely home suddenly seems too far away. The weight of Morris on my shoulder makes me stumble, and Morris topples. I catch us both before I fall completely to the ground. I right Morris, shudder, and plunge forward. Working the fields has made me strong, but not strong enough.

After what feels like hours, I'm nearly past the century oak tree that edges the neatly swept front yard when I hear a guttural, cheerless laugh.

"Well, I'll be," a voice says.

I jump. Morris groans, stumbles.

Benjamin Blakely sits with his back nestled against the oak, a steaming cup of coffee clutched in his hand. He chuckles. "Looks like my big brother got hisself in a little cat fight. Those your claw marks on his face?"

Morris clutches my shoulder and I flinch. I know it's his automatic reaction to Benjamin—the clenching of his fist—but it hurts. "You think you could help me out here?" I bellow.

But Benjamin shakes his head. "You got him into this scrape, I reckon you can get him out." He slaps his knee and laughs.

"Horse's ass," Morris croaks.

I'm so thankful he's coherent that I laugh, and tears fill my eyes.

Mary Scarlet comes running up the lane, skirts flying, followed by their Aunt Tabitha.

"We saw you coming down the lane holding Morris. What happened?" Mary Scarlet asks, lacing an arm around Morris, sharing my burden.

"He ran into the barbed wire that Benjamin struck right at throat level."

"Well, I'm sure he didn't mean to hurt anybody," Mary Scarlet says.

Benjamin erupts in laughter. "You've got big ole brains and itty-bitty sense, brother. That's what Daddy always said about you. I reckon he was right. What an idiot. You saw me string the wire, and then you went and ran into it?" He guffaws, spilling hot coffee on his lap.

I hope it burns a hole in his pants.

Benjamin's words are lost on Morris. He loses consciousness before we reach the front stoop.

Mary Scarlet and I lay him down on the porch floor as carefully as we can. Tabitha calls to Dr. Davidson. He bursts through the door and scrunches down beside Morris like an elderly elf. I'm amazed that he's able to do so—he has to be at least ninety years old. He unwinds the bloody shawl.

Mary Scarlet takes one look at the gaping wound and hurries inside. She returns with her needle, thread, and a matchstick to sterilize the needle. Morris has taught her well. Though some doctors still don't hold with cleaning their instruments, Morris is a believer in Dr. Lister's theories. Morris says the British doctor is saving thousands of lives with his new ideas about instrument sterilization.

Benjamin slinks up the walkway and hovers on the steps, a big stain on the front of his pants like he's wet them. A wad of tobacco swells in his cheek, and he spits every now and again, perilously close to where Dr. Davidson works to clean the wound.

"Stop that," Tabitha says when a yellow stream spatters against the tin wash basin.

Benjamin leans his head back and stares Tabitha down. She looks away.

When Benjamin spits again in nearly the same place, Dr. Davidson rises, and in a single motion, showing elflike dexterity, he straddles Benjamin, knocking him to the ground. With his scalpel in one hand and a bloodied cloth in the other, he says in a voice remarkably calm, "Son, I would hate to have to use this on those fat lips, but if you spit like that again close to my patient, your lips are coming off."

And then he pushes off, settling back in to doctor his patient.

"Okay, little bantam rooster," Benjamin says, and picks himself up off the wood porch floor. He's shaky when he puckers his lips to spit again. He backs down the steps and ambles away.

"Dang bully," Dr. Davidson mutters and douses Morris's face with another clean bowl of water. He picks bits of wood and lichen from the wound with his tweezers. "You got any codeine in that medicine bag of your'n?" he asks Morris.

Morris doesn't answer.

"It's gotten so dang expensive that I'm out of it," Dr. Davidson says. "Reckon I'll have to use opium." He prepares a glass syringe, ready to inject Morris.

"No, sir, if you don't mind," Morris says, surprising all of us. He points to a packet in his medical bag.

"What's this?" Dr. Davidson examines it, pinches it and puts it to his tongue. "That new-fangled aspirin? You think it will help?"

"I don't know, but I've treated too many patients that get addicted to opium to want to use it on myself," Morris croaks.

I wish that he'd allowed for the opium. Opium would let him sleep through Mary Scarlet's neat stitches. Tears are streaming from his eyes. On stitch number thirty-six, he passes out from the pain. Mary Scarlet stitches a neat line from his forehead down to his chin, forty-seven in all.

"Looks like you laid him out on your Singer and set to work," Dr. Davidson says, admiring her stitches.

Mary Scarlet finishes and ties a final, careful knot. I cover Morris with a clean quilt. He awakens, and I give him a shot of whiskey and place a pillow under his head.

Mary Scarlet brings her quilting basket outside and sits in the rocking chair close to Morris. She sets to work piecing her latest quilt, a Lone Star. I watch her face relax, and I think about the joy on the faces of Mama and Eva as they stitch their latest quilt creations. I think about the dreams they stitch into their quilts, the confidences they share. My own hands are too rough from picking cotton and hoeing to sew and piece. The thread catches and tangles on my callouses.

Mary Scarlet and Eva set their quilts in their hope chests. I envy their peace. My hope chest is the land.

When Dr. Davidson decides Morris is ready to be moved and helps us settle him in his bed where he sleeps soundly, I thank Dr. Davidson and head home to milk Moses. We'll have to talk about Morris's medicinal garden idea tomorrow.

I pass through the woods between the properties. Briars catch at my skirt, and the walk feels long and lonely without Morris. I have too much time to think, and the longing I feel for the way things used to be pains me.

I long for my family to stop changing. I long for Papa to be the man I remember from when I was a little girl. No one confuses Papa with St. Nicholas anymore. His once kind face is angry, and spidery red veins riddle his nose and cheeks. And he despises me.

The only one I know who drinks as much as Papa is Benjamin Blakely. That thought leads me down a long, dark road of pain, and I force myself to think of something happy.

Morris is my bright spot. His passion for medicine matches mine for farming. I farm in my sleep. I spend hours daydreaming about how to improve my yields, how to make enough extra so that I can sell the excess and buy more land. Twenty acres is not nearly enough.

My obstacle is Papa. Morris's obstacle is Benjamin. It makes no sense at all to me that John Calvin Blakely picked worthless Benjamin to be the executor of his estate. Why not Morris, or even Mary Scarlet?

Just last week, the Blakelys were forced to sell fifty acres to pay Benjamin's fines for disorderly conduct. He does that when he's drunk.

And what if Benjamin, just out of spite, chooses to keep Morris's land, the land that's adjacent to ours?

But the worst thing that could happen is this: Benjamin decides the land should be divided between himself and Mary Scarlet. Mary Scarlet sides with Benjamin, and claims that since Morris isn't their Daddy's blood, he doesn't get any of the land.

Morris would have to leave Falling Waters and go to Cairo, Georgia, where his mama left him property. Now my fears come back. What if he decides to move and start a medical practice there?

It's why the medicinal farming right here in Falling Waters is such a good idea. If my cotton crop fails, I'll have the herbs. If we can make it work, Morris will stay. I need Morris to stay.

Chapter 8

Fall 1898

Falling Waters, 1888

On this perfect October morning, the sun streams golden on fields of white. I stand on the porch and shield my eyes. Cotton as far as I can see. Joy rises like a bubble in my chest—pure, unadulterated joy. I've done it.

I calculate the time it will take me to pick the field. I pray that the storm threatened by the blood-red sky at sunrise will wait until my field is clear. If Eva and Maisie and Emma will help, it might take us the better part of the day. Maybe by sunset we can have it all gathered and safe in the barn. If all goes well, tomorrow morning I will be in line at the cotton gin, along with the rest of the farmers of Falling Waters, Florida. I can just see myself silhouetted against my mountain of cotton.

They are wrong. All of them. They'd said I couldn't do it. But here it is, sparkling white-gold. Ready to be picked.

Papa. My heart hurts thinking about him. I want him to be proud of me. Instead, my shining field of cotton is the embodiment of his deepest fear. *You have shamed me before the entire town.* The day after our unfortunate encounter with Benjamin's barbed-wire fence, Papa disappeared down the road, his wagon rattling with the stove he's been trying to sell since May.

Papa's war is against me. I remember the first morning Papa realized I wanted to farm.

"Why do they do it?" Papa asked, followed by the creak of the wooden floor and the rustle of Mama's skirts. "*Danke,*" he said to Mama as she handed him his mug. Papa sipped his hot chocolate. "Why is it that these people have no respect for culture?"

I gritted my teeth. I knew why *they* had no respect for culture as defined by Papa.

For Papa, culture meant visiting art galleries, going to hear the symphony, reading Shakespeare. I, too, was a fan of culture. I loved art, and I loved hearing a symphony, the tinkling bells, the giant timpani, the heart-wrenchingly sonorous voice of the cello. And I loved hearing my Papa reading Shakespeare aloud long into the summer evenings.

But we were inhabiting a different space in time. We were no longer a train ride away from Hamburg, nor were there productions of Shakespeare in the town hall. We were in Falling Waters, Florida, where every day brought with it a struggle simply to survive. To this, my Papa seemed oblivious.

"I tell you, wife. One day, we will move to a real American city and introduce our girls. How else will they meet proper husbands?"

In the old country, hosting teas and visiting with calling cards was the way families connected and husbands were found. I wanted to shake my Papa. Why couldn't he see that farming was how you made your way in America? And why hadn't he noticed that when you farmed, you had no time for coming-out parties or nights filled with dancing? Girls met their husbands at church or school.

It hurt my heart to know that when Papa finished his chocolate, he would do what he did every morning: look out over his unplowed land—the mark of a gentleman—and, with a satisfied sigh, walk out to his shop to engage in what he considered a proper profession as an artisan.

As angry as he made me, my heart ached for my Papa. I was proud of his work. He made lovely woodstoves, cast in black iron and inlaid with blue and white porcelain story tiles depicting scenes from Shakespeare.

Papa's tragedy was that the Falling Waters housewives didn't have any use for such fancy cooking stoves. They cooked in the family fireplace. The few who could afford Papa's woodstoves asked politely, "Do you have one with scenes from the Bible?"

It wasn't that my Papa was against the Bible. How could he be? He was surrounded by Mama's favorite Bible verses cross-stitched on blankets, potholders, aprons, and even the dresser scarves she made

51

for the washbasin and water pitcher. Papa just loved Shakespeare more.

Falling Waters housewives yearned for well-made cast-iron skillets for baking their cornbread. When customers mentioned their need, Papa gave them pots and skillets for free and said, "Pah! These are nothing. The art is in the woodstove. One day, you will see."

Of course, they didn't. But they were happy for the free skillets.

"Will you sell a stove today, Papa?" little Eva asked, sipping her breakfast milk and taking a bite of Mama's delicious *schnecken*, the brown sugar and cinnamon still warm from the oven.

Papa squared his shoulders and held himself like the Prussian soldier he'd been. "In America, anything is possible."

What Papa meant was that in America it was possible to pretend like you were still in the old country.

He looked at me expectantly, waiting for agreement. "Yes, Papa," I said.

My soft, sweet mama smiled. She brushed a stray hair from his forehead, gazed at him with loving eyes, and took a sip of her chocolate.

Did only peasants farm—as Papa maintained—in Mama's Holland?

One day, I wanted to be the mistress of a large farm where I could grow enough food to feed my family and have enough money left over to buy sugar and new shoes at the general store. Then, Mama wouldn't have to sew for other people and hide it from Papa.

When Papa was safely out the back door and headed down the path to his workshop, I couldn't help myself. "Mama," I said, "will you ever tell Papa why it is you sew so much?"

Mama smiled, looked over at the hand-cranked Singer, and said, "Papa would be heartbroken if he believed his wife helped support his family. He is a proud man. And besides, I enjoy sewing!"

I tried to hide my frustration. The last thing Mama needed was a contrary child. And the truth was that Mama did love to sew. But I had seen her tired eyes in the wee hours of the morning as she hemmed yards and yards of voluminous black mourning dresses. "I don't believe I'll ever be as kind as you, Mama."

Mama's face flushed. Embarrassed by my compliment, she took my hand and squeezed it. "You are a good girl, my Annie Laura."

I didn't feel like such a good girl. I knew in my heart I was betraying Papa with my dream of a farm. I turned away from her so she couldn't see the truth in my eyes. Mama faced the front window and gazed at the sun tickling the massive pines with dew-drop sparkles.

Out of the corner of my eye, I watched Papa slip quietly in the back door and reach out to retrieve his forgotten chocolate. Sometimes Mama teased him for forgetting things, and he didn't like to be caught. I pretended not to see him.

Mama said, "Wouldn't it be fun to grow our own vegetable garden right out in the front yard?" She said it like she was suggesting a new game we might play. But the truth was this: Mama and I had both seen the cupboard. There wasn't much food left.

Mama glanced at me for confirmation, and I nodded but did not smile.

I snuck a glance in Papa's direction. He looked ready to explode. I took in a little breath of panic, and Mama saw Papa. His face had gone red, and his fists were clenched.

"Otto!" Mama said brightly, a little breathless. She moved quickly to him, but not in time to stop the tirade.

"So, while I'm not here, you talk about me."

"We aren't talking about you, Papa." I rushed to Mama's defense.

"This is not about you, Annie Laura. This is about your mama. Are you so greedy that you want more? Don't I make enough money to buy what we need?"

"Of course you do, Otto," Mama said, with the placating tone of a mother soothing a fussy baby.

"Haven't I told you over and again? Peasant work is beneath my girls. I'll not have you dirtying your hands in the soil."

Mama buried his blustering in a close hug and patted his back. "Of course you are right, Otto. I just thought it might entertain the girls for a bit."

"Oh. Well," he said, mollified by Mama's gentle pats, "it might be fun for little Eva. No harm in a child pretending to garden."

"She will have such fun!" Mama enjoined.

Papa pulled away and shook a finger at me. "But Annie Laura needs to spend her time on schoolwork."

I nodded my agreement, relieved that the storm had passed.

Falling Waters, 1898

If I'm lucky on this morning, these many years later, Papa will return when the field is cleared of cotton. We will have food in the pantry, maybe even new shoes for Eva, Maisie, and Emma. Papa will pretend he doesn't see the cleared field. He will pretend he doesn't know where the money comes from. And we will continue as we always have since coming to America: living off the land. I pray Mama's baby will wait for us to pick all the cotton before it makes its appearance.

I pull on my leather gloves, the best protection against prickly cotton barbs. They are costly but necessary. Hands ruined by barbs can't pick cotton.

"Annie?"

I look down into five-year-old Maisie's bright, brown, expectant eyes. She has pulled on a pair of Papa's leather gloves that reach up to her elbows.

"I'm ready to pick cotton," she says, and mashes a straw hat on her head.

I straighten her hat, stifle my giggle, and draw her close to me.

"Thank you, Maisie. I need you today."

She smiles, proud to be needed for grown-up work.

I know I will find Eva still buried in the feather bed, a blanket over her head. I tried waking her up an hour ago. Trying to get Eva out of bed to help is like trying to get our old rooster to throw a welcome party for a young cock.

"Papa said I could sleep in." Eva rolls over in the bed and covers her face with Mama's Wedding Ring quilt.

"Sure you can," I say. "And Maisie can have two new pairs of shoes."

"Papa said he will buy me whatever I want."

"Okay," I say and walk from the room.

Eva knows Papa lets the drink talk for him. She bangs around the room making as much noise as humanly possible so that I will register how little she wishes to help pick cotton.

I can't blame her. Picking cotton is grueling, painful work, and certainly not on the self-improvement list of a thirteen-year-old girl whose hobby is poring over fashion magazines at her best friend's house. For once I give thanks for those magazines. I know it is only the cut-out picture advertisement of beautiful, soft leather shoes that finally propels Eva out of bed.

Mama stands on the front porch, her apron high and tight across the new baby growing beneath it. She has on gloves and a hat as well.

"No, Mama. You are too close to birthing that baby. You need to stay right here and take care of Papa," I say, though I think Papa left early this morning, and what I'm really thinking is that I would like to kill Papa for giving Mama this baby, and he certainly doesn't deserve to have her taking care of him. Morris's warning reverberates in my ears. *Another baby will kill her.*

Mama laughs. "If I'm going to reap the benefits, I'm going to do the work. Your papa left before sunrise."

I'm relieved. The last thing I need on this day is Papa's judgmental eyes. I also know there will be no changing her mind. I can see it in the set of her square jaw—the same jaw I see when I look at myself in the mirror.

I smile uneasily. "Okay," I say, "but could you please promise me that if you get tired you will go inside and rest?"

Mama nods. She puts her hand to her belly and a whisper of pain flits across her face.

"What?" I ask.

"Nothing at all," she says. "Baby is just moving, ready to get out in the world, I suppose."

Mama loosens her collar and I know that she is not speaking truth.

"Mama, please stay in. I'm going to worry about you. It'll slow down my picking."

"Having a baby has never stopped me before, and I don't plan on letting it stop me today."

Mama gave birth to her last baby, Maisie, when she was thirty-five. Mama is now forty years old. Too old to be having a baby even without Morris's warning.

I should force her to stay inside. But how? Now, I wish I'd taken John Sebring and his wife Maggie up on their offer to help me get this crop in. I said no because it was important to me to prove I could do it without help. If they were here now, Mama might stay inside.

It's too late for regrets. I have a field of cotton to pick.

I stand, wipe the sweat from my face, place a hand on my aching back, and shield my eyes to look out over the field. Noon sun shines high and hot over the sparkling cotton, but the sky on the southern horizon is dark. The promised storm is brewing.

Little Maisie and Emma work like Trojans, heads down, hands flying. Eva and Mama pick together. I wish Mama would go inside, and I wish Eva would pick a little faster. We haven't even picked a third of the cotton. I won't be stopping to eat.

Sharp cotton stalks bite through my worn leather gloves. I ignore the sting. Soon, my hands will go numb and I won't feel anything. I pick through the thorny stalks and toss the soft cotton into the bag slung across my shoulder. It's nearly full. I walk to the end of the row and dump my load into the wagon bed. The cotton pile measures almost one bale. I'm determined there will be two.

I lean into the next row of picking.

"Annie!" Eva's voice is high pitched and panicked. This is not unusual. High drama is her best friend.

I sigh. She is probably asking to take a break, as if she hasn't already taken enough breaks.

"Annie!" This time it's Maisie. Her terror-filled tone forces me to stand up straight. I search the field for her voice.

When I catch sight of her, I throw down my bag of cotton and run.

In the far north corner of the cotton patch, Maisie, Emma, and Eva are huddled around an inert form on the ground.

Mama.

She is lying like the babe in her own womb, her hands clutching her stomach, her feet drawn up close. She has fallen right smack in the middle of a row of white cotton, the stalks reaching for heaven.

"Run," I say to Eva. "Get Morris."

To her credit, Eva doesn't hesitate. She throws down her nearly empty bag and runs.

I need to give Maisie and Emma something to do before they notice the bloody water pooled around Mama, leaching into her spilled bag of cotton. My heart pounds, and I taste fear.

"It's okay," I say with false brightness.

Maisie studies the blood. She looks at me with eyes older than her years.

"Mama will be fine," I say. "Morris is going to take care of her. Right now, would you run to the house and get me a dry towel and one dipped in water?"

Maisie nods and she and Emma run for the house.

"How long have you been having pains, Mama?" I ask.

She shudders, her jaw clenched, and I know she is having another pain.

When the pain releases her and she can breathe again, she looks up at me and smiles. It's a heartbreakingly sweet smile.

"Oh, not too long. I reckon this one is going to come faster than the rest of you did. I was hoping to get to sunset before things got bad, but…" She grits her teeth and groans.

I look around at the field of white. I feel a curl of anger rise in my chest. I squeeze my gloved hands until the leather creaks.

57

Mama relaxes and looks at me like she can read my mind. "Don't hold it against your Papa, Annie. I'm so sorry."

Hot tears rise and choke me, tears of rage coupled with fear.

I stroke her forehead and hold her hand through the next pain. She whimpers like a hurt puppy, and my tears drip on her face. She doesn't seem to feel them.

I lose track of time. Maybe a few minutes have passed. Maybe an hour. But when I look up, I see Morris loping across the field, his long legs casting shadows as he crosses the unpicked cotton like some mythical god.

Without a word, he picks Mama up in his strong arms and rushes her to the house. I follow. Morris lays Mama on her bed, methodically washing his hands, pouring water liberally from the washstand pitcher.

"Eva's gone to get Aunt Tabitha and Maggie," he says. "You're going to need some help."

"I don't need help," I say. "I can take care of what's mine, but Mama needs help." I feel scared and angry and defensive.

Morris's eyes are filled with compassion.

I feel my tears rise again, and I fight them.

"No, Annie, you need help. That pride of yours…"

I can't look at Morris. I look away and straighten the sheets on Mama's bed.

"No." Mama stops Morris from saying the words his lips are forming. "It's not Annie's fault. She begged me not to pick." Another pain grips her.

But it is my fault. All of it. I feel a sick spinning in my own head, and I'm back in Cairo, Georgia, those many years ago when Morris helped Mama give birth to Eva. The moments are nearly the same. Only this time, I'm responsible for my Mama's fragile life, not Miss Harriet's.

I look up into Morris's gentle blue eyes. "I'm sorry," I say.

He looks puzzled, maybe thinking he should have been the one apologizing to me. His words have been uncharacteristically harsh.

"No, I'm sorry," he says. "I shouldn't have said those things."

"That's not what I'm talking about." I look down at my hands as if they belong to someone else. They shake along with my entire body.

"You're exhausted," Morris says. "When was the last time you ate?"

But I know that it isn't food I need to cure my shaking—this trembling comes from my very soul. I recognize it. It's familiar. It's the guilt I've carried for nearly a decade, and, coupled with my fear that Mama is going to die, the pain is so deep, so wide, so strong that I can't force the words from my mouth. They fill my body, and to speak them will remove some vital part of me, the part of me that drives me forward, that nourishes my incessant need to keep doing, doing, doing.

Mama's eyes close as she rests between pains.

Morris takes me by the shoulders. "What is wrong?" he demands.

But I shake him away.

Tabitha comes in, and I'm thankful for the interruption She takes one look at Mama, picks up a cloth, wipes the perspiration from her forehead, and places the dry end in Mama's mouth.

"Bite down on this when the pain comes again," Tabitha instructs her.

Mama nods.

"It was my fault, all of it," I say through chattering teeth.

"What?" Morris asks.

"Your mama and daddy," I begin. The words inside of me are fighting to break free.

"What?" He has his hands on Mama's belly. He doesn't understand. He doesn't know that his own parents would be alive right now this minute if it weren't for me. Morris would have saved them both. "Go get some clean bedsheets," he says.

My vision blurs. I can no longer see Mama or Morris. All I can see is that day thirteen years ago.

Cairo, Georgia, 1885

I was young, too young to have witnessed Morris's real daddy being knocked out by Benjamin Blakely's slingshot. But there was more horror to come.

"Your mama needs sweet drinking water," Morris said as we knelt by Mama's side at our campsite, and I went, numbed by the blood. I'd never seen a birth.

And because I was numb, I forgot to tell Morris what Benjamin Blakely did to his birth daddy. I didn't tell him about the dull thud and the daddy he'd never known falling into his mama's arms. I didn't tell him about Miss Harriet asking me to go get Morris. I didn't tell him that instead of going to get him, I had found him tending my own mama, and then I'd forgotten what I'd been sent for.

But I remembered as soon as I got close to the stream and saw the flames licking the sky in the place where his mama's house should have been.

I remembered when I saw John Calvin and Benjamin Blakely hastening from the crackling flames, the old wood house like tinder wood, going up before anyone could stop it.

And then I heard it. The screams. The blood-curdling screams of Morris's mama.

I threw my water bucket down and ran to Miss Harriet's back stoop. I jerked at the door that had been nailed shut from the outside, pulling with strength I didn't know I had. The door made a cracking sound and opened. But when it did, the whoosh of air only set the flames higher.

Through a heat so intense I didn't believe anyone could survive it, I saw Miss Harriet on the floor with Morris's daddy Elijah in her arms, struggling to pull him across the floor to safety. She looked up at me like a doe startled by a hunter. And then the flames reached the roof, and it caved in right on top of her. I screamed.

In that moment, I knew I was responsible for this horror. I knew that if I had brought Morris here like his mama had asked, none of this would have happened. I backed away from the burning house, snatched up my bucket, and ran for the spring.

Someone laughed. I looked back, and there was Benjamin Blakely, perched up in the tree like a hoot owl. His daddy must have run off, but Benjamin stayed behind. He seemed mesmerized by the flames licking the sky, high as the pine trees. But there was something else in his face, too. Was it sadness? Fear?

Frightened for my own life, I prayed that he wouldn't see me, because if he did, just as surely as I breathed, he would push me into those very flames. I didn't see the pine root snaking across my path. I fell headlong, my bucket clattered against the root, and Benjamin Blakely gazed at me, unmoving, like an owl studying his prey.

"If you speak of this," he said, the crackling fire punctuating his words, "my daddy will kill your mama and your daddy and you, just like he done Mama and her lover." He spat when he said *lover*.

I backed away from Benjamin. *Get water get water get water*, the words a singsong in my head. But for what? The cabin was burning, and there was no hope of saving anyone.

And then I remembered Mama. I bolted to the spring, filled my bucket with water, and ran as hard as I could back to where Morris was getting ready to wash my new baby sister Eva.

I handed the water to Morris.

He thanked me kindly.

I avoided his eyes.

For years, I blocked the memory of that burning house until it faded, shoveled underneath years of hard work, of pressing forward, of making life come out of my fields.

And that was it, wasn't it? I, the person responsible for the deaths of two human beings, thought bringing life to the land would erase it all.

It hadn't.

If I had just brought Morris back like Miss Harriet asked me to, she would be alive, and Morris would know his real daddy.

Falling Waters, 1898

61

I look up into Morris's eyes, and know I will have to tell him the whole story. He will hate me for the rest of my born days, but I must.

"I'm fine," I say. "I'm going to head back to the fields so you and Tabitha can take care of Mama like you ought."

He must have heard something in my tone because he doesn't argue with me.

But I can't pull myself away from my mama.

Tabitha and I hold Mama's hands through the next pain.

After the pain subsides, Morris speaks tenderly to Mama. "Do you mind if I examine you?"

Mama nods, and Morris places gentle hands on her belly. He presses his lips together.

Something is wrong.

"Mrs. Brock, your baby needs to be turned. The head is up."

"I know," Mama says. "But it's too late to turn him." Mama longs for a baby boy to please Papa. Another pain grips her.

When the pain releases her, she says, "It will be fine, Morris. You will do a good job delivering him. Annie," she says looking up at me, "I am in safe hands. You go and pick your cotton. I'm so proud of you."

Before I can respond, another pain grips her. Morris's face goes white.

I shake my head, *no*, but Morris fixes me with a look that urges me to do as my mama said.

"Eva has gone to fetch Maggie up to the house. She'll be here soon," Morris says.

"Okay." I smile down at Mama. "When I see you next, the field will be picked, and I'll have a brand-new baby brother." But my words feel like wood coming out of my mouth. I don't believe the baby will live. The look on Morris's face has told me as much. "I love you, Mama," I say.

She smiles, grits her teeth and moans.

I walk straight to the cotton field and start picking. I pick to forget. I pick to make a bargain with myself that if I get the field picked, I'll talk to Morris, tell him everything. I pick for Mama and the new baby and make a bargain with God. *If I get this field picked before the storm moves in, can you let Mama live? If I get it under the barn before the storm comes in, do you think you could make the baby live, too?*

I don't wait for an answer. I pick a row clean before I notice Mary Scarlet Blakely in the row next to me, picking silently. I stand and look out and see John Sebring picking as well. When did Morris summon them? I don't deserve any of his kindness.

I pick cotton. I pick until my hands are numb, and the drone in my head shuts out my fear and blocks out all thoughts of Mama. I will Papa to come home. I want him to come home. I want him to see Mama's agony. I want him punished.

I don't look up again until sunset, when the wind swirls around us, rustling the oaks that mark the edge of my fields. When I finally look up, I see a handful of young men, picking. I can't tell who they are, but I am thankful for them. I suspect they are friends of John Sebring. He is the only person I know whose sweet, magnetic personality can bring friends in to pick cotton and think it's fun. I recognize them as town boys. Picking cotton is a lark, something they will tell stories about when they go off to college.

The clouds gather angrily along the skyline just before sunset, darkening the few patches of cotton that are left and blotting out any orange glory that might remain in the setting sun. We are nearly finished. The promised storm has held, though the wind whips the cotton like snow, blowing it out of the wagon.

We pick quickly and dump the remainder of our bags into the wagon.

I have done it.

But not alone.

"That's a fine wagonload, Annie Laura," one young man says.

They help push the wagon deep into the barn so the rain won't damage the bales. The top of the cotton mountain brushes beneath the barn door, scattering cotton-snow all around.

"First snowstorm of the winter," one of the young men says, unscrewing a silver flask. "Here's to a white Christmas," he adds, and the rest of them laugh. They pass around the whiskey.

"Thank you all," I say.

Mama's piercing scream shatters the good cheer. The young men scatter, and I run to the front door of our house, terrified of what I'll find inside.

Chapter 9

Aunt Tabitha holds a squirming newborn in her arms. She wipes its tiny face, neck, chest, and arms with a damp cotton towel, expertly wrapping the exposed body parts as soon as she has cleaned them. Soon, the baby is washed and wrapped in the clean white blanket Mama painstakingly embroidered night after night by candlelight, tiny white-on-white leaves, bows, and flowers for her new baby.

Tabitha hands the baby to Mama. Weakly, she hugs the baby to her chest, her arms quivering with the effort. She kisses its tiny forehead and says, "Laura Viola. Her name is Laura Viola," and then she hands her with shaking hands to Tabitha. Her face whitens, and she closes her eyes.

My heart hurts. She couldn't give Papa his baby boy, so she names another girl child after Papa's mother. Oh, Mama!

"Are there any more clean cloths?" Morris asks.

Mama opens her eyes and reaches for me. She speaks, but I have to place my ear against her mouth to hear. "The papers," she says. She watches my face eagerly.

"What papers, Mama?"

"The gold piece," she says.

And suddenly I know. She is speaking of the packet of papers left behind by Morris's papa those many years ago, the one I hid in my apron but never gave to him.

"Yes, Mama?"

"I translated them," she whispers. She closes her eyes again.

I feel such shame that I can barely look at her. "Don't worry, child," she says between labored breaths. "You are not to blame."

"Oh, Mama," I say, and take her cold hands in mine.

She shakes her head as if I'm not understanding properly. The effort seems to drain her.

"Give them to Morris," she says weakly, but her eyes are now open wide, and she waits for my answer.

"I will, Mama. I will give the papers to Morris." She settles her head against her pillow, closes her eyes and sighs.

When Morris comes back in, his arms are filled with Mama's old cleaning rags. They are bleached white. He takes one look at Mama's face and gently lifts her wrist for a pulse. He then works like a madman to staunch the blood that fills the bed.

But Morris can't stop the flow. Mama is bleeding out, her blood filling the bed that has both given life and taken it away.

"Bring your sisters in and say what you have to say," Morris says, his lips a tight, angry line. I know Papa to be the focus of that anger. Morris had warned him clearly that another baby would kill her.

Damn Papa to hell.

I call Maisie, Emma, and Eva in, clasp their hands, and we gather around Mama.

"Lay your hands on her," I say.

Small, cotton-pricked hands envelop Mama.

"You feel these hands, Mama?" I ask, but she doesn't answer, and I pray she can hear us. "We love you. And we thank you for being such a good mama, for loving us so hard, for making our childhood so happy, for being the kind of mama we hope one day we can be. Oh, Mama," I say, and can't find any more words.

"I love you, Mama," Maisie says and kisses Mama's cheek.

Lightning strikes with a loud jolt. Thunder roars, and rain pounds on the tin roof. It's so loud I can't hear what Eva is saying.

She puts her hand on Mama's forehead, "She's so hot," she says. "MAMA!" she screams. "WAKE UP!"

Tabitha shushes Eva and takes her out of the room. Eva wails and screams. She kicks her way out the front door and runs screaming into the storm.

Mama's forehead wrinkles, and I lean down to her. "I'll take care of us, Mama. I promise. You don't have anything to worry about. You go on and rest now. You taught me what to do, and I'm going to make you proud."

Mama's hands grip at the covers. Her chest pauses its gentle up and down movement.

And just like that, she is gone.

Maisie touches Mama's cheek and looks up at me with wide eyes. Emma is watching me too.

The rain quiets for a moment, and Maisie says, "Where did Mama go?"

I don't know how to answer. I want to lie. But I realize that my precocious baby sister understands that Mama is dead.

Morris rescues me. "Well, her body is here," Morris says, "but her spirit, it's gone to be with your Oma, and all those who went before her."

"Like a party?" Emma asks.

"Yes," Morris says, "something like that."

"Oh," Maisie says. "Can we go, too?"

"No, my sweet child," I answer, and gather them in my arms. "You two have to stay here and help me take care of our new baby."

Aunt Tabitha, tears streaming down her face, stands in the doorway.

"Would you like to hold her?" Aunt Tabitha asks.

Maisie nods, and Aunt Tabitha leads the girls out of the room of death into the kitchen where the woodstove burns warm and cheery. Eva is back inside and sits silent beside the stove, her wet hair dripping on the pocked-wood floor.

Aunt Tabitha pulls the rocking chair close to the stove, helps Maisie sit down, and hands her the baby. Emma nestles beside her. Tabitha keeps a close eye on Maisie's handling of the newborn. But she doesn't need to. Maisie's pudgy arms cradle the baby gently but securely.

"I hate that baby," Eva says, her brow furrowed, her fists clenched. "She killed Mama."

Maisie shakes her head. "She didn't kill Mama." She turns to the baby in her arms, leaning close to the little face. "I'm going to help take care of you, don't you worry. I'm going to tell you all about your mama who had to go away to a party when you got born."

Tabitha smiles and relaxes in the cane-backed chair she's pulled up beside Maisie.

Eva rolls her eyes.

A knock on the door heralds John Sebring and Maggie, rain drenched, their own baby nestled in Maggie's arms.

Morris speaks softly to them, and Maggie nods. "I'll nurse the baby," she says. "I've plenty of milk for them both."

We wash Mama, lay her out in a clean nightgown, and leave a candle burning beside her bed. Tomorrow morning, we will move her to the kitchen table for the viewing.

As for me, I only want to get past this day and this feeling.

But the pounding in my chest tells me that no matter how busy I stay, I'm going to carry the guilt of Mama's death to my grave. If I had gotten help with the cotton, Mama might have lived.

And there is more. I have to find Mama's translation of the letter and confess my sins to Morris. After telling him my truth, he will be glad to leave Falling Waters. He will head to Cairo and beyond, and never look back.

And there's this. How long will Papa stay gone? Surely he realized before he left that Mama was near her time. Will he stay away on purpose?

Chapter 10

Papa misses the rain that continues for three days and nights. He misses Mama's funeral and then her burial in the sticky orange clay. He misses our feeling of surprise that the world continues. How can people ride by on wagons on their way to town to buy sugar or calico for a new dress when our world has ended?

Mama was my center. She brought hope, laughter, and joy. Mama was always there for me, a silent witness to my work on the farm—the work that keeps us fed and clothed. And somehow, as long as Mama was here, as long as I knew there was someone out there who understood the enormity of what Papa insists on ignoring, someone who understood why I do what I do, someone who loved me for it, appreciated it, and gave me daily words of encouragement, I was okay with Papa's charade.

Papa still pretends to believe he's supporting our family. Will I allow him to maintain his "pride" without Mama?

I don't know.

On the fourth day after Mama's funeral, the sun casts its harsh glare on the empty cotton fields, reminding me of the cotton I must sell if my family is to survive.

So I shield my eyes, hitch our mule Dolly to the wagon filled with cotton, and try not to think about how proud Mama would be if she could see our fine, white gold. "Oh, Annie Laura," she would say. "You've done it again—you've warded off shame." I blink away my tears, pick loose cotton from my hair, and hear Mama's words whispered in the last moments of her precious life. "Tell Morris the truth."

It has to happen today. Mama was right.

Can a heart that is already broken break again?

Have I always enjoyed Morris's affection so much because I knew it was short lived? I haven't been able to read Mama's careful translation, her beautiful script a testimony to the love she had for setting things down on paper and making things right. I fear what the packet might reveal.

Today is the day I will talk to Morris. As soon as I've taken care of my business in town with this cotton, I'll find him. He will be faced with the truth about me. For me, it will be another death. Can I bear it? Perhaps I'm immune to the pain. Perhaps this cold nothingness I've felt in my soul since Mama died means I will never feel anything again.

I turn Dolly and my wagon full of cotton onto the dirt road leading to town where my crop will be ginned, baled, and sold. I look to my left, and a horse and rider hurtles towards me.

It's Morris.

I take a deep breath. I'm not ready for this. I need to sell my cotton first.

He pulls back on his reins and rides up alongside me.

Things always seem to happen in their own order. I don't get to choose.

"That's a pretty load." Morris's tone is uncharacteristically curt.

I nod. "Thank you," I croak, unsettled by his sudden appearance and our shared knowledge that this cotton was bought with my mama's blood. The main reason I wanted it sold before I faced Morris.

And now self-doubt cascades over me like a mighty gulf wave. Maybe Papa is right. Farming cost me Mama's life. What kind of person would choose a livelihood that threatens the lives of those they love most?

Morris squints at something in the distance, not noticing my nervousness. "I'm heading out today."

"Heading out where?" I ask, jolted out of my apprehension.

"You haven't heard, then?" He studies me, shame written across his face. "Of course, you haven't."

What have I missed?

"What I mean is that with your mama dying, the new baby to feed, and your papa having disappeared, I don't reckon you've had much time to go to the general store and hear the gossip." There's a bitter tone to Morris's words, one I've not heard before.

My insides curdle. His horse gives a little stutter step. Morris steadies his horse, dismounts, and tethers him to the side of my wagon.

"Mind if I come up?" he asks. His tone is both resigned and apologetic. I feel something shift in the air as surely as the moody Florida weather has shifted from hot to cold. Morris is pulling away from me, and I don't know why.

"Sure." I look away. If I don't see him pulling away, maybe it isn't happening.

Morris climbs up into the wagon and sits beside me. Stray cotton blows from my bales and dots his unshaven face. I brush it away. When my hand touches his face, he reaches up to take it.

"Mind if I hold your hand while I tell you this?"

I rest his hand over the folds of my apron. Holding his hand gives me such peace.

"Some bad stuff has happened over the last few days," he says. "I don't know why. I really don't." His big hand shakes, and I look up at his face. His eyes are wide as if he's seen a haint.

I've never seen Morris scared. He is my safe harbor.

"What is it?" I ask.

His brow creases, and he points to the document bag tied to his saddle horn.

Is the shine in his eyes a reflection of the sun, or are those tears?

"What is it, Morris?" I ask, hardly able to find my voice. A nameless pall blankets me. I reach for him, and he takes me in his arms. His entire body trembles like a century oak loosened from its base by a late summer hurricane. I know he will speak when he can.

"Is it Mary Scarlet?" I ask. "Is she ill?"

Morris stiffens. "It is Mary Scarlet," he says, spitting the words from his mouth like rancid meat.

I slide away, frightened by the intensity of his outburst. My skirt catches on the rough wood of the wagon bench. He loosens it for me.

"They've taken the land," he says, "and sent the sheriff to force me to leave with nothing but the clothes on my back and my horse. It seems that Mary Scarlet also mortgaged my office on Main Street, a building I paid for."

"What? How could that be? What about the medicinal herbs?"

Morris smacks the wagon seat, spooking Dolly. I pull back on the reins.

"I knew I should have investigated all of her secrecy. It was right under my nose. What an idiot I am."

And suddenly I remember something that happened nearly a year ago. I had been headed to town, the proud owner of the land of my dreams, but uncertain how best to care for it.

1897

The brown leaves of winter were nearly gone, and there was the hint of green in the deep woods and cypress swamps. Spring rains would come soon and fill the dry swamp with water and bring the trees back to life. It was hard to be anything but happy in the face of such cheerful radiance.

I was on a mission and needed advice on the best way to spend the extra money I had saved from the fall harvest. My goal was to make the land as productive as possible. I wanted to talk with Morris. If I could catch him between patients, I knew I wouldn't be disappointed. He always gave me the best advice.

I passed the general store. I needed to price the tools and ask around about another mule. But first I would check in on Morris. I wanted his advice. As my Oma said, *advice from a wise man is worth its weight in gold.*

Morris kept hours on Mondays and Wednesdays, but the rest of the week he traveled the countryside seeing to patients, or he journeyed to Cairo, Georgia, to work his land. Mary Scarlet kept his books and made appointments in his Main Street office.

The office was small with a reception area in the front and an exam room in the back. Mary Scarlet also used the office as a storefront for the small stock of fine sewing supplies she sold from a large cardboard box.

Morris joked that more people came into the office to buy thread than they did to get any doctoring. Mary Scarlet only carried the finest notions. She imported from England, and her needles didn't rust like the cheap ones sold by the tinkers and hawkers.

I opened the door with its tinkling bells. "Afternoon, Mary Scarlet," I said. The smell of ether and lye soap wafted over me as I entered.

Mary Scarlet didn't look up but sat at her desk studying a large piece of paper. It was unusual to see her read. Usually she was tallying figures, stitching a quilt, or neatening her notions.

"What are you so busy working on?" I asked, genuinely interested in what piece of writing could hold Mary Scarlet's attention such that she hadn't even noticed the tinkling bell that heralded my entrance.

She jumped like a schoolgirl caught passing notes during lessons. "You scared me," she said, half smiling when she saw it was me. She stuffed the paper in the desk drawer of the massive oak desk.

"I haven't seen you in a month of Sundays." Her voice sounded falsely bright. "What brings you to town?" She adjusted her bun nervously and folded her hands in front of her.

"I was looking for Morris," I said, trying not to look at the top desk drawer. Did Mary Scarlet have a secret admirer sending her letters?

Morris appeared from the exam room, wiping his hands on a clean white towel. His eyes brightened when he saw me, and he leaned forward and kissed my cheek.

Mary Scarlet's eyes widened, and her eyebrows rose nearly to her hairline. She seemed taken aback by this familiarity.

"Well, well," she said, "I had no idea."

My face burned, but Morris was nonplussed. "I always kiss a pretty lady," he said.

73

I laughed. I was far from a pretty lady, but it was nice to hear Morris proclaim me one.

He held out his arm and said, "Could I take you for a stroll around our lovely downtown area? I promise to avoid the hog and horse dung."

I laughed.

"That sounds wonderful, thank you." I took Morris's arm.

Strangely, Mary Scarlet breathed a relieved sigh, and before the *thank you* evaporated, she had her hand on the desk drawer.

Morris and I set off down the wooden sidewalk. When he glanced back into the window of his office, I followed his gaze. Mary Scarlet had pulled the paper from the top drawer and was studying it again. She chewed on her pencil like it was sweet Indian grass.

"I don't know what Mary Scarlet has going on," he said, "but she and the sheriff have become tight as bedbugs in a boarding house."

"The sheriff is married," I said, slightly horrified.

"I don't think it's anything like that," Morris said. "It seems to be more about shuffling papers and having hushed conversations. When I come in, they stop talking. It might be about Benjamin. He stays in trouble with the law."

"Why don't you ask her about it?"

"I did. She said I was jumping to conclusions. She said all she was doing was making friends with the sheriff so that the next time Benjamin got into trouble, she could help get him out of it."

"She would do anything for him." I felt sorry for her. The Bible verse *Don't throw your pearls before swine* came to mind.

"Yes, she would," Morris said. "I just hope Benjamin is the motive, and that she doesn't get mixed up in the sheriff's dirty land deals."

"I don't think Mary Scarlet would do that," I said. "But I do think that she would protect Benjamin from anything and everything, for good or for ill."

"I don't understand it." Morris said. "He has been nothing but cruel to her since the day Mama died."

His words jolted me, and I searched for something to say. "Well, she has gotten less attached to him in the last couple of years."

"True," Morris agreed, not noticing my discomfort at the mention of his mother's death. "But that's not what you're here in town for, is it?" he asked, placing my hand more securely on his arm. He helped me down the rickety steps leading to the street and led me to the church grounds where it was quiet and peaceful. We sat on a stone bench.

I forced my mind away from that horrible day when Miss Harriet and Elijah perished in the fire. "I need advice," I said.

Morris's eyes widened in surprise.

"I need advice about the farm," I said. "I saved some money from the fall harvest, and I'm wondering if I ought to spend it on a new mule and plow."

My thoughts tumbled out all in a rush, and Morris listened like my words were penny candy.

I blushed at his attentiveness. It was hard to think about the mule and the plow. Instead, I wanted to touch the dimple that punctuated Morris's smile, and maybe run my fingers through his curly brown hair. I noticed the chest hair peeking from above his shirt and wanted to loosen the buttons and rest my hands against his strong chest.

"Well," he said.

I jerked myself out of my imaginings and listened to what he was saying.

"I think you're right. A mule and plow would make it so that two people could work the land. If you hired two men, twice as much work could get done."

"I wasn't thinking to hire two men," I said, focusing on the hiring of men instead of the man in front of me. "Maybe just one boy."

"I think two. That would leave you free to take care of the cow, the chickens, and the hogs as well as the kitchen garden. It might also give you some free time for a medicinal herb garden!"

I couldn't even think in terms this big. Hiring two men? I had never considered such a thing. What a difference that would make.

"And something else," Morris said, "You might consider hiring a family to sharecrop."

I had feared that one day my family might be forced to sharecrop. It had never occurred to me that folks might sharecrop my land. But Morris was right. I had enough land to let. If someone else could see to the clearing of a good bit of the land and the planting, I could take care of the animals and expand the kitchen garden. That would solve some of the land-clearing problem, too. I could grow herbs, but they would need the shade of the century oaks and pines, and probably the protection of the swamps as well. Maybe I could grow a variety of medicines, and maybe the medicinal herbs at his disposal would convince Morris to sell his land in Cairo and stay here for good.

I needed Morris here.

In an impulsive move that I knew ran the risk of seeming forward, especially given what I had been thinking a few minutes ago, I took his hand, entwining my fingers in his. "Where do you suggest I find the hired help?"

He looked down at our hands, his large hand shadowing my smaller, calloused one, and he smiled such a sweet smile that I felt my insides quiver. I could almost forget about the farm, the land, and my dreams when I considered those kind, crinkly blue eyes.

"Let me see what I can do. You go find yourself a mule and plow."

The birds' morning song matched the cheery notes welling in my heart. Was this what love felt like?

1898

But that was then, and this is now, and now feels like a nightmare.

"Mary Scarlet knew," Morris says, "She bailed Benjamin out of jail so many times for his drinking and disorderly conduct that she

76

ran out of money. She had to mortgage most of the land for ready cash."

Cold fear grips me. Was that what my tenant farmer's wife was talking about when she said Benjamin would own my land? My brain swirls; the possibilities are frightening. If Morris has no land, he will have to move.

Morris jumps down from the wagon and paces back and forth, kicking the dusty clay that rises in swirls and eddies around his boots.

"But that's not all," he says. He squints up at me. "She mortgaged your land as well."

"What could possibly give her the ability to mortgage my land?" I ask, my mouth dry, my voice raspy.

"I'm not a lawyer, so I don't understand it," Morris says. He grasps the sides of the wagon. "What I do understand is that we need a lawyer to straighten it out. Surely if your father is alive, they can't touch your land."

"What do you mean? How could they ever touch land that I own?" I feel like the earth is collapsing beneath me. The only thing certain in my life is my land. I hold the deed. I know it's mine, all of it, bought and paid for. All I have to do is keep up with the taxes, and while that thought can be daunting, it is doable. This makes no sense.

Morris tries to explain. "The land your papa gave you is the land in question. Somehow, Benjamin was made your guardian."

I feel like I'm going to retch. "That's not possible," I say.

"As best I can figure it out, this is what happened. Since your father doesn't read English, the sheriff was within his rights to appoint you a guardian—at the sheriff's discretion—who could read it, just in case your father passed away. Until you are twenty-one, Benjamin is your guardian."

I want to laugh at the absurdity of it all. Surely this is a joke? Morris's white face tells me it isn't.

"How? And when? When did all of this happen?" I ask.

"Right under our very noses. Do you remember the papers Mary Scarlet had on her desk a while ago?"

"Yes."

"That was the beginning of the plan. As of now," Morris continues, "I don't have the cash to pay a lawyer. I've been evicted from my own home. So I'm going to have to head out, go to Cairo, run my practice from there until I can get ahead enough to pay the lawyer to straighten this mess out. Meanwhile, you are here, doing what you do. But watch Benjamin, Annie Laura. He wants to hurt you. I don't understand the vendetta he has against you and your family. That fire we thought your daddy started in a drunken fit last year? That wasn't your daddy. It was Benjamin. He told me so, gloating at his victory over me. He stood at the porch with the eviction notice in his hand and told me he would make you and your family pay."

"What are we paying for?" I ask, but as soon as I say it I can see young Benjamin, many years ago, urine running down his legs. I can remember Papa's horror and his words, "Never shame a man, Annie Laura. He will never forget."

And he hasn't.

"You need to get your cotton on in." Morris loosens the reins and mounts his horse. "We'll talk more about this later." He touches the brim of his hat and rides away.

I head to town. No one is going to take my land away. No one.

Chapter 11

After visiting the post office to pick up our mail, I lay Papa's letter in the now empty wagon—the only evidence of the bales of cotton are the leftover bits and pieces caught in the rough of the wood. Selling the cotton wasn't nearly as satisfying as I had hoped. Still, the price was good, better than I expected. I've made enough to buy my family everything they need and Eva her new shoes.

But I'm nervous. If my land is taken from me, then what? At W. T. Tiller's General Store I make my decision: I'll buy only what we can't live without and save the rest of the cotton profits for land. I purchase seeds, sugar, flour, calico, coffee, cocoa, and gloves. Eva's party shoes will have to wait.

I wish I'd saved Eva at least half a bale of cotton. She so wanted it for spinning yarn to crochet into a bedspread and tablecloth for her hope chest. I think she wanted that as much as she wanted the new shoes.

I can't think about it. All I can allow myself to think about is how to make sure my family survives. One day, I'll be able to give Eva what she dreams of, and not just what she needs. What's left is enough to buy five acres, just in case I have to start over again.

I read Papa's letter. He's on his way home. Anger turns my mouth bitter. My last memory of Mama is of her grasping the sheets, holding on to life.

The baby lives, but Mama is dead. The anger and bitterness I thought I'd gained control of blossoms.

It's a good thing Morris insists on being the first to greet Papa when he gets home. "Your papa expects more of you than you have the energy to give right now. Compassion, not anger," he says.

Compassion? I don't think so. I'm angry at Morris for even suggesting such a thing. And, yes, Papa expects the most from me—I'm the oldest child.

I expect even more from him. Maybe even perfection.

But he's my father. If not perfect, he's at least supposed to be really close. Isn't that the point of parents? To show you how you should behave? Aren't parents supposed to be living examples of the best of human nature? Models for their children?

The day Papa arrives, I stand at the back door. My stomach is filled with knots. It's Morris who will give Papa the news that Mama is gone. It's like experiencing her death all over again. I watch as Morris greets Papa where the dirt road ends and my land begins. Papa's face is joyful, as if he carries with him the good news that will save us all. His joy is heartbreaking. My throat closes and my eyes fill.

Across the kitchen garden and beneath the towering oak tree is the mound of clay topped with wilted gardenias and a roughly hewn cross.

I watch as Morris lays a hand on Papa's shoulder and speaks. I see Papa back away, shaking his head. Then he turns as if getting his bearings. He sights the gardenia mound and runs towards it, leaving Morris standing beside Papa's horse and brightly colored wagon, the garish red and yellow flowers a leering reminder of happier days.

I watch Papa prostrate himself on Mama's grave. I imagine his tears bringing those wilted gardenias back to life. Let him be, I think. Let him lie there and cry until his tears are gone.

But when I look up after wiping away my own tears, I have to push opened the screen door to make sure I see what I think I see. What is Papa doing?

Oh, dear God, no.

Red clay flies high in the air. Papa digs like a dog locked in a fenced-in yard. I snatch up my shawl and fly down the steps. Morris leaves the horse and wagon and runs to Papa. By the time we both get there, Papa has buried himself halfway in the yellow-orange clay. Morris wrestles him out of his hole, but Papa wiggles back. I grasp his arm, but he is as slippery as a baby at bath time. Each time we wrestle him out of the hole, he slithers back in.

I want to laugh and cry at the same time.

"No!" Papa bellows when Morris manhandles him away from the hole, the echo resounding and filling the newly clear-cut pasture. A month before, trees would have absorbed his sorrow; now there is nothing to soften his pain, just the burned-out hollows of smoldering stumps. The land smells of death.

"Let him go," I say, and Morris does.

I kneel down. His fury dissipates as quickly as it rose. Papa gazes into my eyes, pleading. For what? Compassion? Understanding? Grace?

My lips tighten. I grit my teeth until my cheek muscles twitch.

He recoils, as if I've slapped him.

"My Gott," he says, "*Ich habe dies getan.*"

"Yes, Papa," I say evenly. "You have done this."

He examines his hands, as if studying each particle of wet clay. He looks up at me again. And this time his face is filled with such sorrow and shame that I avert my eyes.

I hear the barely perceptible sound of wet clay being dribbled into a shallow hole, and, wordlessly, Papa begins the slow labor of refilling Mama's grave.

I watch until I can't, and then I reach to help Papa push the clay back into the hole. At the rate he is going, we will be here until tomorrow. Morris stops me before I can shove the viscous orange mess back into the grave.

"He has much he needs to say to her. Let him do this alone."

He's right. Morris takes my hand and leads me away. When I look back, Papa works slowly, deliberately, refilling the deep hole he has dug. He replaces the clay handful by handful, the lumps of clay trickling in like sand through an hourglass.

My heart hurts for my mama, my papa, for all of us. Morris is right. I have to be led by compassion, not anger. Papa is far from perfect. But he is doing the best he can. As are we all.

The next day, Morris prepares to leave, though I will him to stay. I can't bear the thought of his going back to Cairo now. But he has a plan, and a lawyer friend in Cairo.

"If I don't go now, I may never get the land back," Morris says. "I've talked to a few people. The Falling Waters sheriff has gone crazy, and there is no stopping him except through the proper legal channels. I know it is slow, agonizingly slow, but it is the only way this is going to work. You have to trust me. If I thought uncontrolled fury would change anything, I would stay right there. But it won't. Let me do this right, Annie Laura. Please."

I know he will be back with his lawyer as soon as he can make enough cash to pay one. I also know Cairo, while filled with the painful memories of his mama's death, is the one place Benjamin and Mary Scarlet will not follow, will not revisit for all the world.

Well, I think, stopping myself like Emilia in *Othello*, the two probably would do it for all the world. They have a greedy streak, there is no doubt, but even their greedy streak would tread cautiously in a place like Cairo.

And I let him go. Just like that. I don't tell him about the packet of papers safe in Mama's nightstand. I've not read them yet, though it was Mama's dying wish that I should give them to Morris. I don't tell him about the gold rock. I can't bear the thought of losing Morris forever.

Instead, I wave a feeble goodbye and turn to my fields. Time to start the spring planting.

As soon as I finish the day's planting, I'll read those papers. And then I'll decide when and if I will give them to Morris.

Working the soil refreshes me, as it always does. When I finish what I can for the day, I search for Papa. He needs to know why Morris left.

I hope to find him holding the baby, but I don't. He hasn't acknowledged her, as if she is the one responsible for Mama's death. Instead, I find Papa shining up the tile running along the side of a stove he has just completed, and I ask him about the transaction with the sheriff.

"We own the land," Papa says. "I gave it to you…it is your land." He says these words slowly as if explaining to a five-year-old.

"Yes, Papa, I know that," I say, "but remember what you said those many years ago about shaming a man?"

"No, but perhaps you could remind me?"

"Remember when you wanted to talk with Benjamin about throwing the rocks at me?"

Anger turns Papa's face scarlet. "Yes," he says. "Yes. It's coming back to me."

Chapter 12

Falling Waters, 1888

I had been on my way to school after yet another tense moment with Papa over my wanting a farm. This was before I made friends with Maggie and John Sebring.

"Did you know, Bertha," Papa said to Mama, "I've discovered that to get ahead in America, you have to be smart. You must read smart, speak smart, and look smart. Otherwise, how will Annie Laura catch one of our good German boys who has come to America to make his fortune? See?" He snatched up one of my notebooks. I made a panicked grab for it, but Papa held it high, teasing me with it.

My heart beat hard. If Papa were to look inside...

"Look at our girl. She has all her books ready, even her hand-made English dictionary. She is going to learn to be an accomplished lady, and when we present her in society, men will swoon over her." He beamed proudly and lowered the notebook.

"I must go," I said and took the book from his hand. Papa was so wrong.

I grabbed my satchel and rushed out the door. "Bye!" I said before saying something I would immediately regret. I hurried away in mortal fear that Papa would wish to look inside my homemade book.

I clutched it to my chest. It was a dictionary, true enough. It had English words in it: Hoe. Corn. Cotton. Sweet Potatoes. Mule. Plow. Beside each word I'd drawn a careful picture, and beside the picture I wrote in German everything I overheard or learned from every farmer I met in Falling Waters.

Papa would be furious if he ever saw it. And even more furious if he discovered that I was friendly with those he deemed "peasants." It would anger him that they liked me—even though I was German and a foreigner—because I was interested in everything they did.

They were more flattered than irritated when I pestered them for information about the best way to grow crops.

It was a relief to be at the edge of our property and on the dirt road leading to school. I inhaled the sweet morning air, a balm to my soul, and ran towards school as quickly as I could.

To be honest, there was another reason I was eager to get away from home and hurry to school. Morris Blakely was standing in as our substitute teacher for a few weeks. Papa said it was probably because people couldn't afford a doctor, and the town council had voted in a teacher's salary. Morris was the only man in town who had been to college.

Thinking about Morris made me feel ashamed. I'd stopped thinking about Miss Harriet and Elijah when we settled down here in Falling Waters. The only one who knew my secret was Benjamin Blakely. But less than a year ago, the Blakelys had come right here to Falling Waters and bought the land beside us. The land was sold in thirty-acre plats. We had one plat. The Blakelys had nearly a hundred acres of rich farmland. I yearned for such a farm.

I hadn't found the courage to tell Morris about his real daddy. I was resigned to live with the guilt of knowing that if only I had remembered to tell Morris about what was going on at his mama's house the day Eva was born, Miss Harriet might be alive today. And Morris might have his real daddy.

Morris would hate me if he ever found out, and though I knew it was selfish, I didn't want Morris Blakely to hate me. My face felt hot thinking about him. He was taller than all of his students by a full head. When the boys went outside to play baseball at recess, though he was the teacher, Morris Blakely was the first one out. He liked to pitch. He could throw twenty straight pitches that only John Sebring Corley could see, and every now and again he could even hit one. Morris Blakely could also hit the ball clear to the church steeple, no matter who was pitching.

I wasn't the only girl in school who blushed when Morris called on me to read. The girl who sat next to me could barely get past the first sentence, he made her so nervous.

A sound snatched my thoughts away from Morris Blakely. Something was whining most piteously, then yelping in earsplitting terror. I hitched up my skirts and ran towards the sound.

What I saw stopped me cold. A puppy struggled high in a magnolia tree. His legs were tied to a branch, and he hung upside down. How in the world had he gotten there? What demon had so cruelly tied him up?

It only took me a moment to see the perpetrator.

Benjamin Blakely stood a few feet away, watching the pitiful struggle and laughing. Rage grew inside of me. Mary Scarlet stood beside him. To her credit, she wasn't enjoying the show half so much as Benjamin. But neither was she making any move to save the puppy.

"Take him down, Benjy," she said. "He's hurting. It's not funny anymore."

As if such a thing could ever be funny. I made my way through the brush, aiming to climb the tree and save the puppy. They hadn't seen me yet. Brambles tangled my skirt. I shook it free and ducked behind the palmettos.

"Ok," Benjamin said. "I'll do just what you want."

I didn't like the tone of his voice, and the grin on his face was sickening. Quick as a rabbit, he pulled a slingshot out of his back pocket and began loading it with small stones.

Before I could think, I tackled Benjamin, yanked the slingshot from his hands, and threw it as far as I could. I sprinted to the magnolia with its abundance of low-lying branches and climbed up quickly. My breath came quick and heavy, and I kept my eye on the puppy. I expected Benjamin to grab hold of my skirt and pull me down, but he was too busy searching for his slingshot.

"You'll pay for this, Annie Laura Brock," he snarled. I knew his threat to be a promise that I would probably endure for the rest of my life, but I didn't care. Rage propelled me up the tree quick as a squirrel. I reached the branch just below where the puppy hung suspended.

If I untied the puppy, he would fall and probably die on the ground far below. I stood on the branch beneath him and lifted my skirt, spreading it to form a safety net. I reached up, holding my skirt, and held on tight to the branch, and with my free hand I reached for the puppy.

My foot slipped, and I fell hard on the branch. The branch swayed but didn't break. I stood again, this time leaning back against the trunk for balance. I spread my skirt beneath the puppy once again, balanced myself, the sweat now trickling into my eyes. I blinked hard and reached for the ties. The puppy wriggled still more, making it hard to get my fingers around the knots.

The knots were secure, and it was slow going. I talked to the puppy, soft and low. If only I could hold him up—I needed another hand.

When I was finally able to untie the last knot, freeing the puppy from the cruel bondage, he landed in my skirt with a pitiful, high-pitched, rapid-fire barking. It was more squeal than bark. His tiny legs were probably broken from his struggle trying to loosen himself. Thank the lord he had not been able to get loose. It was a long way down to the ground. He would have freed himself to his death.

I looked down to see what was happening on the ground. I had to protect the puppy and get past Benjamin. I would take the puppy home for Mama to tend. I would be late for school, but I didn't care. Benjamin was still rooting around in the palmetto bushes and brambles looking for his slingshot.

I looked to Mary Scarlet for help. She wanted to save the puppy, too.

But when she saw me looking at her, I was sorely disappointed. Instead of helping me, she turned on me quick as lightning. "That's our property," she screamed. "You keep your hands off our property."

I was so surprised I nearly dropped the puppy out of my skirt. Hadn't I just heard Mary Scarlet plead for Benjamin to free the puppy? Why did she turn on me? I still had several branches to go before I made it to the ground.

Benjamin found his slingshot. I slid down the trunk. Mary Scarlet gathered stones.

I was an easy target.

I pulled the puppy close and wrapped him as tight as I could in my wool skirt. When the first stone hit the tree trunk just above my head, I knew Benjamin Blakely was aiming for me. He meant to kill me. I scooted to the far side of the trunk and maneuvered my way slowly down. The stones hit the trunk, *thunk, thunk, thunk.*

Benjamin moved to my side of the tree. I moved to the other side again, nearly dropping the puppy. Benjamin had run out of stones. I tied my skirt around the puppy more securely. Sweat dripped down my brow, though it was a cool day.

I could hear Mary Scarlet running across the pine straw-laden woods, scrambling for more stones.

"Hurry up, stupid," Benjamin hissed. "She's almost down. What are you, blind?" he jeered. "Can't see that pile of rocks over there?" He pointed and spat in the direction of a pile of wicked-looking stones glittering in the morning sun.

I made it to the bottom branch. I was almost to the ground. The puppy was safe, and I was alive.

And then something thunked against my head.

When I came to, the sun was glaring hot.

"Come on, now," a gentle voice said. "Wake up, there's a girl."

I jolted awake. Something burned my nose. Smelling salts. I sat up, and the sharp pain in my head laid me right back down.

"Where is the puppy?"

"Ahh, lie there for a minute, I'll be right back." I recognized the voice as Tabitha Blakely's. She was Morris's stepsister, although he called her his Aunt Tabitha, and she had helped Mama deliver Eva.

The magnolia tree rose above me like a giant soldier. I winced at the sun's brightness and shut my eyes against it. Why was Tabitha here? Where was the puppy?

I touched my face where the pain was. It was wet and sticky. Blood leaked from my forehead and trickled down my cheek. A moment later, gentle fingers probed my face. I heard the swish of water, and Tabitha lay a cool, damp cloth to my wound.

"Hold on for just a little bit longer," Tabitha said, "and it will stop hurting so badly."

There was something on the cloth besides water. It pulled the pain away as surely as a towel wicking water from a washed floor.

"Can you stand?"

"I think so. Can you help me find the puppy? I think he must have gotten away."

"I'll look for the puppy. Let's get you home."

Tabitha helped me up, her hands surprisingly strong for someone so small. She wrapped her arms around my waist and helped me walk. My ankle hurt, too. I couldn't put any weight on it, and I leaned hard on her skinny shoulders, grateful for her help. I had to trust that she would find my puppy.

"I'm sorry," I said, afraid I'd hurt her.

"It's fine," she said. "My shoulders are strong." She said it in a way that seemed to mean something deeper, but I didn't know what. We made our way to my house.

Mama came running down the lane towards us, skirts flying. She ran so hard, her hair jolted loose from its hairpins.

I started crying as soon as she held me. Just melted like candle wax in the warmth of her embrace.

She settled me inside the house on the settee, pushed a pillow under my head, and gazed down on my forehead.

"What happened?" Mama looked up at Tabitha for an answer, but Tabitha seemed unable to speak.

Did Mama recognize her? Did she remember her as the woman who helped save her life at the birthing? Three years wasn't such a long time, but I wasn't sure Mama had been awake for much of the time Tabitha tended her.

Mama pumped water into a bucket, carried it into the house, and set it down beside me.

"Would you mind bringing me those warm cloths drying on the stove?"

Tabitha darted to the stove. She seemed happy to have something useful to do.

Mama lifted the cloth from my forehead. Her delicate hands looked thinner than I remembered. I was so close to her that I could see how her bones protruded at her neckline in a way I'd never noticed before.

Tabitha stepped across the creaky wood floor.

"Mein Gott," Mama said, her voice ragged. "What happened to her?"

Mama never said such things, and her words scared me. She pulled the cloth gently from my head, held it up in the sunlight, saw me looking, and snatched it away. But I saw the thick red blood. I must have fallen harder than I remembered. All I could remember was wrapping the puppy up and climbing down the tree.

"What happened to the puppy?"

Aunt Tabitha, who had shrunk into a corner of the room, looked away. "What puppy?"

My anger made me rise too soon, and my head pounded. Suddenly Tabitha didn't seem so kind. Tears coursed down my face. The puppy. Someone had to find him or he would die.

"I found Annie Laura on the road," Tabitha said to Mama. This was a lie. I remembered waking up underneath a magnolia tree yards away from the road.

"I think a horse must have ridden by, kicking up loose stones, and one must have hit her in the head. I don't know," the woman said.

Mama's brow furrowed. Tabitha spoke a rapid southern dialect, and Mama hadn't completely understood what she said.

"No, ma'am, that is not what happened at all." It hurt my head to talk, but white-hot anger made my words flow freely.

Mama's face clouded over, and I could hear what was coming as soon as Tabitha left. *Don't be rude to your elders. Respect them. They have lived more years than you and have reasons for what they say and do.*

Tabitha set her jaw and turned away. She was lying. Why?

Now my head pounded so fiercely that I couldn't see. I took a deep breath. I spoke slowly, quietly. The sound of even my softest voice hurt my head. But I remembered everything clearly now, and I was going to tell Mama the truth. "I was walking to school, and I heard a puppy yelping. When I ran to the tree, Benjamin Blakely had tied the puppy up in the tree by its legs and was laughing as it struggled to get down." I paused. I had to finish. Mama deserved to know the truth. I took a breath and steeled myself against the pain pounding in my head.

"I climbed the tree and got the poor puppy down, and on my way down, Benjamin used his slingshot to hit me in the head with a stone. I must have passed out because that's all I remember until this nice lady bathed my wound and helped me home."

At least Tabitha had the decency to look ashamed.

Mama waited for her response.

"Ah, yes, it is as she says," Tabitha said. This time, she too spoke slowly. "I am so sorry." She bowed her head in shame.

"These children, Benjamin and Mary Scarlet," Mama said, enunciating each syllable, her English careful and slow, "they are yours?"

"I raised them, but they are my father's children," Tabitha said, looking out the window. "Their mama, she died."

My face burned. Tabitha looked at me. Did she know my secret? Did she know that I was responsible for the death of Harriet Blakely? My fear threatened to swallow me.

"Their mama was your sister?" Mama's voice was gentle, full of compassion.

"No, not my sister." Tabitha stiffened. "My stepmother, though I was older than she. "Here," she said, her motions now quick, as if she couldn't leave our house quickly enough, "you take this liniment, and use it on her head twice a day. It will take all that swelling down."

91

Tabitha's concern seemed genuine. So maybe she didn't know about my part in the death of her stepmother. Still, I couldn't look at her.

"And you stay away from Mary Scarlet and Benjamin." Tabitha's words, spoken quickly, were directed at me. "Morris is good. But those two, they are nothing but trouble." She touched my face with a work-worn but gentle hand. And it was then that I noticed the bruise on her cheek and another on her arm. Someone had gripped her so tightly that they'd left the mark of their hand.

"Yes, ma'am," I said and tried not to stare at the bruises. "Why are they so mean?" I asked. I couldn't help myself.

Mama always told me I was too direct, but I believe if you want the truth, the only way to get it is to be direct. And I wanted to know how someone as nice as Miss Harriet could have produced a son as mean as Benjamin.

"It is a long story," Tabitha said. "Maybe one day I can tell you." She smiled and turned to Mama. "I'm sorry your little girl was hurt," she said.

"Won't you stay for some cookies?" Mama offered, her kindness suffusing the blue in her eyes until they looked like soft cornflowers on a snowy hill.

"No, ma'am, but thank you. Maybe another day." She turned to me. "I'll find your puppy."

Tabitha walked out the door and slowly down the lane.

"She is carrying someone else's burden," Mama said, watching her walk away. "I hope she lets it go before it kills her."

"Yes," I said, lonely with my secret but relieved that Tabitha would look for the poor puppy. I needed to tell someone what I knew, what I had done. Mama would be the best person to tell, but I was afraid she would think it was her own fault for having a baby that very day and keeping Morris away from his parents. It was Mama's life Morris had saved while his own parents were dying. I could never, ever let Mama know.

I slept for an entire day and night. I was jolted awake by three-year-old Eva's voice.

"Papa!" Eva shouted and beckoned me to the window. Her silky black hair bounced up and down. "He's home. Look, Annie Laura, look!"

Papa came whistling down the lane leading his horse and wagon. We all three gathered at the window, Mama, Eva, and me. We peered out, squinting our eyes in the bright afternoon sunlight. Was the wagon empty? Had Papa sold a stove?

"It is empty!" Mama cried, jubilant. I hugged her and saw a tear sparkling in her eye. I took her hand, and we followed Eva outside to greet Papa.

"Papa," Eva said, "you sold your oven!"

"Either that," Papa said, swooping Eva up into his arms, "or the bandits stole it!"

Eva giggled. "No, Papa," she said.

"Papa, bandits can't steal a stove, especially not your stoves. Your stoves are too heavy and much too tall," I said.

"Not even a very tall bandit?" Papa said, teasing.

"No, Papa," Eva said quite seriously.

"It would take three bandits to steal your stoves," I said.

"What about my workshop and my tools?" Papa teased. "How many bandits would it take to steal all of that?" Papa pointed to his little workshop behind the house where he made his magnificent woodstoves.

We all laughed except for Mama, who worried. "Don't talk of such, Otto," she said. "Don't invite evil in."

Papa put little Eva down gently and walked to Mama, enveloping her in his arms. "Ach, my little beauty," he said, touching her hair so gently, so intimately, that I felt embarrassed. "I would never let such a thing happen. And besides," he said, moving to the wagon, "I've found us a guard dog!" He lifted a tiny bundle from the wagon bed and placed it gently on the ground. The puppy wiggled with delight and then sat down on its haunches.

"I think he is injured," Papa said. "I found him on the side of the road, and I was afraid he would starve or some wild creature would eat him for lunch. He doesn't walk well."

I ran to him, took the puppy from his arms, and hugged him. "Oh, Papa," I said. "Thank you, thank you!" We would need to doctor him, but he was safe and warm here with us.

Papa looked down at me. "I thought of you when I found him, my girl. I know what a gift you have with God's creatures, and I thought if anyone can heal this puppy, my Annie Laura can." Papa leaned down to kiss my forehead, but I ducked before he could kiss the throbbing wound.

"What is this?" Papa said. "Too big to kiss your papa?" and he laughed a jolly laugh.

"No, Papa, she's hurt," little Eva said. "Look!" She pointed to the bandage on my forehead that I'd tried to hide with my hair.

"My girl," Papa said, "what happened?"

"A mean boy shot her with a slingshot like David shot Goliath," Eva said.

Papa's merry demeanor turned suddenly angry. "Who would do such a thing? Who would shoot a stone at my little girl?" And he patted his vest pocket where he kept his pistol.

"I brought down Napoleon's brother," Papa said. "I will kill anyone who has dared harm my little girl. Where is he? Where is the *ratte*?" Papa stormed down the lane, dropping the reins over the horse's patient head. "Where is he?" he raged. "Where?"

"Papa!" I said.

Mama hurried after him.

"Otto," she said. "Sweetheart." She grabbed him by his coattails and swung him around to face her. "Stop this nonsense," she said soothingly. "We must tell you the story, and then we will decide rationally what ought to be done."

"I know what ought to be done," he said. "Whoever did this ought to be beat within an inch of his life, and as soon as I find out who he is, I will do exactly that."

I knew in my heart that Papa would find Benjamin Blakely. He would track him down, and when he was finished with him, Benjamin Blakely would be my mortal enemy. For a lifetime. I shivered.

Chapter 13

Falling Waters, 1888

"I will take you to school today," Papa said early the next morning before the sun was up. He drank a steaming cup of Mama's cocoa. The smell of chocolate filled the house. "And I will pick you up as well," he added, swiping his hair out of his eyes and shoving it securely into the jaunty cap he placed on his head.

I didn't want to spoil Papa's good mood, but I didn't want him taking me to school or picking me up in the afternoon. I wanted to be the same as the other kids at school. Papa insisted on speaking German to me, even in front of other people. It embarrassed me, but Papa said, "Be proud of your heritage. Never forget your motherland." I was too young to remember Germany. *America* was my motherland. If he saw my face register anything but pride, he would fly into a rage.

Mama said Papa was like a schoolboy who had not yet learned to control his moods. She was right. He could go from cheerful exuberance to frightening anger in a matter of minutes. When he grew moody, Mama fed him. If that didn't work, she encouraged him to go for a walk.

"Walking in nature. Breathing in God's clean air. That is what makes life worth living," Papa said. But the same nature that gave him joy also irritated him. The mosquitoes, for one thing. "If harnessed," Papa said, "these creatures could pull a wagon loaded with two stoves." Sometimes Papa came home from his walk refreshed. Sometimes he came home angrier than when he left. That meant he had hidden the silver flask in his coat pocket.

"Papa," I said, "thank you, but my ankle is good as new. See?" I walked a fast, painful circle around the kitchen table with a smile on my face to prove it. "Besides," I said, talking fast now that I had his attention, "you sold a stove yesterday. Have you an idea what your next one might look like?" I hoped to get his mind off me and on his work. Papa was in heaven crafting his elegant cast-iron wood-stoves. He whistled as he worked, and sometimes he became so lost in his creations that he forgot to eat. Pouring the bubbling hot iron into the molds, fitting the pieces together, and affixing the lovely tiles he had imported from Germany made Papa very happy.

"Ten years old and already telling your papa what to do. Do you hear that, Mama? She already knows how to keep the man of the house busy!" He pulled me close and hugged me. He smelled like Papa—shaving soap and fresh tobacco. I breathed him in and pulled away.

"What is it, my little slave driver? Are you so worried about your papa? I'll have you know, I have a new stove made and ready to go," he said. "I can afford to take a rest." He patted his waistcoat pocket to indicate that it was full of money from yesterday's sale.

I ate my breakfast as slowly as possible. I savored my cocoa. I cut my bread into careful squares and slathered it with the fresh butter Mama churned the day before. And the best thing about it? The milk came from the cow I had raised and hidden from Papa. He didn't know about the cowshed Mama and I had built while he traveled far and wide trying to sell his stoves. We'd built it in the very back of our property where he never ventured. I touched the lovely wooden butter mold, carved with flowers and entwining leaves. I glanced over at Papa, hoping he would forget his offer of taking me to school. The butter was warm and smooth on my tongue. If Papa found out about my cow, he would stomp angrily into the house for an endless argument with Mama. I could hear the argument as if it were real and not in my imagination. "But Otto," Mama would say, "fresh milk is necessary for Eva and Annie Laura to grow strong."

"Pah," Papa would say. "Peasant chores. The next thing you know, she'll be making cheese."

And he would be right. I couldn't wait to learn how to make cheese. Papa overlooked the pertinent fact that he'd yet to make enough money to hire any servants.

I finished my breakfast, washed the dishes, and walked back to the bedroom I shared with Eva. I looked back at Papa still sitting at the table reading yesterday's newspaper. He made no signs of going into the backyard to work on a new stove.

I reached for the silver brush Oma had given me when I was a little girl. I ran my fingers over the cool silver engravings. The dresser set was a miniature version of my mother's own set. The tray was porcelain, its dainty roses pink and moss green. In the tray lay my silver-edged comb and a tiny rosebud-painted dish, just the right size for catching stray hairs. I saved the hair for friendship lockets. I was hoping for a new friend soon.

I peeked through the cracked door, hoping Papa had found something else to do. But he hadn't. He pulled on his officer's frock coat, still lovely though a little tattered, and searched for his leather gloves. It was cool outside, but not cold enough for the coat. Papa wore it even if it was warm outside. "It makes me look respectable," he said, but I didn't think so. How was a Prussian military officer's frock coat going to help him look respectable in America?

I took my time brushing my hair. It slipped through my brush easily. I wished for curls. Curls always made your hair look thicker, and I longed for thick hair like Mama's. I placed the silver brush back on the tray and arranged all the pieces of my dresser set in a neat line. I had thought of another way of diverting Papa's attention away from taking me to school.

"Papa, have you forgotten what day this is?" I asked from the bedroom. This might do the trick. "You must stay home to greet Black Peter to make sure he has toys for Eva."

"And you, my Annie Laura," he said. "*You* are not too old for Black Peter!" Papa said.

His words brought me out of the bedroom, and I smiled, partially relieved at least. A small part of me had suggested that Papa stay home because I was worried I might be too old for St. Nicholas and his helper, Black Peter, to bring me treats.

"Black Peter!" Eva said. "He comes today, Papa!" and she danced a little circle on the rag rug. "And, St. Nicholas, too? Where will they stay? Will they live in the courthouse until Christmas?"

"Sit down, now," Mama said when Eva nearly knocked the iron kettle of cocoa from her hands. Mama repositioned her kettle pad and righted the kettle, filling Papa's colorful blue, green, and tan porcelain stein. The stein was made for beer, but Papa liked it filled with hot cocoa. He took it with him when he made trips in the cart. He liked Mama's cocoa hot or cold.

"Black Peter will not be here until late this afternoon, just before sunset. I'll get home from school, and we'll make decorations and bake treats," I said.

Eva looked out the window. "But it's dark now," she said. "Is it sunset?"

"No, my little pet, it is just before sunrise. You have a whole day to help your mama with her chores," Papa said.

"Are there chores I can help with today, Mama?" Eva asked.

She wanted as many good points as she could earn. Then, Black Peter would be sure to leave presents for her. I knew Eva was not entirely convinced she was deserving of gifts. She was an impulsive child. Like Papa, she was quick to speak, quick to act. It got her into a world of trouble with our quiet, careful mama.

"Black Peter will bring you plenty of gifts. You are a good girl," Mama said.

"I am?" Eva asked.

"Of course you are," I said. Papa sat drumming his fingers on the intricately carved mahogany dining table. Eva played with her doll on the burgundy settee. She had draped a quilt over Papa's reading chair and stool and was pretending it was her house. Papa stood and washed his hands in the rose-painted porcelain washbowl, and dried his hands on Mama's colorfully embroidered towel. He rested his elbow on the top of Mama's pie safe and surveyed all of us.

"I am a happy man," he said. "I have work I love, beautiful girls, a lovely wife. What more could I ask for?"

"Nothing more, Papa," I answered. But I could think of many things. For Papa to act more American. For Papa not to take me to school today. And most importantly, for us to have land. Papa did not believe in buying land. He only wanted enough room for a house and his workshop, wagon, and horse. Affordable land parcels were sold in thirty-acre plats. We needed another plat.

I watched Papa, hoping against hope that he would suddenly remember something he had to do. But he was not to be deterred from his mission. He would see me safely to school. "Come along, little one," he said.

I hugged Eva goodbye while Papa hitched the horse to the colorful wagon. Papa had hand-lettered the words "Brock Woodstoves" on the side and then painted a perfect model of one of his stoves, with birds and leaves wrapping around the edges of the wagon. When I was a little girl, I thought it was lovelier than any paintings I had seen in stuffy New York galleries. Mama colored it all in. She was good with a paintbrush, and now the wagon was bright red with blue, green, and yellow birds, leaves and curlicues, all outlined in black. When I was little, I got cheerful just looking on it, and believed the brightly painted wagon helped Papa sell his woodstoves.

Now, the wagon was an embarrassment.

It had puzzled Papa when he first came to Florida that most people used their fireplaces for cooking, and the cooking fireplaces were in the central room in the house. Most people were too poor to build a separate kitchen. As a result, their houses were blisteringly hot in the summer. He saw their discomfort in the summer heat as an opportunity. If he could get them to understand how much cooler a woodstove was, since the fire was blazing in an enclosed space rather than heating up the entire room, he could help them cook better meals and keep cool in the summer.

At first, Papa went house to house with his stove set up in the red wagon and demonstrated cooking on the stove. He showed how, all at the same time, you could cook a ham and buttered corn on the stovetop, a cake in the oven, and even have bread rising in the warming oven.

The warming oven was the feature that sold Papa's stoves. With the warming oven, women didn't have to wait all day for their bread to rise. It cut rising time in half. Once Papa introduced them to this wonderful invention, those who could afford it bought a stove.

Husbands caught on to building an outside kitchen to house the new stove. Because everyone stayed cooler in the summer, Papa's stoves were a hit at first. Most people told their friends about them and he sold even more. But soon, everyone who could afford a stove had bought one, and Papa had no one else to sell to. He traveled all over the area, in ever-widening circles. But the results were no good.

The closer we came to the school, the taller Papa sat. His face put me in mind of the picture sitting on our fireplace mantle of Papa as a Prussian soldier. That face would scare a dragon.

Papa scanned the road to the left and right. I knew he was on the lookout for the person who had hurt me. I prayed they were already in school. I had tarried as long as possible. But I hadn't tarried long enough.

I saw them before he did. I clutched my book bag. Papa clucked to the horse.

We drew closer. Unaware of his audience, Benjamin gave Mary Scarlet a little push, then another. To get out of his way, she stepped closer and closer to the shallow creek that ran beside the road.

"Stop it, Benjy," Mary Scarlet said.

"Stop it, Benjy," Benjamin mocked. "You and whose army is going to stop me?"

Intent on his goal of forcing Mary Scarlet into the water, Benjamin didn't hear our wagon until it was too late.

"Would you like a ride?" Papa said, his voice level, but I could feel the tension in his body. Papa could not stand bullies. Especially those who tormented girls. I wasn't about to tell him this was the same boy who had put the lump on my head.

Benjamin jumped at Papa's voice, scrambling to keep from falling into the creek. When he saw who was driving the wagon, he sneered. "We don't need no ride from no foreigner."

"But thank you," Mary Scarlet was quick to put in. There Mary Scarlet went, trying to smooth things over for her brother. When she saw me in the wagon, she hung her head. But Benjamin shot me a look of pure hatred.

I squeezed Papa's hand, trying to implore him to be quiet, to leave well enough alone.

Papa slowed the horse down next to the Blakely children. He remained silent. Benjamin looked annoyed, and I knew he was wondering what was taking us so long to get by him. I saw a flicker of concern cross his face when he realized Papa had matched the horse's pace to his.

No one said a word.

The silence was punctured only by the clop, clop, clop of the horse's hooves on the packed clay road. My stomach hurt.

What would Papa say? What would he do?

The Blakely children slowed their pace, and as they slowed, so did Papa. When they stopped, Papa stopped.

The silence was unbearable. I started to speak, but Papa squeezed my hand to silence me.

Papa laid the reins carefully on the wagon seat. He climbed from the wagon. He stood, towering above Benjamin Blakely. He laid his hand on the pistol belted around his waist.

He waited. Seconds ticked by. A crow cawed. Finally, Benjamin burst out, "What do you want?"

Mary Scarlet was already crying, silent tears running down her face.

Papa just looked at Benjamin. Then he walked close, so close that he could touch Benjamin if he breathed just right. Benjamin whimpered.

And then the morning breeze caught the acrid smell of urine.

I looked down to see where the smell was coming from. I thought it was Mary Scarlet at first, but then I followed her eyes to the ground. The urine made clean rivulets, forming a damp pool around Benjamin's filthy bare feet.

Papa climbed back into the wagon, his soldier's face gone. He picked up the reins, and without looking at Benjamin he said, "Son, the next time you feel the need for some target practice with your slingshot, aim for a man." Papa shook the reins, and we jingled away.

How had Papa known it was Benjamin's stone that left the mark on my forehead?

We rode along silently for a while. "It's not good," Papa said, his voice full of remorse, "to shame a boy. I only meant to frighten him. Not shame him."

I wasn't the least bit sorry. Benjamin Blakely deserved everything he got and more. "Well, I think he deserved it. He needs to be so scared that he will never hurt anybody again."

"Yes, my child, but the problem is that I didn't just frighten him. When you frighten a boy, he stays away. When you shame a boy, he carries the grudge until he dies. I fear I have only created more trouble for you, my child. I am sorry."

I pondered this as the horse trudged down the road to my school. "Why does Mary Scarlet defend him?" I asked. "He is so mean to her."

"You never know what goes on inside a family unless you live there," Papa said. "I suspect his family holds secrets that we can't even guess at. They seem to have plenty of money."

"Why, then, is Benjamin so filthy?" I asked.

Papa shook his head. "I don't know. But I do know this: I fear the sort of trouble that boy will make."

Chapter 14

1898

Papa remembers that day. "The boy wet his pants right in front of you, me, and his sister. The shame of it for him. I knew he would try to pay us back. I hoped that he would eventually forget about it, but I see that it's not to be."

"No, Papa, it isn't. So now we must hire a lawyer. Do you know anyone?" I ask, hoping that in his travels he has befriended a lawyer. Papa makes friends easily.

"I might," Papa says, rubbing his beard thoughtfully. "I just might." He drops his tools, wipes his hands on his apron, and hurries to the barn. He's saddled the horse and is on his way before I can ask him who his lawyer friend might be and where he lives.

After Papa leaves, I know I can't stand idly by while our land is taken. I have to do something. But what? How can I stop Benjamin and Mary Scarlet? What can I say that might change their minds?

Something Morris said earlier rings in my ears. "John Sebring Corley is the only man living in this town who understands Benjamin and Mary Scarlet." But how can that help? Can John Sebring convince Benjamin and Mary Scarlet to change their minds? It doesn't seem likely that there has to be a way.

Working the soil helps clear my thoughts. I can prepare part of my ground for a medicinal garden for Morris. Maybe once I've worked for a while, I can think of what to say to John Sebring. The thought of visiting John and Margaret this evening sets my heart to rest. As does the idea that maybe, just maybe, by the time the medicinal garden flourishes, we'll have it all worked out and Morris can come home to me.

I choose an uncleared area in the northern portion of my land, the spot with the most shade, pick up my axe and hoe, and head in that direction. The birds call to one another, checking to see which of their friends was hearty enough to make it through last night's storm. Mockingbirds mimic blue jay calls, and squirrels chirp back. Crows caw. I can't wait for spring when the robins and cardinals will come back and brighten the woods with their songs.

When I reach the area I plan to use, I hold my axe and lay down my hoe, overwhelmed. I seem to have forgotten that this land is an old-growth forest, an oak hammock. The hundred-plus-year-old oaks and pines loom, menacing, blocking out the sun. How can this ever be a medicinal garden? The family who had owned the original land grant believed that these woods were too dense to clear. It's why they were willing to sell it cheap. But I had bought the land, knowing that a dense wood meant rich soil. I take a deep breath, say a quick prayer, and set to work.

I start with the least tree-shaded area, and inch by inch I clear bramble and brush. The palmettos are the most stubborn. I attack what must have been a 300-year-old root. I wonder what this palmetto has seen during its long life span. Was there once an Indian village here on this land? What had the Indians planted? Maybe corn, but I knew the natives hadn't cleared much land. They had respect for the hundred-year-old oaks, the cedars, and the cypress knees.

As the day warms, the birds stop singing and the squirrels grow quiet. I shed my shawl, hang it over a tiny cedar, and continue working.

Crackling leaves warn me that someone is approaching. I pause and look up, but the sparse sun shines directly in my eyes, and the person, whoever it is, appears as nothing more than a shadow.

"What's a pretty little lady like you doing way out here in the deep woods all by her lonesome?"

I jerk as if slapped. It's Benjamin Blakely. He laughs.

I tighten my grip on the axe. I can't show any fear. I speak through gritted teeth. "What do you want?"

"I just want to help you out a little," Benjamin says, moving close. Too close. "Maybe plow some of this virgin forest."

The implication of his words makes me want to retch.

"Well I don't want your help, and I don't need any trouble," I say, hoping the trembling in my knees ends and that my voice remains calm. I step across the palmetto to a pine tree. I lift my axe and swing it hard. The pine tree between us lurches, vibrates ever so slightly, and Benjamin steps back.

It's exactly the reaction I hoped for. But now I have another problem. What if he lunges forward while I work to pull my axe from the tree, its sharp edge lodged deeply in the new passageway of the soft, virgin pine?

The sweat trickling beneath my arms reeks of fear.

Benjamin Blakely moves a step closer. Then another. I struggle with my axe. He laughs.

He doesn't see the hoe lying in front of him. Nor, for that matter, do I. He takes a lazy, sauntering step as I struggle with my axe. He reaches for me and falls forward. I grunt and heft the axe up out of its soft bed, sap tears running down the bark. I hold my axe and stand over him.

I press my advantage. "I don't have time for your foolishness, Benjamin. Go on and worry someone else to death. I've got work to do."

He scrambles up and away from my axe. When he is a safe distance away, he calls, "I'll be back when it's time to plow," and disappears into the vine-tangled woods.

My hands shake, but I attack the pine with my axe as if it's Benjamin Blakely. The pine will fall, I'm sure of that. Finally, my hands bleeding and my dress soaked, I hear the tell-tale creak. I step back to see which way it will fall. The pine needles sway in the wind like a woman's hair, and slowly, oh so slowly, the tree begins its descent to the ground, hesitant at first but increasing its speed until it hits with a massive shudder, the earth shaking beneath its force.

When it falls, I cry, the tears streaming down my face and watering the ground where the tree lies. I can almost hear her whispering, *I will never die. You can cut me down, you can burn me up, but do you see the trees I've planted around me?-Baby pines, falling from my boughs, buried in the earth, then springing forth, new, green. From now till the end of time, I am here.*

After being scared out of my mind by Benjamin Blakely, I need my friends. I need their sweet calmness. I need to be in the midst of their happy family to remind myself that even in the darkness, there is always light.

I saddle Dolly and set out to visit John and Margaret.

John sits on the front porch untangling his casting net. He travels down to Anderson every week, casts his net in St. Andrew Bay, and comes back with a wagonload of mullet to sell at Saturday Market. Sometimes, he has time to scallop, and scallops are my favorite. I love steaming them until their shells pop open and dipping the sweet meat in my own butter. It's like eating candy. I trade John and Margaret eggs for the sweet meat. John loves gardening, but neither he nor Margaret loves taking care of chickens.

John likes to tell stories as he untangles his nets, and I'm in desperate need of a story tonight.

He offers me a seat, and I wipe the sweat from my brow with my apron. "I need you to tell me what you know about Benjamin and Mary Scarlet," I say. "They've taken Morris's land, and are threatening to take mine. I fear Benjamin might follow Morris and hurt him."

I neglect to mention my encounter with Benjamin.

"You don't have anything to worry about on that count," John says. "Benjamin is about as likely to go back to Cairo as he is to jump down the chimney when the winter fire is burning."

"I don't understand it," Margaret says, anxious concern for her fretting baby keeping her from offering me a cool drink. "What happened up there that's so hush-hush, neither one of you want to talk about it?"

My face gets hot. "Do you want me to hold her for a minute, Margaret?" I offer, reaching for the baby, longing for the comfort of holding her in my arms.

"No, but thank you, my friend. I just made a pitcher of lemonade," she says. "I would love for you to get a glass."

I understand. This sickly baby is so fragile, so precious. Margaret wants to hold little Bonnie as much as possible before she is snatched away by whatever lingering illness will not leave the infant alone. The only advice Morris could offer John and Margaret was to feed and love her well. Poor Margaret.

"I can get it for her," John says, pushing away from his net.

"No, don't you bother," I say. "I know where the cups are, and I know where you keep the lemonade. You sit there with your wife and baby and warm up your voice. I want to hear a story."

"Just make yourself to home," John calls, as if I need encouragement. Their home is as much a home to me—maybe more so—than my own. Margaret is the sister I chose.

I walk into Margaret's cool, neat kitchen. John has built her shelves all the way around the room where she displays her plates, her teapot, and the lovely flowers that she grows from cuttings. Margaret loves nothing more than walking through someone's yard or even the woods, finding a plant or flower she loves, taking a cutting and coaxing it to set out roots and grow. She has rooted everything from roses to wild blueberry bushes. Her backyard garden looks like a jungle, but, transplanted into the house, the flowers adorn the tiny cabin with color and life.

If only Margaret had the same luck with her baby. I look at the oak cradle John made in the months before Bonnie's birth. He polished it until the wood was smooth of burrs and the golden oak gleamed like sunshine.

Margaret has done everything possible for little Bonnie, but the tiny thing has what Morris deems "failure to thrive." She can't gain weight no matter how much Margaret nurses her. They've tried supplements of goat's milk, rice paste, and cream, but the infant grows weaker by the month, and I fear that one bout of the grippe will take the baby away from John and Margaret forever.

I pour myself a glass of Margaret's delicious lemonade made from the lemons of their own tree. Back out on the porch, John has launched into his tale about Cairo, Georgia, and the Blakely family.

"I was living up in Cairo, then. Mama and Daddy had bought a little farm, enough to support the three of us. Mama's people were all from Cairo. Mama was pretty old for marrying, almost forty. I was their only baby. You know, after the war with the North, there weren't many men to go around for the young women of Cairo."

"Did you get lonely?" Margaret asks, cuddling her tiny baby girl.

"No, because there were plenty of cousins for me to play with. Mama had an older sister, my Aunt Harriet. She married young, way back the first year of the war. When her husband Elijah went off to fight, they had only been married for a week. He didn't come back. Morris was born nine months later."

I try to imagine Morris as a child. But it makes my heart ache to do so. I miss him already.

"My Aunt Harriet was a beautiful woman. Every single man in town—that is, the few that the war left alive—tried courting her. After twelve years, she gave up hope on her husband ever coming back again and married a man with enough land to support her— John Calvin Blakely."

A blue jay shrieks in the front yard, startling Margaret. The angry jay is hidden by the lush green live oaks marking the separation between John and Margaret's land and downtown Falling Waters.

I ignore the bird and focus on John. Something he said triggers a memory. Something I had heard one night in the woods when the crazy preacher tried to scare Mary Scarlet. It was the day Maggie and I became friends, the day Eva and I waited for Black Peter.

1888

When Benjamin stayed away for the rest of the school day, pouting because Morris had punished him in front of the entire class, I was relieved. Papa would be picking me up from school, and the last thing I wanted was another encounter between Papa and Benjamin.

I could hardly wait for Papa to pick me up after school that day and introduce him to my new friend. Maggie's home was only a half-mile from the school, and I had promised her that Papa would take her there. Maggie reluctantly agreed. I didn't understand her reluctance. Perhaps she was nervous to ride with Papa, whom she'd never met?

Maggie and I stood in front of the schoolhouse on the newly built wooden sidewalk and waited. To our left was the freshly painted Methodist church, and to the right stood the courthouse. Falling Waters was an up and coming town, or so Papa said. The smell of new wood sometimes drowned out the smell of the hogs that wallowed around the city's well.

I wanted my new friend to meet Papa. I knew she would love him once she met him. He was such a dear, kind man. It hurt my heart to see how some people treated Papa in this town. Didn't they know he was a decorated war hero? Didn't they know he was an artist? He was even a medic in the Prussian Army, though he didn't have a license to practice medicine.

After what felt like an eternity, Papa pulled up in his brightly painted wagon. I helped Maggie up, and Papa's brown eyes danced with joy.

Before we could ride away, Mr. Morris Blakely came hurrying out of the schoolhouse door. My face felt hot.

"I was afraid I was going to miss you," he said to Papa. He grabbed Papa's hand in a warm handshake. "I have not gotten a chance to say hello to you," he said. "I wanted to tell you what a scholar your Annie Laura is turning out to be."

Papa gave him a broad smile and returned the handshake with gusto. "She loves school," he said. "She loves learning."

"And she knows Shakespeare!" Morris said. "Much better than I do!"

"It's because Papa loves Shakespeare," I said.

Morris smiled at me, and my heart melted right then and there. "Well," he said, "I don't want to keep you, sir. I just wanted to say hello and welcome. We are lucky to have a family like you here in our small town."

Was he apologizing for Benjamin's appalling behavior?

I smiled, grateful for his kindness. His blue eyes crinkled, and his curly hair formed a wiry halo around his head.

"See y'all tomorrow!"

We waved and Papa steered the wagon towards Maggie's house.

We rode past fallow fields that had once been white with cotton and golden with corn. Soon, the ground would be sown with new seed, but for now the fields rested and waited. I could hardly wait until I had my own fields. I could imagine myself seeing to the planting and tending. It would take some hard work clearing the land beside our house—that is, if I could figure out how to buy it—but I was up for some hard work.

When the split-rail fence marking Maggie's daddy's property came into view, Maggie said, "Thank you so much. You can stop here."

Papa said, "Please, let me take you up to your house. I don't mind."

Maggie's face reddened. "No, I don't think so, but thank you so much."

Papa nodded his understanding. But I didn't understand.

Just beyond the fence, a little child with a springy mass of yellow-white curls appeared. She jumped up and down and yelled, "Daddy! Our Maggie is home. Santa brought her!"

Papa and I laughed. It wasn't the first time a child had accused Papa of being Santa Claus. He was prematurely gray, white headed, really. Mama said it happened during the war. She said he left for the war with coal-black hair and came home an old man. Besides his hair, however, there was nothing about Papa that was old. He was barrel chested from lifting the heavy equipment it took to build the lovely iron woodstoves. And he was jolly when he wasn't drinking from the silver flask.

110

A man strode towards us, slapping the split rails. He was tall and thin and must be Maggie's father, though he looked nothing like Maggie. Where she was blonde, he was black headed. He drew closer. I didn't like the look in his strange brown eyes. They were emotionless and angry all at the same time. The smile on his face was confusing. It didn't match his eyes at all.

I understood exactly what Maggie had been talking about when she said her daddy would kill Benjamin Blakely. I suddenly feared for the life of my own papa, though I didn't understand what this man could possibly have against him.

The man slowed his pace, eyeing Papa.

"Thank you so much," Maggie said to Papa and me, her voice quavering. "Now, you can go on. I know your mama is missing you."

But for Papa, it would be incredibly bad manners to drop the daughter off without speaking to her daddy. He wouldn't drop a woodstove off in that manner, much less a child.

Papa climbed down from the wagon. Maggie placed a hand over her mouth. I felt the hair rise up on the back of my neck. Papa held steady.

"What kind of contraption is that?" the man asked, pointing to the brightly colored wagon. "What are you, a band of gypsies or something?"

"No, sir," Papa said, "I am Otto Brock, and this is my daughter, Annie Laura." Papa held out his hand.

The man spat on the ground. It was clear he would rather have spat on Papa.

"We don't need your kind in these parts," he said. He turned his back to Papa and walked away.

Papa's hand dropped like an autumn leaf.

Yet another family who didn't like foreigners. I couldn't understand it. Maggie's own grandmama was German born.

The man stalked back to his house, and Maggie followed, her head bent low.

She didn't even look back. My heart fell. Had I lost my new friend already? I felt the tears well in my eyes. Such hope I had felt.

"Don't worry, my little one," Papa said. "She will be your friend, and a good one. She is just obedient to her papa."

How did Papa know exactly what I was thinking?

"And we must get home quickly," he said, smiling and giving the horse a gentle slap with his reins. "Black Peter will be there and gone, and we will have missed him!"

"But Papa, he doesn't even know you. Why are people like that?" I asked.

"I don't really know." Papa pointed to the wildflowers growing along the side of the road, purple, yellow, and white. "I do know this, though. I wouldn't trade living in this country for anything. Where in Germany could you find such flowers on December 6?" Papa jingled the horse's reins, and we clip-clopped home.

Eva met us at the end of the lane. "Is Black Peter with you?" she asked.

"No," Papa said, "you must wait inside for him. You must answer the door!"

Eva ran as fast as her fat little legs would carry her back towards the house. If she must be in the house when Black Peter came, in the house she would be.

"Do you need me to help you, Papa?" I asked.

"Help me?" Papa smiled. "Oh, no, my child. I don't need your help. Black Peter needs mine. All I need for you to do is get the cocoa ready and lay it out on the porch for our Black Peter. When he smells Mama's cocoa, he will be certain to come running with his bag full of candy for you and Eva!"

I jumped down from the cart. I hoped Black Peter would bring me some farming tools. Maybe something to dig with, and my own plow! With a plow and the family horse, I could be ready for spring. Of course, a plow wouldn't fit in my shoe, but a good pair of gloves and a bag of seeds might.

I looked out over the front stoop into the daunting vine-tangled woods. Before I could have fields, I needed to clear the woods. That would take weeks. Who would help me?

"Annie Laura! Come in, come in! Mama has the cocoa boiling!" Eva pulled me by my blue wool skirt into the house. The smell of freshly baked stollen wafted through the air, and I breathed in the heavenly scent. I loved Christmas season. There was the baking of sweets and goodies, the excitement of Black Peter, and the advent calendar with its tiny boxes stuffed with lovely treats.

I deposited my shoes behind the front door in the neat row Mama demanded. As a good Dutch housewife, Mama did not allow for dirt in the house, especially if it was unnecessary. Only guests were allowed to wear their shoes in the house. It was my job to sweep the floor clean after they left, and scrub it, too, if the shoes had tracked in horse manure.

I ran with Eva into the kitchen where Mama stood over the stove watching the steam from the kettle reach the ceiling. Only when the steam reached the wooden ceiling of the kitchen would Mama take it off the eye of the woodstove and make her cocoa. Otherwise, she said, it wasn't boiling hard enough.

I saw that the woodstove needed cleaning. The cinders were overflowing. "Mama, you've done a good bit of cooking today."

And if the cinders didn't tell enough of the story, the delicious scent of gingerbread in the air let us know Mama had been cooking even more Christmas treats.

"Did Eva take a good nap?" I asked.

"Yes," Mama said with a smile. "I had time to bake two batches of gingerbread and a pan of stollen!"

It was going to be a heavenly night.

"Thank you, my angel girl," Mama said after I emptied the messy cinders into the lye bucket filled nearly to the top with rainwater.

"I think I hear Black Peter coming down the lane."

Eva nearly jumped out of her pinafore. I had to fix it back up onto her shoulders and tie it securely at her back. Eva wriggled the entire time.

"Let's go hide in the woods beside the trail and wait for him," I said.

"Be careful of the snakes and wolves," Mama said.

"Don't worry, Mama. Mr. Morris Blakely said the snakes mostly sleep in the winter, and we don't have wolves in Florida!"

"Still be careful." Mama studied my face and smiled. "I believe you're a little sweet on that teacher of yours!"

"Mama!" I giggled and took a firm hold on Eva's hand. We ran to the woods, Eva's shawl trailing and dragging through the sandy clay until it was mottled with burrs and leaves.

When we reached a woody alcove far from the house, but close to the road, I saw that we were in the front acreage of the Blakelys' land. It was no matter. No one ever came over here except hogs. They came up to wallow in the cool dirt, but they were domestic hogs, not the kind that you found in the woods that ran wild and could kill you in a stampede or with their wicked tusks. The formal entrance to the Blakely farm was another half-mile up the dirt road. This part of their land was mostly woods.

"Shh," I said. "Hunker down and wait. They will be coming up the road in just a minute. Black Peter is here even in Florida, helping Saint Nicholas deliver his presents. Listen!"

We sat waiting, breathless. Even though I was nearly grown, I was excited to see St. Nicolas and Black Peter. We strained our ears to hear. It was silent except for the cawing of crows and the sound of the early December wind whistling through the pine trees. In Florida, it was a gentle, whispering whistle, not like the wind up north. Here, the pine trees rustled like ladies' skirts, and the wind was gentle on our faces.

"I hear something," Eva said.

"Shh," I said. I heard it, too. It wasn't a jangling of bells, nor was it the whispering wind. It was something else.

Someone was crying.

I put my finger to my lips. "Shh, don't make a sound. You stay right here and wait for Black Peter. I'm sure he'll be here in a minute!"

As if on cue, we heard the bells, and Eva burst from the woods to see a man dressed in red with a long, white beard. It was St. Nicholas looking suspiciously like Papa. He was accompanied by a black man dressed up in fancy red clothes. The black man had a cloth bag filled with candy and strapped to his side. Eva hurried down the lane to greet them, and Black Peter began throwing tiny gold coins. I couldn't help but follow.

We picked up coins as quickly as we could, knowing that inside we would find delicious chocolate candy.

As quickly as they had come, Black Peter and St. Nicholas disappeared around the bend.

"Where are they going?" Eva asked.

"They are going to visit the other children. But don't you worry. We will put our shoes beside the bed tonight, along with a carrot for the gray horse, and in the morning, won't you be surprised to find a gift inside your shoe!"

Eva wriggled with excitement. "Does he come every day?"

"Every day until Christmas!" I said. "Go inside, now, and tell Mama the good news. I will be back in a moment."

Eva ran to the house without a backward glance.

I watched her climb the front steps, and then I turned to investigate the crying.

Chapter 15

1888

I avoided the dry, crackly leaves and sought the silent beds of straw to muffle my footsteps. Closer and closer I moved to the poor soul whose identity I had yet to discover. I knelt behind a giant oak, felled by the violent storms of summer. It would take two men to reach around its circumference. The oak hid me well.

The sun had set, and the western sky was bathed in a sea of fiery orange. The smell of wood smoke wafted through the air along with the sound of crackling lighter wood.

I peered over the edge of the oak and saw Mary Scarlet Blakely seated on the far side of the fire, weeping into her hands.

I cleared my throat and stood, not wishing to startle her.

Mary Scarlet looked up, wide eyed, fearful, the fire reflected in her eyes. "Go away," she said, her voice pitched low, as though she were afraid someone would hear. She looked fearfully into the woods. "They're coming, go!"

I felt my heart beating hard, and I slid behind the oak tree. Over the crest of the hill just behind Mary Scarlet came her father and brother. John Calvin and Benjamin Blakely were dressed for deer hunting. They carried guns, their game bags nestled against their sides.

They led a man dressed in white, beating on a tambourine. His eerie chanting made cold chills run down my spine.

"I the LORD thy God am a jealous God," the man intoned, his accent heavily German, "visiting the iniquity of the mothers upon the children unto the third and fourth generation. ...a jealous God, visiting the iniquity of the mothers upon the children unto the third and fourth generation... a jealous God..."

The man chanted it over and over.

"You stay hidden, do you hear me? Don't you show yourself no matter what," Mary Scarlet hissed.

As the white-robed man came near, I could see the spittle flecked into his beard. He looked like the visiting preacher who spoke at our church every so often, the one Mama didn't like.

I wanted to stand and stop him because he was getting the verse all wrong. He left out the most important part, what Mama and Oma had made certain I understood: *shewing mercy unto thousands of them that love me and keep my commandments.*

I wanted to shout these words to comfort Mary Scarlet, who huddled on the ground just a few feet away, her arms wrapped around her knees, her head down. My God was merciful. Whatever awful deed Mary Scarlet had committed that made it necessary for a preacher to come visit her privately, God could forgive.

"Satan's spawn," the man shrieked. "SATAN'S spawn," he shrieked again. He stood directly above Mary Scarlet now and circled her with his shrieking. "A jealous God, visiting the iniquity of the mothers upon the children unto the third and fourth genera-tion…Satan's spawn."

I felt ill. Why was he screaming at Mary Scarlet?

That was the other thing that told me he wasn't a man of God. Mama said you could tell the difference by their kindness. Not the scary kind of kindness where they wanted something out of you, but real kindness, like Mama had.

I wanted to comfort Mary Scarlet. But her panic-stricken eyes warned me to stay away. Her shoulders quivered. Now she was cry-ing hard.

Somewhere a dog barked. The man beckoned Benjamin and Mr. Blakely to join him.

The three circled Mary Scarlet, chanting the words *sins of the mother* over and over in a macabre dance, and I grew frightened. They circled closer and closer.

"Stand up, daughter of Satan. Stand!" the man screeched.

Mary Scarlet stayed where she was. I knew she probably did not have the strength to stand. If I were in that circle instead of Mary Scarlet, I knew I couldn't have stood.

Mary Scarlet's father prodded her with the butt of his gun. "Stand," he hissed.

She unfolded herself and stood like a thin undergarment on a clothesline. Her face was white, blanched from crying and sheer terror.

"You speak when the man asks you questions, do you hear me, girl?" Her father prodded her again with the gun butt.

Mary Scarlet dropped her head.

"Who was your mother?" The man spat the word "mother" as if it were a curse.

"Mama," she whispered.

"Louder," the man said. "The Lord God wants to hear her name so that he, the almighty, knows on whom to rain his judgment and wrath unto the fourth generation."

"Say the whore's name. Say it," her father growled.

"Whore's name, whore's name, whore's name," Benjamin echoed.

Mary Scarlet reared back and drew herself up. "She was your mother, too," she shouted.

Benjamin's hand shot out and would have made cracking contact with his sister's face, except the preacher man grabbed it.

"Vengeance belongeth to the Lord God Almighty," he said, and dropped Benjamin's arm as if it, too, were dirty.

Was I the only one who noticed?

But Mary Scarlet saw. She wiped away her tears. She looked the man directly in the eye and said, quiet but forceful, "Harriet Elizabeth Blakely was my mother, and my father, too."

Benjamin and John Calvin froze.

"Blasphemy!" the man shrieked. "Daughter of Satan, you blaspheme the holy name of the Virgin Mother. There must be sacrifice. You, daughter of a whore, you have blasphemed the holy name of the Virgin Mother. You have rained coals and fiery brimstones upon all of us who stand here. You have made us sinners, and now, blood...must...be...shed."

The macabre glint of his spittle shone in Mary Scarlet's hair.

"Unsheathe your dagger," the man said to Mr. Blakely. The fiery glow showed John Calvin's face blanch white. He stood still. Had he brought this so-called preacher man out to scare Mary Scarlet? Was he regretting it? I was pretty certain by the look on his face that he didn't want to make her bleed.

Benjamin sprang forward, his knife unsheathed. He grabbed Mary Scarlet by the hair, and her neck glistened white as her father's face.

Just then came the sound of trampling hooves, and a herd of wild boar screamed through, chased by an unseen predator, dissolving the circle of humans in their chaotic scramble to avoid the flames.

John Calvin sprang into action. He shot one of the boars as it flew by, and then he slit its throat. Blood flowed to the ground. He dipped his hand in the warm gooey mess and smeared Mary Scarlet's face.

"Blood has been shed. The sacrifice is made," he said, visibly shaken. "Let's go home." The hogs disappeared into the twilight.

The blood bath woke Mary Scarlet to a new anger. She leaned in to the man in white who had been thrown against her in the scrambling hooves and hissed, "Blood has been shed. Long before this day. Ask him about it," she said, pointing to her father. "And ask this one, too. He believed my father's lies about my mother. He said she was a liar, a manipulator, not to be trusted. He filled our heads with it from the time we were babies. But do you know who the real liar and manipulator is? You are looking at him." She pointed at her father. "My brother is a twisted shell of a person because he believed Daddy's lies about our mama…"

John Calvin Blakely reached in and slapped her face so hard that it knocked her to the ground.

"Your mama was a whore, girl. Don't ever forget it. That makes you Satan's spawn. You best be grateful we even took you in."

"At least I'm not a murderer," Mary Scarlet hissed.

I heard her words. So Mary Scarlet knew.

But Benjamin hadn't heard her. He was too busy shouting, "Your mama was a whore."

"Shut up," John Calvin said, recoiling from Mary Scarlet's words and lashing out at Benjamin. "She was your mama, too."

Benjamin fell back like his father had slapped him as well. "No, Daddy. I'm yours," he said, pleading, trying with his words to erase the mother who had carried him and loved him.

"Devil's spawn," the preacher man muttered, ignoring the chaos between the father and his children. And then, as if the words inflamed and empowered him, he said to Mary Scarlet, "Your womb is cursed. Any child you bring forth is cursed, as you yourself are cursed."

"We're finished here," John Calvin said, pushing the preacher away. "She's a hopeless liar, just like her mother. If we stay here any longer, she'll try to manipulate you into believing the things that grow in her own mind. She's sick."

The man in white writhed. "It is not finished," he squawked. "Blood," he said. "Blood."

"You want me to cut myself? Is that what you are asking? All right, I will." Mary Scarlet whipped a knife from her apron pocket and slashed her arm.

I gasped when the blood poured down from the wound and dripped at Mary Scarlet's feet, making pink blotches on her apron.

"I swear," Mary Scarlet said, her voice even, "by the blood on this ground that the only liar out here is standing beside you." She pointed to her father. "Daddy poisoned us against our own mama. Benjamin believed his lies, and now Benjamin is a twisted shell of a human. But they didn't work with me, Daddy. Not with me. I know who my mama was. I visited her every chance I got, and I've never forgotten her kindness and her love for me.

"There is some kind of evil surrounding you, daddy. Because when I was with you, I believed your lies about her. Other people and my own eyes told me different. My mama was a good woman. The only mistake she made in her life was marrying you. You married her for her money and her land, and in return you brought her nothing but pain and heartbreak. I remember her crying all the time when she lived with you.

120

"But you know what, Daddy? She was happy away from you. Away from a man who didn't love her, who didn't give a damn about her. She was happiest when I was there, and the few times Benjamin came to visit her. She knew love, Daddy. Not from you, but from me and from her first husband. I saw him. I saw them together. And they loved each other. My brother Morris is a love baby.

"Did you hide the letters her husband sent her so she wouldn't know he was coming back? So you could marry her and get her land? You did, I know. I found them. You thought you had burnt them. And I saw with my own eyes what you did to him. You are the one that will burn in hell, Daddy. Not me. And you will burn harder because you pulled Benjamin down with you and tried to pull me. But this blood right here? It's mine. My blood is purified by my truth. I'm swearing by it. You are a liar and a thief. You stole our childhood. You killed our mama. And then you killed her husband."

John Calvin Blakely stood silent. In the firelight's eerie glow, he shrank back, but then he moved forward, arming himself once again with the comfort and familiarity of his own lies.

"No one will ever believe a word you say," he said. And then the men and Benjamin walked away.

I moved slowly and kneeled beside Mary Scarlet, who looked like she was about to faint. I ripped my petticoat and wrapped her arm.

"Your words are true, Mary Scarlet." I said. "I knew your mama. I knew her kindness. And I saw her husband Elijah."

Mary Scarlet leaned on me and was so quiet that I was uncertain whether she had heard me or not.

I led her to the spring that divided our two properties.

It didn't seem enough to merely rinse the bloodied arm. We both needed to immerse ourselves in the icy, cleansing water.

We rose from the spring bonded beyond death.

Chapter 16

1898

I sit listening to John Sebring weave his tale of the history of the Blakelys as Maggie tries to nurse the baby and her husband knots his cast net. According to Mary Scarlet, her daddy married her mama for *her* land and money, not the other way around.

"John Calvin Blakely had outlived his own wife and most of the men of his generation," John Sebring says. "They had nearly all died in the war. He was still a handsome man at fifty. His wife and kids had taken good care of the land during the war and prospered when no one else had. Some say they worked for the Yankees, but I imagine it was just a rumor spread by bitter people. People who aren't willing to work for their money are always resentful of those who are."

Or maybe the story went horribly wrong. If John Calvin Blakely had all that prosperous land, why would he have married Harriet for her land and money? Was it simply greed?

The baby mews and Margaret tries feeding her again, but she turns her little face away and whimpers a feeble cry. Mama's new baby girl, though four months younger, is almost the same size as tiny Bonnie, and already her cry is lustier.

Margaret catches me staring at the baby and smiles a beautiful, tender smile. "Isn't she the most beautiful baby ever?"

"Yes, Margaret, she is," I say. There is nothing else I can say. But the pain in John Sebring's eyes tells me that he knows his baby is weak and probably not long for this world. He lays a gentle hand on Margaret's leg, puts down his net, and scoops his tiny daughter into his arms. He nestles her against his chest and continues his story.

The baby settles, lulled by the deep rumbling bass of John Sebring's voice reverberating against her cheek. Margaret's careful flower and vine embroidery filling the baby's soft white cotton batiste dress are a testimony to her love. The delicate white fabric contrasts with the worn chambray of John Sebring's shirt.

"The rest of this story is not happy, so prepare yourself. I'm glad Bonnie is too young to understand."

Margaret picks up her embroidery hoop and her latest project, another lovely dress for Bonnie. The baby has so many white gowns embroidered with delicate white flowers that she hardly ever wears the same one twice.

"A long time went by and Aunt Harriet couldn't get pregnant. It was rumored that a war injury had rendered John Calvin impotent. Excuse me for speaking of such," John Sebring says. "John Calvin needed more children to work his land."

"No harm speaking the truth," I say.

He nods and continues. "Now you have to understand that the rest of this story comes from my mama, who never liked John Calvin Blakely a lick. I myself don't hold anything against him. He seemed fine by me. He provided for his family and all; he just wasn't real friendly."

John Sebring looks off beyond the line of oaks and into the field as if searching for something. "A few years later, after Aunt Harriet became pregnant with Benjamin, John Calvin left for a few months. No one knew where he went, but he didn't come back until almost a year after Benjamin was born. Morris and John Calvin's sons from his first marriage worked the land and kept food on the table."

John Sebring straightens the folds of Bonnie's gown.

"Morris loved baby Benjamin, and Benjamin loved him. It was like Morris was his daddy instead of his half-brother. When John Calvin returned, Aunt Harriet became pregnant again, this time with Mary Scarlet. Aunt Harriet loved those babies with all her heart. My Margaret here makes me think of my Aunt Harriet, but only in that way, no other."

John pauses to watch his wife, her hair covering the embroidery she holds close to her eyes so she can see it in the gloaming.

"A few more years passed. John Calvin was nearly silent during those years. But soon, a horror unfolded."

The April breeze that has been so balmy and warm turns suddenly cool. The sun has dropped behind the horizon. John doesn't light the lamps. He gazes at the faded western light. I follow his gaze. The lightning bugs dance in the bushes beyond the swept yard. The only sound is the thin, raspy breathing of the baby snuggled safe in her father's arms.

"I'm not sparing you any details, though what I'm about to tell you is not fit for a lady's ears."

I clutch my apron, wad it, then smooth it over my knees. I can't bear to look John Sebring in the eyes. Does he know my part in this drama? My heart is beating hard. I try to vanquish the memory.

"One day, John Calvin walked into the sheriff's office to report a killing. When the sheriff asked who had done the killing, John Calvin answered, 'I did.'"

This confession brings me up short.

John Sebring continues his story. "John Calvin walked the sheriff to a smoldering hut way off the road on a piece of property owned by Aunt Harriet and her first husband. The sickening smell of roasted, charred meat filled the air.

"There on the stone floor of the hut lay a man, his body burned beyond recognition.

"To the sheriff's horror, across the room from him stood eleven-year-old Benjamin Blakely, grasping his mother's braids in both hands, forcing her to stare at the burnt figure.

"Her eyes were shut tight, and she was moaning, rocking back and forth, though Benjamin's tight grasp left her scant room for movement.

"She was tied to a chair, her knees, wrists, and ankles bloody from an earlier desperate struggle to free herself and save the man she loved.

"'Let go, son,' the sheriff said to the boy.

"'Daddy told me to hold her so she could see what she done,' Benjamin said."

"Oh, my dear God," I say. These are the only words I can utter.

John continues as though he can't stop. "John Calvin had forced Benjamin to stand at the window and witness his mother's sin with the man she had married so long ago, returned from war.

"John Calvin had then eased into the room, and when the man saw him and stood, hiding Miss Harriet behind him, John Calvin Blakely shot him in both knees, one after the other, and doused his lower body with kerosene. He then tied Harriet up and called Benjamin in to hold her by her hair, forcing her to watch.

"John Calvin Blakely, a man big as a timberjack and strong as an ox, kicked the man's legs into the fireplace then stood on his hands while the man's lower body writhed in the flames.

"This is the story John Calvin Blakely told the sheriff," John Sebring says. "The sheriff, a strong man with a strong stomach, threw up into the bushes outside the stone hut before he could cover the dead man and untie my Aunt Harriet.

"Once untied, Harriet put the rest of her clothes back on, walked down to the creek, tied seven stones in her petticoats, jumped from the diving rock, and drowned herself.

"Benjamin followed her, crying for his mama to hold him, screaming he was sorry. When his mama jumped in, Benjamin went in after her. If the sheriff hadn't heard his screams, the boy would have drowned, too. Benjamin dove in over and over again, screaming 'I'm sorry I'm sorry,' until the sheriff was able to swim in and catch him, pulling him to shore and holding him until he stopped struggling and started sobbing."

I feel tears prickle for the child who had been Benjamin Blakely.

John Sebring continues, "John Calvin Blakely donated his wife's land to the church, put his children in a wagon, and drove to Falling Waters, Florida, where he died four years later."

John Sebring stands, shaking his head. "I hope never to have to tell that story again." He takes his sleeping baby girl into the house, lays her in her cradle, and walks down the road into the dark night.

My mind reels, and I call out to John Sebring. "So John Calvin thought the babies—Mary Scarlet and Benjamin—were fathered by Harriet's first husband, Morris's daddy?"

John turns back and nods.

"And that's why he killed him?" I ask.

"Yes, that's the way the story goes," he says.

125

For weeks after, John Sebring's story makes me wonder. Am I still at fault for the deaths of Elijah and Harriet? If I had sent Morris back, would John Calvin have hurt him too? Probably not. But he might have. And in that case, maybe, instead of killing Morris's daddy, I actually saved Morris.

I know that in many ways, I'm trying to justify my silence. There is still the matter of the packet of papers I've still not shared with Morris. When he returns, I tell myself, we will talk.

We have to, or the weight of this story is going to kill me.

With Mama gone, I'm forced to spend a lot more time than I wish inside the house. Eva had taken over the majority of Mama's heavy chores the month before she died. I hadn't even noticed, I was so preoccupied by my cotton crop. It's made me see Eva in an entirely new light.

And now, there is our new baby sister, Laura Viola, to tend to. I hire a wet-nurse, Isabelle, a girl whose baby died at birth. Tabitha recommended her to me the day Mama died.

I'm finding that keeping Emma and Maisie entertained and out of trouble can be a full-time job. And there is so much more to be done. I'm not certain how I'm going to handle it all. The fields need caring for. I tried my hand at mending, but I'm no good with the needle. I keep catching threads on my rough fingers. When Margaret comes over and offers to help, I'm beside myself with joy.

But I wonder how Margaret will feel about Mama's healthy baby, thriving under the care of Isabelle. I'm surprised to find that Margaret and Isabelle are old friends.

"Isabelle!" Margaret says when she sees her. "I haven't seen you in years!"

Isabelle ducks her head, cuddles Laura Viola, and then looks up shyly at Margaret. "We were just girls back then, weren't we, Margaret?" she says.

Margaret turns to me. "We've known each other since we were five and sharing syrup-filled biscuits for lunch. Remember, Isabelle? Every day we checked to see who had the biggest one."

Isabelle smiles, the brightest smile I've seen since she took up residence in the corner of our living room beside the baby's cradle.

"Can I see your baby?" Isabelle asks.

Margaret unwraps baby Bonnie, who seems even smaller and thinner today. Margaret misses the look of concern that crosses Isabelle's face, but I don't.

Maisie scampers into the room, her face glowing with the warmth of the sunny day. She takes one look at Bonnie and says, "I'm sorry your baby is so sick, Miss Margaret. Do you think she will let Mama hold her when she goes to be with Jesus?"

I close my eyes and take a deep breath. The very room stands still.

Tears sparkle like stars in Margaret's eyes. "I hope she will, Maisie. Aside from your sweet mama, the only person I would rather have holding my baby girl in heaven is Jesus himself."

It's the first admission Margaret has made that her baby is not long for this world. I don't not know what to do or say, so I say nothing. Margaret senses my discomfort.

"It's fine, Annie Laura. I'm just enjoying her as long as I have her. Morris has done everything he could to help her, and she's still not gaining weight. I believe she is just a little angel sent to me for a moment. As soon as she has shed her earthly bonds, she is going to fly right back up to heaven and into your mama's open arms."

My heart aches.

"It's why I'm so selfish with her," Margaret says. "I don't want anyone else holding her. I want as many memories with her as I can grasp." Margaret smiles and pats her baby girl, then holds her up in the air. Little Bonnie offers a wan smile but looks adoringly into her mama's eyes. A breathy little "coo" escapes her lips, and I think Margaret is going to melt with delight.

"Did you hear her?" Margaret says. "She's trying to talk!"

We all laugh with Margaret, rejoicing in this tiny sign of normal.

It's a happy moment in the midst of our sadness. Emma stands behind Maisie, and both smile at baby Bonnie. Isabelle holds Laura

Viola, plump and full of her morning feeding, and Margaret, glowing like a blue-eyed Madonna, lifts Bonnie high in the air, hoping for a repeat of the magical coo. She is not disappointed.

The room dissolves in delighted giggles. Eva comes in from the bedroom she has been tidying. "What is all the laughter about?" she asks. "I feel like I'm missing someone's birthday party!"

"Come join us," Margaret says. "I did bring some teacakes. Maisie, do you mind getting them out of my bag?"

"I'll make some coffee," I say.

"And we'll have a surprise birthday party for babies," Margaret says. "We are going to celebrate all the joy they give us with every coo and smile."

"Yay!" Maisie and Eva say, clapping their hands. I know their mouths water for Margaret's teacakes. No one could make them like Margaret.

Maisie carefully unwraps the light, fluffy cookie cakes, and Eva places them on Mama's rose china. We all sit at the table, and I pull down the matching china teacups. When the coffee is done, I pour everyone a cup, including the little girls. I fill their cups with sugar and cream first and then top it off with a little coffee.

"A surprise birthday party!" Emma exclaims. "I like surprise birthday parties!"

I look around me, surrounded by the faces I love, and my heart sings. What a perfect impromptu moment of joy for all of us.

Chapter 17

That night, after everyone has gone to bed, I take the packet of papers from Mama's nightstand and read them.

The first paper is all I care about. It's a land deed in a place called Zuid-Afrikaansche Republiek.

A few weeks later, Morris returns one last time to Falling Waters to pack up his medical equipment and carry it back to Cairo. We only have a few moments alone together—it seems that everyone in town wants to speak with Morris before he leaves. He's a good doctor and a kind teacher, and there is hardly a person in town whose life he hasn't touched.

He comes to see me early one morning before the dawn breaks, already on his way back to Cairo. I wait for him, the packet of papers with the gold rock clutched in my hands. Today is the day. If I'm going to be able to live with myself, I have to tell him the truth.

My heart pounds.

"There's something I have to tell you," I say. "Something I've needed to tell you for a long, long time. Something that is going to make you rethink your feelings about me."

Morris watches me. Something flickers in his eyes, something I don't quite understand.

I lay the packet on the ground. I can't think while I'm holding it.

"A long time ago," I say, but my words falter. He takes my hands and moves me to a fallen log. We sit down.

"I did something. Or I didn't do something that I was supposed to have done. Something that would have changed your life."

Morris watches me with kind, steady eyes. "Whatever it was," he says, "if it was a long time ago, you were probably too young…"

"No," I say. I place a finger on his lips. "You can't talk, please. This is really hard for me to say, and if you stop me from talking, I'm afraid I won't be able to tell the whole story."

"Okay," Morris says, and takes my hands in his.

But I pull them away.

"I have to do this alone," I say. "I was getting water from the spring," I begin, and dole out the entire sordid story. I look into the woods as I speak because I can't look up at him, can't stand the thought of what I know he might do, the gradual pulling away, the judgment in his eyes, the anger. He can hate me. I might never see him again. He will go to Cairo and live his life. I steel my heart. I can stand it. I can. And now, I feel an overwhelming relief. I have said what I had to say.

I look up at him.

He is looking down at his hands. He doesn't meet my eyes.

The silence grows big between us until the chasm is so wide it will be impossible to cross.

"I wish I could have met my father," Morris says.

His words fall like raindrops on a tin roof, rattling my soul. I wait for recrimination. But he has none.

"You were a little girl, Annie Laura. Nine years old. Your own mama was giving birth to your baby sister and bleeding out. How could you be expected to relay a message that didn't seem life threatening? Because when you left that cabin, no one was dying. My pa had suffered a thunk on the head, that was all. It needed tending, but he wasn't going to die of it."

The way he speaks the words makes it sound as though they have been walking around in his head for a long time.

A hawk circles above us, his lazy swooping glide forcing us to look up into the painfully sunny blue sky. Morning has broken, harsh and bright. The hawk's circle eddies and flows, and soon he flies away, out of sight. "His prey has been granted another day of life," Morris says.

I nod. As have we all.

"I didn't know Benjamin hit him with his sling shot," Morris said. "I didn't realize Mama had taken him inside the cabin to take care of him."

My forehead wrinkles. Morris sounds like he knew the rest of the story.

He looks at me. "Benjamin said his daddy caught my whore mama in bed with another man and burned the house down around them. I left it alone. I didn't want my mama's name dragged through the mud."

"You knew?" I ask.

"Most of it," Morris says. "John Sebring happened on it. He was in the woods checking his traps. He told me about it after John Calvin died. He said he feared if he told me before, I would have killed him myself."

"You knew I was there?"

"I knew that much—"

"I'm so sorry, Morris. I know you might never forgive me for killing your parents."

"You didn't kill my parents. John Calvin Blakely did that."

"If I had told you like your mama asked me to, it wouldn't have happened."

"That, or I would have been killed in the fire with my father."

My heart thuds. And in that instant, I know Morris is right. If I had told him that day, he would have been in the burning house too. John Calvin Blakely knew Morris wasn't his son, and there was no love lost between them.

"So you probably saved my life," Morris says.

"You're very generous," I say. Hope, as gentle as a baby's sigh, breathes into my heart.

He nods. All this time, he knew. Or he knew most of the story, anyway.

"John Sebring told me what Benjamin said—that John Calvin would kill your family if you told anybody. That secret must have eaten you up, Annie Laura. I'm sorry."

He is apologizing to me. It isn't right.

"You have nothing to be sorry for," I insist.

He looks away, up into the sky, as if searching for the hawk. Though the sky is painfully bright, the day is cold. I shiver.

He puts his arm around me. "You're cold," he says.

I move in to him. Forgiven. I feel so relieved that I take a deep, shuddering breath. What trials we have both been through. He has known all along. Had forgiven me a long time ago.

We sit in silence for a while, and then Morris trembles, a deep, hard tremble. When he takes a deep, gasping breath and shudders, I don't look at him, giving him his privacy. But he grips me in his arms, pulls me close to him, and sobs deep, quaking sobs.

"I didn't know the man who died with Mama was my daddy," he says.

When his grief is spent, he glances at the brown cotton fields, denuded of their crops. He swallows. "I'm not in much of a position to make promises," he says.

I smile. "If you were in a position to make promises, what would you say?"

"I would say that as soon as I can take care of you, I'm coming back."

I smile so big that my eyes nearly squeeze shut. My smile wipes the serious right off his face. He smiles back. "Will you wait for me, Annie Laura? I don't know how long it will be, but will you wait?"

"I'll wait," I say.

"I know how much you love the land, and I want to be able to buy you enough land to farm. I want..." He stumbles over his words.

"You want?" I say for him.

"I want to marry you, Annie Laura. I want our children to run free on their own land. I want them to learn the ways of the earth. I want you to teach them the secrets of growing and producing, of creating bountiful harvest, and loving the land while you do so."

If I were any other girl, I'd be thrilled at this proposal. But I'm me, and though I love this man more than I can ever love anyone, I have a lot to do before I can think about getting married. I have to care for my little sisters, keep them fed and clothed because it doesn't look like Papa is going to be much help. But I do believe that if I hold out long enough to keep them healthy and whole, there's a rainbow out there, and no matter how far away it is, it's still a bright promise that my story will end happily.

132

"I love you, Morris Blakely," I say. "I'll wait for you until I'm an old woman if I have to."

He laughs, takes me in his arms, and hugs me to him.

And then he pulls away. Places a finger beneath my chin. Lifts my lips to his. And ever so gently, he kisses me. I shudder, lean into him, and give myself to him completely.

We stand, locked in each other's arms until the horse shakes his head and Maisie calls out to us.

"I love you, Annie Laura," Morris says.

"Write me?" I ask.

"Often," he says. He mounts his horse again, turns, tips his cap, and rides off into the morning light.

And then I remember the parcel.

Chapter 18

Once Morris receives this packet, I know I won't see him for a year or more. The passage to the Transvaal will take a month at least. And from there, who knows how long it will take him to find his father's gold mine.

Because that's the secret the packet held, the truth Mama wanted me to share with Morris.

But my heart had to unburden my truth first. And in the unburdening, I had forgotten the packet.

After Morris finds the mine, how long will it take him to secure his claim? It's been over a decade since his father left the Transvaal to return to America. I'm pretty sure his plan was to rescue Miss Harriet from a loveless marriage and take her to his new home.

My heart hurts at the thought of losing Morris for so long.

But Morris is now just a speck in the distance, and I could bury this knowledge.

After all, who knows if the gold mine is still in operation? Or still belongs to his father? Or, for that matter, if Morris would even want to go?

But my heart knows better. Morris needs money, needs an income, needs to be able to be independent. Am I an evil person? Am I so selfish that I would keep Morris from his patrimony just to keep him close?

What is wrong with me? I rush out the door.

"Morris!" I call. But Morris is gone.

I run to the barn. Papa has taken the horse. All that's left is my mule. Daisy stands in her stall munching lazily on her breakfast of hay. It's going to be tough to talk her into running after Morris's horse. She has a strong sense of self-preservation, and if she thinks she is going to have to pull a plow all day long, she's not about to waste her breath running beforehand.

"Come on, girl." I pray that putting the saddle on her will convince her this is not a plow day. She watches me with patient brown eyes. Curious, but patient. Maybe she'll be agreeable and help me catch up with Morris.

I mount Daisy and talk gently to her. "Come on, girl. Don't let me down." I ride her to the dirt road and urge her forward. She speeds up some, but not as much as I need her to. She's doing a jarring fast walk, not the smooth gait she is capable of. Perhaps she's trying to determine whether we are still headed to a field to plow. She continues at this pace until we pass the last of our own fields.

As soon as we pass the fields, she seems to sniff the air like she's making a decision. And she does. I urge her forward, and she moves into her smooth gait.

We've already lost too much time. Morris is far ahead of us. I can only hope that he might stop in town to recheck his medical supplies before they're loaded on the train to Cairo.

I hear the train's whistle and know I'm too late. My chance of being able to catch Morris is slim to none.

Part of me says, *At least you tried. You can tell him that if you don't catch him. And then you can mail the packet.*

But what if the packet gets lost in the mail?

No, I will have to personally deliver the information, even if it means taking Daisy all the way to Cairo. I whisper a thank-you prayer for Isabelle. She'll tend to Maisie, Emma, and the new baby, and can be trusted to take care of everyone until I return. Eva will help her.

However, as soon as we pass town and head out onto open road, Daisy slows her gait. This is new territory. She has no idea how long we will be traveling—nor do I—and she isn't about to sacrifice herself.

Surely Morris won't be able to keep up such a fast pace? Surely he will stop somewhere to let his horse drink and graze?

Daisy ambles along for what seems hours, in spite of my frequent encouraging kicks to her sides. Truth be told, we've been on the road for an hour at the most.

My stomach rumbles, and Daisy slows even more. She must smell water. She turns off the road, and had I the will I would steer her back, but I've given up hope of finding Morris and feel that allowing her to drink is the humane thing to do. She takes me down a trail, and I have to trust her. My mule would never wander unless it was for her own benefit. Sure enough, within a few minutes I can hear running water. The dense brush clears onto a pool as blue as Morris's eyes and just as clear. There are several of these springs around Northwest Florida, but finding one always feels like finding a treasure chest.

I hop to the ground and let Daisy drink her fill.

A horse whinnies, and I looked across the spring, perhaps twenty feet, to see the brown horse that belongs to Morris. My heart leaps. But where is Morris?

Fear twists my thoughts. Has Benjamin come for him and, finding him alone, killed him? I look around, but Morris is nowhere to be seen. *Calm yourself, Annie Laura. The poor man probably just needed to relieve himself.*

I drink from the spring. The water is clear and cold, and tastes as lovely as it looks.

I hear a rustling across the spring and look up to see Morris holding his brown saddlebag steady while he pats down something inside. He doesn't see me.

Not wanting to frighten him, I wait until he is finished with whatever it is in that saddlebag that has his attention.

The horse whinnies again, and this time Daisy offers up an answering bray.

Morris, startled, reaches for the revolver at his waist and trains it on me.

"Whoa!" I say. "It's just me!"

"Annie Laura?" He peers across the spring, squinting. "Is that you?"

"It is," I say, and I can't keep the thrill out of my voice. Even though we have only been apart for a few hours, I am deliriously happy to see him again.

"Just a moment, let me get around there." He takes his horse by the bridle and leads him into the dark, swampy overhang of cypress, magnolia, and oak before reappearing on my side of the spring.

"What is it?" he asks, worry lines etched deeply in his forehead.

"No, it's fine, everyone is fine." His kindness and concern melt my heart and make my next words very difficult.

"I have something I meant to give you before you left."

He seems taken aback. "Something that required you to follow me down the highway, nearly to Cottondale?" Fear replaces worry in his face. "Have you lost your land? Are those papers kicking you out, too?"

"No, no, nothing like that," I say. "Papa is on the road right now looking for a lawyer to help us straighten out the property issue. I don't think it's going to be a problem."

Morris looks skeptical. "Then what was so important that you followed me down the road riding Daisy?"

We both laugh at this. I love my Daisy, but Morris knows her stubborn ways.

"Let's find a place and sit down. And don't worry. This is nothing but good news." My face and heart do not match my words. I feel Morris studying me. My biggest fear is that Morris will become a rich man, and many years will pass before he is able to—or wants to—see me again.

Morris ties his horse to a nearby tree and unbuckles the blanketroll secured to the saddle.

"I found some gingerroot," he says, patting his saddlebag. "Rare, but good for all sorts of complaints. I've never seen it in this part of Florida. I think someone must have planted it a long time ago in a backyard garden, and then moved on."

I smile. He is eager as a young boy to show me the root, and I take a moment to admire it.

I look around and consider the possibility that this could have been someone's backyard long ago. The difficulty of making a living in Florida—the harsh climate, the mosquitoes and snakes, not to mention bears and panthers—must have made pioneering here a daunting task. It is hard enough for us in these modern times.

Papa had moved us to Florida only because Falling Waters could be reached by rail, which meant there was a town and, therefore, some protection from the wild beasts, though little protection from the heat and mosquitoes.

Why am I so determined to stay here? It's because I have made my own way. I've been successful despite all the odds—including my Papa—being piled against me. I'm a foreigner. I'm a woman. And I'm young. But none of that has mattered. I've done what I set out to do, and no one can take it away from me.

Morris spreads the blanket and we both sit down, me clutching a bag containing the packet and the gold.

"So," Morris says, teasingly, "are you going to show me what you have there?"

I peel my fingers away and hand it over, my heart pounding and my face hot.

"You don't look as though this does, in fact, bring good news," Morris quips, pulling open the packet.

The gold rock spills out onto the dark green blanket. It shimmers in the sun. "What's this?" he asks, picking up the rock. "Fool's gold?"

"No, I don't think so. I'm pretty sure it's real."

He studies it, his forehead wrinkling again. "Whose is it?"

"Yours." I smooth down my skirt and hold my own hands.

"I don't remember losing it," he says.

"Just read." I can't contain my fear, and my words sound angry. He backs imperceptibly away, my tone a blow.

"All right," he says.

And he reads.

It takes him a while, long enough for the cardinal mama in the tree above me to travel back and forth to feed her babies ten different times. I watch her because I don't want to see Morris's delight once he realizes the rich heritage his father has gifted to him.

He finishes reading, places the packet of papers in a neat stack, and slides them back into the bag. He holds the gold rock in his hand.

He sighs, closes his eyes and wets his lips. He looks down at me, catches my chin with his forefinger, tips my face up to his, and kisses me deeply.

It's both tender and passionate.

"Take the gold," he says, pressing the glittering rock into my hand. "Secure your land with it."

"No, Morris. The gold is for you to buy passage to the Transvaal. You must go immediately. I've held on to this far longer than I should. First as a girl, fearful of what you might think of me, and these past few weeks as a woman afraid that it meant the end of us."

Morris nods and looks away. The little cardinal flies one final trip, away from her nest and back again, and her baby birds hush their peeping, full at last.

"I'll come back for you, Annie Laura. Will you wait?"

I nod. The tears rise from somewhere deep inside me, swell my throat, force their way into my eyes and down my cheeks. I wipe them with my sleeve, and Morris clutches me to his chest. I drink in the smell of him and quiet my own sobbing until I hear the certain, calming thud of his heart, thrumming against my ear. *I'll come back. I'll come back. I'll come back.*

And I know he will.

Morris writes me from New York, just before he boards the transatlantic ocean liner that will take him first to England and then to the Transvaal. The journey will take the better part of a month, but he assures me that the gold piece has been enough to pay for his passage and travel expenses.

Papa seems distressed when I tell him Morris's news. "Yes, your mama told me about his opportunity. Has he gone yet?"

"I received this letter from him today. He's gone."

"I have friends from the Prussian army who invested heavily in the gold mines," Papa says. "Some did very well. Others sold their holdings for less than they paid."

"Still, free land is free land. If he makes nothing from the mines, then he can sell the land and come home."

Papa smiles. "You would like that, my Annie?"

I blush. "Yes, Papa, I would."

"You wish to marry this Dr. Morris Blakely?"

"One day, yes." It's funny how when something gets taken away you realize how desperately you want it. Such is the case with Morris. I miss him so much already and look forward to the day when he will return home. Then, maybe, Papa will be satisfied with his ability to support me, and we can marry.

"He is a good man. He will take good care of you."

"Thank you, Papa."

Papa folds the newspaper he still receives off the train every day without fail, the German news, usually two weeks old, but news nonetheless. "The German papers are reporting Dutch concern about the invasion of the English into their land in the Transvaal. They worry that another war will break out soon."

"War?"

"Where there are riches, there is always war."

"How soon?"

"Nothing has been officially declared."

My heart drops. War? What if Morris arrives there and, because of a war, he can't get back?

"Wars never last forever," Papa says, as if reading my mind.

Chapter 19

May 1899

I walk alone through the still woods, a basket of teacakes on my arm for my sharecropper and his boys. They love sweets, and I want them to eat them while they're fresh. The boys work hard, and the Lord knows their mama's not going to feed them.

The May day is hot, the air oppressive and still. An annoying trickle of sweat slides down my back. I pull my hair up off the nape of my neck and twist it into a bun.

In the great silence, I can hear myself breathe. I look up and around, listening for the sound of a friendly bird, but not even a mockingbird sings. All I can hear is the crackling of the dried-out pine straw beneath my feet. I look up in the tall loblolly pines for some friendly squirrels—there is always at least one leaping from branch to branch—but even the squirrels are gone today.

Maisie would say, "Maybe they're all having a squirrel party somewhere." I wish she were with me. I would welcome her sweet chatter. Holding her little hand would take away the strangeness and the silence.

A thin plume of smoke rises like an arrow above the pine tree before me.

Fire.

Fear paralyzes me until I realize that it's too far away to be on my farm. It looks to be in the direction of town. The still air is now my friend. The fire—maybe someone burning their trash—will stay wherever it is.

Suddenly, an explosion rocks the woods. The century oaks quiver. I put my hand on a sappy pine to brace myself. What was it? The only sound I know that loud is the cannon that gets fired on the Fourth of July in remembrance of the war—the war that ravaged this land in the years before my family came. Is this the beginning of another war?

I pull my hand away from the tree and try to wipe the sticky pine sap onto my skirt. I'm shaking.

A horse pounds down the sandy path toward me, its rider leaning forward, urging the steed to breakneck speed. Seeing me, the rider reins in his mount.

My heart climbs up my throat. Morris! He's home! I clutch my basket, pick up my skirts and run toward him, my heart pounding.

I can already imagine him hopping down off his horse, lifting me high, swirling me around so that I'm safe in his arms. And announcing he will stay! Joy makes me giddy.

But it's not Morris. "Fire downtown...get help!" the neighbor says.

Disappointment strangles me, then makes my words come out small. "I'll get Tom and the twins and find Papa."

Tiny clouds of clay-dust rise behind him. Another explosion rocks the woods, shaking the trees and me. I pray it isn't near the schoolhouse and all the children. Tom and his boys fly by, their bare feet making soft thudding sounds.

"Get some buckets," Tom calls.

The church bells gongs *emergency*, and I run for buckets and my papa.

As I near the house, the smoke over the horizon grows, now a writhing cloud shadowing the sun. The entire town must be on fire. I pound up my wooden stairs. Another explosion, and the solid oak front door shudders.

I look behind me and see that Papa has already saddled the horse. He waves and rides away, wooden buckets thumping against his saddle.

It's then that I remember Margaret and baby Bonnie.

"Papa, wait!" I call, but it's too late. Papa disappears down the road.

Margaret's house borders the town and is probably in danger of being burned to the ground. John Sebring is not due to arrive until later this evening—he's on his way back from fishing in Anderson. I have to help her. I think about saddling my mule but realize she will

142

balk if she even smells smoke. I'm left with one choice. I run down the sand and clay road for Margaret's house. *Get me there quickly. Please, Lord.*

The formerly quiet wooded road is now crowded with men headed towards town, most on foot but some on horses and mules. They're armed with buckets and gunny sacks to beat down the angry blaze. I hurry through them, weaving between hooves and bare feet.

I'm pushed back by the sheer force of these men, determined to get to town to save their loved ones. But I'm propelled forward by a strength I didn't know existed, and the familiar faces around me congeal into an anonymous mass of strangers that I must push through.

When I cross over and into the woods, I understand the risk I'm taking. The tangled growth hides rattlesnakes, wild hogs, and an occasional bear, but I'm not scared. I figure on the critters running away from the fire, not towards it, and forge ahead. This is the quickest way to my Margaret.

I hear someone cut into the woods behind me. At least I'll not be alone. I look back, but whoever it is must fear discovery as he, or she, ducks out of my vision when I glance back. Perhaps the person is running away, not wanting to risk his own life to fight the fire. I don't have time to stop and ask why.

Dense growth and vine-shrouded trees make navigating the woods difficult even on a sunny day. Today, the sun is hidden behind layers of billowing smoke, casting a thick cloud over the nearly impenetrable woods.

But the path is familiar to me. Margaret and I frequent the narrow path, even though Papa warns us against it. He says the woods are too dangerous. But Papa came from the old country where the woods were filled with carnivorous wolves, and we are grown women.

I think of the fun-filled afternoons Margaret and I spent here in the woods gathering kindling first for Mama's stove, then Papa's furnace, and later for Margaret's little woodstove after she and John Sebring married. The possibility of danger made the foray into the woods exciting, and together Margaret and I were fearless.

An unfamiliar chill runs through me, though the day is hot. Perhaps it's simply because the woods aren't the same without Margaret. Perhaps it's the fire. The truth is, I've never ventured into this part of the deep woods alone. What if Margaret is caught in the fire? Before I know it, I'm all-out running, hoping my memory of the path will keep me safe. Panic sweeps over me and propels me forward even faster.

I hear a sound behind me again, but I don't have time to turn around. I listen hard as I run, but I hear nothing but the sound of my own feet thrashing the now swampy floor. My feet make a sucking sound. I must be close to the spring. The woods darken, and I can't see around me. Am I going in the right direction? I stop, and though I can't see three feet in front of me, I put my hand on the gnarly old oak, as big around as three men, where Margaret and I often stop to rest and talk. My hand on that oak calms me, and I feel safe. I run forward, faster now.

I hear another noise. Thinking I might find a familiar face running along behind me, I turn midstride to look. But there is nothing. When I turn back around, I nearly trip over an oak log lying in my path. I hold tight to my skirts and jump over it. Only I don't see the massive pine root stretching its long tendrils across my path. I land on the root, and my foot slips, turning my ankle sharply with all my weight resting on it.

The pain, sharp and intense, makes me yelp like a hurt dog. I tumble, roll off the pine root and into a palmetto stand. Fronds smack my face, blinding me.

I lie still for a moment and breathe, willing away the pain. Pine trees spread their shallow roots in every direction in the sandy pine woods. They shoot out like sparks from a newly stoked fire, and I curse myself for not noticing them.

I roll away from the palmetto bush. Margaret. I have to get up and go. I jump up, but the pain in my ankle yanks me to the ground.

Flat on my back, tears tickle my ears. I look around me for a walking stick. I get on my knees and crawl among the pine roots. I lay my hand on a fallen branch. Relief courses through me. But it

144

crumbles in my hand. Pine. I need sturdy oak. I fling the rotten mess away and crawl deeper into the woods. I have to find a sturdy branch. Time is running out.

I know that just to my left is a grove of oaks. Papa was particular about the best kind of wood to burn for stoking his fires. He had never thought to ask where I found it. Margaret and I discovered deep in the oak grove, close to the spring, that there was always plenty of strong, new wood blown down by Florida thunderstorms.

I ease myself to a standing position on my one good leg, my back against the sturdy trunk of a massive pine tree. I hobble toward the oak grove. A branch crackles behind me. Probably a scared animal moving as quickly as it can away from the fire. But the thought doesn't comfort me. I ignore my gut and the hair rising on the back of my neck. Sheer panic, I tell myself.

The smoke-covered sun fights a losing battle through the dense oak. I hop along on my good foot. It's slow going, what with all the exposed roots, and I know I have to come up with a better plan. I can crawl faster than I can hop, so I fall to my knees. I don't see the puddle of murky sludge. April storms have left standing water in this section of the low-lying woods.

I yank my skirts out of the sludge and shimmy away from the rank, mosquito-breeding pool. I swat a thumb-sized mosquito away from my eyes. More swarm, and they feast on my arms and exposed legs like I'm a dish served up especially for them. I brush away as many as I can, but more come to fill their place.

I have to find a solid oak stick. Why is this so hard? Normally there are plenty. If I don't find one quickly, I'll have to crawl out of the woods.

What good will I be to Margaret with my bum leg and no walking stick?

I'll defeat the pain. I'll simply stand and pretend it's not there. I'm bigger than this pain. I stand, plant both feet. I walk forward. And sprawl on the ground. The pain makes colored lights swirl before my eyes.

I'll have to crawl to Margaret's house. A branch I can use for a walking stick might turn up on the way. I grit my teeth and hurtle forward.

Dried leaves crackle behind me. Wild hogs? The last thing I need is to tangle with a boar—I'd seen one with tusks a foot long, and teeth to match. I look around for a tree to climb. A branch snaps. I move as quietly as I can to the base of an oak tree. I pick up a large stick for protection, but it crumbles in my hand. My heart pounds.

Whatever it is comes closer and then stops. I can hear breathing now, quick and hard like someone has been running. This is not a hog. I want to feel relief, but something about the silence is terrifying.

"Who's there?" I speak into the silence. "Who is it?"

More breathing. I look behind me. Not a hint of sunlight sparkles through the high branches. I'm in utter darkness. A sense of foreboding sweeps through me. My stomach clenches.

"What do you want?" I ask the silence.

The breathing is right next to me now. I could reach out and touch whoever it is. But I don't. Fear freezes me.

The blow comes out of the darkness. I hurtle to the ground, facedown in the rich black dirt, and something hard lands on my back. I can't breathe. A hand claws at the back of my shirt, snatching it up and away. I struggle against it. Front buttons held my blouse together, but they are tugged so tight the material becomes a noose digging into my neck, choking me. I clutch at my neck, pull down so I can breathe. The man curses.

I know the voice.

The sharp blade of a knife slices through my shirt, touching my skin at the nape of my neck. I'm thrust down flat.

"No!" I scream. I claw and punch. He slams my head, and I taste rich, black dirt. I spit the dirt, push up, kick wildly, strike home. I hear a guttural "bitch." A sharp pain in my head. Then blackness.

Chapter 20

When I wake, the air smells of smoke. I can't tell if it's day or night. Mosquitoes whir around my ears, and the taste of blood is in my mouth. My battered body aches. A rush of memory, and I wish death might come quickly.

I taste dirt and spit it out. The land, my source of strength, of hope, of joy, has betrayed me, a silent witness to my disgrace. I pound the earth beneath me and curse the day I naively believed it to be my salvation.

And then I remember Margaret.

I will crawl to her. I lift my head, and pain squeezes my eyes shut. The pounding drowns out any sound, and I rest my head on the dirt. I take a deep breath and pray for the strength to find my friend.

If I lift my head slowly, maybe it won't hurt so bad. Oh so slowly, I force my aching body up, pull my blouse closed, and bind it with my head scarf.

Something moves close to me. I roll into a tight ball.

"Annie Laura?"

It's a woman's voice, and I recognize it.

I open my eyes, and Tabitha, my Morris's half-sister, draws near.

"I have to go save Margaret," I say.

"Yes, sweet girl, yes. But let's get you taken care of first."

I strain to see her, but darkness has descended on my world.

My head aches. "She needs me." Every word I speak feels like a hot knife searing my brain.

"I saw John Sebring on the road. He's headed for Margaret and the baby."

Relief washes over me, tears form in my eyes, tickle my face. "John Sebring. Yes."

Tabitha helps me stand. Something warm eases down my legs. The thick liquid is not menstrual blood.

I weep.

Tabitha holds me close. "I didn't get here fast enough. I tried. God knows I tried. But I didn't. I saw him break off the road, saw him take off after you, but I was too far back. Road too crowded. When I found my way into the woods..."

My stomach clenches. "Why would you need to follow him?"

"Come on, girl. Let's get you to the spring."

I snatch my hand away. "Why did you feel like you needed to follow him?" I don't care that I can't hear my own words for the pain in my head.

She looks away.

She knew.

"I tried, I did, but I couldn't catch him."

Rage like nothing I've ever felt courses through my body. "How did you know what he was going to do? How could you possibly know and let him go?"

"He was too fast..." She is pleading with me now, her eyes filled with tears, but I don't care. I'm shaking with fury.

"You could have sent someone in the woods, you could have screamed out what you thought he was doing."

"And you think anyone would have stopped and listened?"

She is right, and I know it. The fire, the fear of losing their loved ones, the fear of losing their town was far more important than preventing what might happen to me. I'm a foreigner. It doesn't matter that I've been here since I was a child. It doesn't matter that Mama has baked for them and Papa has kept them supplied with fine-quality match holders, pots, pans, and woodstoves. It doesn't matter that I've worked alongside them, learned their ways, respected them, and built a farm that I believed they all took pride in.

No, because all those things I ignored about them are what has brought me to this day. The way the men look at me when I dare wear long pants to tend my fields. The whisperings: *Why ain't she in the store buying doo-dads like the other women instead of hanging out here on the porch with us?*

I didn't chew and spit, but I hung around with those men, hungry for information on how to build a successful farm. I let my sister and my mama do the shopping, paid for by my sweat. But I built a successful farm. I did it. I listened to those men, despite their jibes, and I learned from them.

And that knowledge? They can't take it away from me. The thought gives me the strength, and the strength gives me compassion for Tabitha.

She has it as hard as I do. She is also a foreigner of a sort, an unmarried female, a spinster, now far too old to ever marry. She is shunned and made fun of. She's raised her half-brothers and -sisters alone, and tried keeping them in line after her papa died.

Only one of them she never has been able to keep in line.

And that is not Tabitha's fault.

I need to direct my anger where it belongs.

"I'm sorry," I whisper.

"No need."

I nod my thanks. "I want to wash myself." I want to wash away the filth. I want to wash away the memory.

Tabitha hands me a walking stick and helps me stand, but the pain between my legs forces memory. I clutch my skirts tightly around me, covering every inch of my lower body, and let Tabitha help me hobble my way to the spring. Her arm around me feels surprisingly safe, and I lean into her.

I don't know exactly how Tabitha guessed his intentions. I don't want to know. I don't want to think about it—I only want to wash myself clean and forget.

When we approach the spring, the full moon brightens the heavy clouds of smoke. I shed my boots, touch the water with my toe, and wash my ankle clean. It throbs, but the water is refreshing. While the day has been still—a blessing that perhaps kept the fire away from Margaret's house and contained to the town—the gentlest of breezes now whispers through the pines.

"Would you like for me to hold your clothes and keep them dry?" Tabitha's voice, though gentle, pierces the silence like a sharp blade, and I shudder.

I feel chilled to the bone, though the late spring evening is dense and warm. I wrap my arms around myself, clinging to the shredded bits that had been my blouse.

"No, thank you, I'll wear them in."

I can't abide the thought of being naked and vulnerable, and I step out into the cooling waters with all my clothes safely on. I inch my way along the sandy bottom that stretches several feet before it drops off. The spring is hundreds of feet deep. No one has ever plumbed its depths. Tonight, I'm tempted. I only need to step off the sandy shelf, and my skirts will do their job. They will pull me down, down, down, catch on a deeply submerged root, and I will be released to Mama, to Oma, to Jesus.

"Don't you get too far out. I can't swim." That's Tabitha with her seer's gift for reading my thoughts.

I ease myself to the very edge of that ledge. I'm weightless, the water closes over my head and shuts me in for being so stupidly alone in the woods. Papa had warned me often enough. "There are bad people in the world, Annie," he had said. "Bad men. Watch yourself. Take care. Never go into the woods alone."

I raise my head above the water, take a breath. I look around for absolution. The silence of the spring is my judge.

Did I bring this upon myself because I am stupidly impulsive? Whatever possessed me to take a shortcut through the woods? Why hadn't I just gone down the road like everyone else?

Not everyone else.

The tears course down my face and mix with the cool spring waters. I slide under the water, wishing never to rise again.

I hear Mama's voice of reason. *No, my Annie, this is not your fault. You went looking for a stick so that you could help your friend save her baby. You are good, you are loving, you are kind. You did not deserve this horror. Whoever did this to you is a sick creature who will suffer the consequences of the great evil he has visited upon you.*

I allow myself to be caressed in the embrace I imagine to be Mama's. Or is it God's? The water spreads my skirts around me, buffering me like a protective shield.

I come up for a breath, look around, and see Tabitha kneeling on the shore. Moonlight streams between the trees, lights the spring and illuminates her silhouette. She looks like some ancient celestial being, her hair glowing, white as the sand on which she kneels.

I hear a rustling in the woods close to Tabitha. I panic and scream at the top of my lungs, "No! Go away. Leave me alone!" I reach an arm towards the deep center of the spring, this time for safety. Can I swim out? Or will my skirts pull me to my death?

"Hush, child. You're safe." Despite her fear of water, Tabitha moves swiftly towards me. Her back is stooped as though she carries a heavy burden, her body unable to bear the pain. "He's nowhere near here—he took off long ago." She reaches for me. "Sweet child, get on up out of that water and come to me."

Her certainty calms me, and I paddle to the shallow water to meet her. Oh, Tabitha.

Our gazes lock. She wants to speak. I can see her mouth working in the faint light.

I watch her. And I understand. "I'm not the first, am I?"

Tabitha stops, waist deep in the water. I shiver, and the back of my head throbs. I touch it gingerly. I remember him cursing me, then striking the back of my head. I remember the voice. I feel weak. The water roils around me and I vomit into the cleansing spring. I escape up onto the sandy shore, away from my own bile.

"Who else?" I ask, my head spinning. "Who else did he do this to?"

Tabitha's eyes are fixed on a star and unutterably sad.

I try to find her star, but I can't, and I vomit again into the white sand.

Chapter 21

I suck in a sick breath of smoke-filled air, gag and cough. Who else? What other poor girl has this man savaged? And why? Why did he do it? I need to see Margaret. I want her beside me, listening intently the way she does, with compassion and complete understanding. She is my friend, and I need her now.

"Do you have your wagon?"

Tabitha nods.

A feeling comes to me like a shadow, uninvited, and I fear the worst. Margaret's house is too close to town. What if the baby and Margaret were napping when the fire started, and John hadn't gotten there in time?

I try to stand on the shore, but my sopping wet skirts pull me down even before the sharp pain of my ankle. If it weren't for this injury, I could have gotten to Margaret. I would know she is safe.

And I would still be me instead of this pained thing that I don't recognize.

But realization like a cold chill passes through me. I'm shivering, the cold working its way from my head all the way down my body.

Hurt ankle or not, the man—who does not deserve to be called by his name—would still have attacked me. If not today, then later. The realization is sobering. What if he had attacked me with my little sisters nearby? What if he tries to attack my little sisters?

I want to kill him.

And I will.

As soon as I know Margaret is safe.

"I have to find Margaret. I have to help her with Bonnie." I speak the words into the darkness.

"I understand," Tabitha says, startling me. "I've got the mule and wagon, but first we have to get you dry enough to walk."

Tabitha lifts the shawl from around her shoulders and places it around mine. My chin vibrates with a will of its own. Tabitha reaches down and grabs hold of my skirts. I jerk away, scrambling like a crab across the sand, my sodden skirts a barrier.

"Oh, child," Tabitha says. "I'm not going to hurt you. See, here? I'm just wringing the water out of your skirts. Otherwise, you won't make it to the wagon. They weigh more than you do."

I shudder. What if I'm too late?

"I'm real thankful it's warm out so you only have the one skirt and petticoat," Tabitha says, gingerly moving towards me, and checking to see if I'm going to let her touch my clothes. "Otherwise," she continues, taking my skirt oh so gently, rolling it up and wringing it out, "I fear you might have drowned in that spring." Tabitha pauses and studies me. "Child, if I could squeeze your pain out the way I'm able to squeeze out this water, I would do it."

She reaches for me again. I can't have it. I can't have anyone touch me. I back away. A buzzing sound fills my ears.

"I've got you," Tabitha says and helps me to a fallen oak. "You sit here for a moment and let the oak tree help dry out that skirt."

After I'm seated, she watches me, seeking permission to touch my skirts. I take a deep, shuddering breath and nod.

"Okay," she says, and maintains eye contact with me as she reaches.

I whimper when she grabs hold and wrings out the sodden mess. She hums a tune I don't recognize, but it soothes me enough for her to arrange my skirts along the massive oak roots, spreading them so they don't touch the ground.

My head throbs. What had he hit me with? I probe gingerly, my fingers tentative. The wound is at least clean, washed in the spring, but the cut is deep, and it stings. I rest my head on my arms and wonder how long I'll need to wait for my skirts to be dry enough to move comfortably. I lean against the massive oak and close my eyes, waiting.

Crackling flames jerk me awake. How long have I slept? Has the fire reached its arms out and found us?

But it's only a small campfire. Tabitha must have built it to help my skirts dry faster.

"You need to move a little closer if you can," Tabitha says. "It would be best if you could just take them off and let me hang them in these here trees, but I suspect you won't let me do that."

I clutch my skirts like they're life preservers.

"Well, here, then. You lean on me and let's see if we can stand close enough to the fire to dry you off." Tabitha takes my arm and stands me up, leading me closer to the fire's warmth.

I stand still and gaze into the fire. "Why?" My voice feels small, but the question encompasses all of me.

Sweat beads on Tabitha's forehead. "He's let evil get hold of him, sure enough," she says. "He hasn't always been this way, though. He was a sweet little boy. And then his mama died and he ain't been the same since." She shakes her head.

Anger rises in me, hot, strong, overpowering. It rises like a wave and crashes down on Tabitha.

"Am I supposed to have sympathy for him because his mama died? Your mama died, Tabitha, long ago, but you help people. And that sweet little boy? He was the one who made his mama die. He had evil in him even then. So don't sit there and try to make me feel empathy for that evil bastard. I want him dead."

"You don't mean that," Tabitha says.

"How many other women, Tabitha? How many?"

Tabitha flinches. She hides her face in the darkness.

"No. You turn your face back so I can see you. How many?"

"Someone is coming," she says.

A dim figure appears out of the darkness. My anger washes away.

John Sebring Corley comes stumbling through the woods. He walks into the campfire's light. He's carrying Margaret and a tiny, inert bundle. He doesn't notice us. He makes his way towards the spring. He's talking to himself.

"I have to kill the flames," he says. "I have to cool them off. They just got too hot, that's all."

We follow him. Tabitha clutches my waist, and I lean heavily on her shoulder.

The moon's light spangles the spring with icy glitter. John Sebring wades in, the heavy splashes of his boots breaking the silence of the night.

Margaret is very still.

"John Sebring," I call. I pull away from Tabitha and crawl into the spring after him.

He jumps a little but turns and smiles.

"I'm glad it's you," he says. His eyes are vacant. "Maybe you can help me out here. Can you hold Bonnie for a minute? I think if I get Margaret in the spring and rinse all the heat off of her, she'll be ok."

I kneel close to him in the water, the bank gentle, the sand soft against my knees. I look on the dark figure John Sebring holds in the water and swallow the sob that rises in my throat.

I reach out for the stiff little bundle nestled between Margaret and John.

John Sebring places the child in my arms. I hold her close, praying that the heat of my body will somehow force her limbs to move, force the baby babble from her mouth, force the toothy grin, the soft hands to touch my face. Oh, God, no. I rock Bonnie, hold her close, frantic with the belief that maybe, just maybe, she isn't gone, and I can bring her back. Tears course down my face. Bonnie's gown is whole, marred by neither burns nor scorches. I rub the embroidery and avoid the baby's cold hands and face.

John Sebring watches.

"You keep on like that," he says. "I'm going to see to Margaret." He moves away from me, taking Margaret deep into the heart of the spring, and I fear his desire is to keep walking and be swallowed up in the watery depths. I understand. The yearning is in me.

"John Sebring?" I call. "It's deep out there, be careful."

But he croons over Margaret. "Come on, sweetheart. I've brought you here to this place you love. Speak to me. Tell me how the water is so cooling on a hot day. Splash like you do and force me to swim and act like a kid again."

He swirls her around, and the ripples he creates lap gently against me. I lift the baby out of danger as if she lives.

John Sebring grows still. He stares at the lifeless form in his arms.

There is a long silence. At last it's broken by heart-wrenching sobs that tear through the night. Birds startle and fly away, tree branches crack, and leaves swirl madly with their leaving.

When his tears are spent, John Sebring turns back to the shore line and seeks my face.

"I tried to save her," he pleads.

"I know you did, John."

"It wasn't the flames that got her, so I knew if I could get her here to the spring, she would be fine and the baby, too. Is Bonnie okay, Annie?"

His tears shine in the moon's light. "When the fire came," John Sebring says, cradling his precious wife in the cooling waters, "I ran for home. Margaret was in the house, the fire blazing all around her. She was sitting in the rocking chair, holding Bonnie. 'She's gone, John,' my Margaret said to me."

John Sebring pauses, arranges Margaret's hair, brushing it from her face, fanning it out in the water around her.

He turns back to me, his face strained with yearning. "I ran in, Annie Laura, quick as I could, but the flames were quicker. I couldn't understand why Margaret was just sitting there in the rocking chair with our baby, letting the fire get them. The doorframe fell in and blocked my way. I had to go around back and go in the through the back door, through our bedroom and out into that blazing front room. I knew it was going to be too late. I screamed for her, 'Margaret! You've got to come on, get the baby and come on.' But when I finally got to her and batted out the flames, she was sleeping like this." And John holds Margaret out to me like an offering.

I fear what I might see, what the flames have done. I don't want to see her face, but John insists. Just as I look, the moon rises large above the oak trees, shining its bright light on her sweet, unblemished face.

"I don't understand. She looks good, like the fire didn't even get her."

"I think it was her heart," John Sebring says. "I think the grief. I don't know how long she had been sitting there with Bonnie gone, not breathing anymore. Had she sat there all day? And then the fire. Maybe she breathed too much smoke, or maybe it was all too much for her. I thought when I got to her and held her in my arms, maybe she would come back to me, but she didn't. She couldn't. Her eyes were on her child when they closed, and I reckon they are still."

I bow my head. *Sweet Jesus. Be with us.*

Why Margaret?

John Sebring rinses his wife tenderly, carefully. He bathes her as though she were alive. I shiver in the cold spring. I can't hold the baby any longer. She's a burden in my arms, so light, but so heavy. Tabitha waits at the shore. She takes the pitiful babe in her arms and helps me to the fire.

My tears are gone, washed away by the spring and the utter sadness and desolation of this night. My pain is nothing next to John Sebring's great loss. What can be worse than losing your beloved wife and baby?

I've lost my dearest friend.

In her wisdom, Tabitha gently lifts Bonnie out of gown and wraps the baby in her apron. She lays the bundle carefully on the ground and hangs the beautifully embroidered baby dress—the one I had watched Margaret create—on a branch near the fire to dry.

By the time the baby gown is dry and the inert body is dressed once again, John Sebring has lifted Margaret from the waters and laid her on the white sand. She glistens in the moonlight like an angel.

I lay the baby down beside her, arranging the white gown, its gentle folds caressing mother and child.

Words must be spoken, and there is no preacher nearby to speak.

I look at John Sebring.

He nods.

"Lord," John Sebring says, his voice shaky, "you gave me this precious gift. I thank you for it. I didn't do nothing to deserve it, but you gave freely. I tried my best to keep them safe. Now, they are yours. Treat them gently. Amen."

We sit until the moon grows small and the stars shine brightly in the black velvet sky. A whippoorwill pierces the silence, its haunting cry calling all souls to heaven. As if cued by the sound, the crickets and katydids begin their chorus. They sing a tentative note, then grow louder, their voices reverberating, rising through the trees to the sky and the stars beyond. The woods sing.

John Sebring seeks my hand. We listen.

Chapter 22

When I wake, it's morning, and I'm cold, so very cold. I hear whimpering, and it's coming from me. John Sebring kneels beside me. I flinch when he tries to pick me up. He doesn't ask questions. He knows nothing of what happened to me. He only knows his own raw grief. His silence soothes me, and I allow him to lift me into the wagon, beside the carefully wrapped bodies of Maggie and Bonnie. Tabitha works at steering the wagon home. John Sebring holds me, both of us shivering. We cradle our grief between us.

"Do you have a wrap?" John asks Tabitha.

She shakes her head.

Smoke blankets the trees like gray snow. It's hard to make out the road.

When Tabitha's mule finds its way to my house, John Sebring carries me inside and places me gently on the couch. I hear him murmur something to Eva. Her eyes are red like she's been crying. Was she worried about me? She hurries to cover me with a blanket and stokes the woodstove. The friendly flames warm my body but don't touch my heart. I fight sleep.

"John Sebring?" It's Mary Scarlet. She has an arm around Eva.

Why is Mary Scarlet here? My eyes are heavy.

"What happened?" Mary Scarlet walks toward him. John trembles and falls into her arms. She eases him down into a seat at the kitchen table. Eva pours him a steaming cup of coffee with a trembling hand.

I fight sleep, but my eyes close anyway, and I see Mama holding Maisie. They sit at the kitchen table. I'm not sure if it's a memory or a dream.

Mama offers Maisie a gingersnap. She points out the window to the trees, the birds, the flowers. Mama says, "God loves you so much, he painted you this beautiful picture. Isn't it beautiful?"

"For me?" Maisie answers. Her face shines with delight.

"For you, Maisie."

"And for Annie Laura? And Eva?"

"Yes," is Mama's gentle response, "for Annie Laura and Eva, too."

"And for you and for Papa?"

"Yes, for Papa and me, too," Mama says, and kisses her head.

"God likes to paint, doesn't he, Mama?"

"Yes, Maisie, he does."

"Mama, why did God take your mama away?"

Mama's voice is thick when she answers the unexpected question. "God took my mama to his home."

"Does it make you sad?" Maisie asks.

"Yes, it makes me sad," Mama says. "I miss her. But I know God has a beautiful home, much more beautiful than ours."

"Because he loves to paint."

"Yes," Mama agrees, "because he loves to paint. So, I have to think that she must be happy there."

"But how can you be happy without your people?" Maisie asks. "Doesn't she miss all of us?"

"Yes, I'm sure she does, Maisie. But you know, her own mama and papa and sisters and brothers are there, and all the people she loves. I suppose she might miss us, but she has plenty of people to keep her company until we come."

Maisie is quiet for a while. "Mama, when you go to God's home, can you take me with you, please?"

And now Mama's voice is clear, but her face sparkles with tears. "No, my sweet angel girl. I'll have to go alone. You will stay and be brave for Annie Laura and Eva and Papa. Can you do that for me?"

Maisie considers this for a few moments, munching her gingersnap. She swallows, takes a sip of the sweet cow's milk Mama has sitting out in the customary little blue tin mug, and says, "Yes, Mama. I will do that for you. I will miss you, but I will remember that one day I will be with you. And I will stay right here and take care of Annie Laura and Papa and Eva. Don't you worry about them." Then Maisie jumps from Mama's lap and runs outside down the stairs and into the beautiful world God has painted for her.

It's a deep sleep, hard and healing, the sleep of death or great shock. When I wake, the sun shines on my face through the open kitchen window. I feel refreshed until the smell of old smoke floats in the open window, and I'm jolted into remembering.

"Where's John?" I ask.

"Tom came and got him," Eva says, shaking the woodstove embers. "They needed his help. The fire was still burning at midnight and they needed manpower to stop it."

Eva hands me a teacup with steaming hot, fresh tea, and I thank her. She avoids looking at me. Does she know what happened?

When I see Maisie and Emma on the floor beside me, I realize they've been keeping watch over me. Maisie's dimpled hand rests on my arm, her head rests on the couch beside me. My throat closes with something I can't explain.

Emma looks up at me with grave eyes. "My mama took your baby sister," she says.

My entire body tenses. "What do you mean?"

"She's not going to keep Laura Viola," Maisie says. "She's just going to mind her so Isabelle can go home and check on her own mama, to make sure she made it safely through the fire."

"That's what my mama said. But she doesn't say the truth sometimes." Emma's brown eyes are wide and serious.

"Don't worry, Emma. Your mama just took my sister home with her. Isabelle couldn't take care of her. She had to go check on her family, see?" Maisie says.

But Emma shakes her head. "No. My mama took her and now she's gone. My daddy came here looking for Mama when you were sleeping. Eva said to him, 'But isn't she at your house?' and my daddy said, 'No, she ain't at our house. She's gone.'"

I look at Eva. Is this true? Is that why she was crying? "What is she talking about?" My words to Eva come out more harshly than I intend, and Eva backs away.

"She told me she could take care of the baby for me for a little bit. That she could sleep in Emma's old cradle. She said she would

161

keep her until Isabelle got back. I figured she was better at minding a baby than I am."

Had I never told Eva about the woman's track record with babies?

"Oh, Eva," I say, "what were you thinking?"

"I'm sorry, Annie Laura," Eva says, her chin jutted out, her hands on her hips. "But you just left me to take care of everything in the house like you always do. I didn't have the first notion of what to do after Isabelle left. The baby lifted a cry that would wake the dead. I was beside myself. And then you took your sweet time coming back," she says accusingly. "Did you find a beau in the woods or what?"

I recoil like I've been slapped. My mouth is dry. I try to speak.

Eva hugs herself. "When Tom came just before you got back this morning, he said he would go looking for her. He said for me not to worry, that I had enough to do tending to this house. He said I was doing a mighty fine job of it, and he would see to his wife and the baby."

My strength is gone. I want to fall back on the couch and sleep. I yearn for the sweet dreamland where Mama is alive. But my yearning is no match for the scene playing out before me.

"It's ok, Eva," I say, speaking words I don't believe. "She will be ok. Tom will find her. She can't have gotten far."

"Mama had her train bag," Emma says. "That means she ran away on the train. She does that sometimes. Then Daddy has to go find her. I'm thirsty."

"I'll get you some water," I say. I can fix thirsty.

I get up and limp outside to get Emma a cool tin cup of water from the well and try to figure out how to get Laura Viola back.

I splash my face in the soothing water, and then dip out a cup for myself and Emma. I turn back to the house, but I'm stopped cold by Papa.

He looks like a wraith. When had he lost so much weight? When had those dark bags formed under his eyes? He looks like death, like how I feel inside.

162

But Papa doesn't even see me. Has he found Mama's baby dead somewhere?

"Papa, what is it?"

"They are gone," he says. "Someone has taken them."

"Someone has taken what?" But Papa's grief has robbed him of language.

"They?" And now I panic. Maisie and Emma? Had they left while I was out here getting water? But no, I can hear them from the front stoop, playing a clapping game, their sing-song carrying across the yard.

Papa looks up as if just seeing me. "No, all of them, Annie Laura. They took everything."

"I don't understand."

He beckons, and I lean on his arm and go with him, the tin water cup sloshing over my hand.

He takes me to his workshop. I'm stunned by the sight. The entire front door has been destroyed with something, and from the looks of the damage, it must have been an axe, and a heavy one at that. If someone was trying to get in, why did they feel they had to cut the door down? Papa never locked his shop. But the savage blows have splintered the wood and left the door in a dozen pieces, littering the packed gray dirt flooring.

Papa kicks the largest piece aside so that we can walk in.

Another hole is cut through the back of his workshop, this one bigger, big enough for a wagon to fit in.

And, indeed, a wagon must have fit in here. All of Papa's tools are gone. All of his molds, all of the spare iron, even the giant bellows. All gone. The tiles imported from Holland, the half-finished stove he had been working on, the matchstick holders that had lined the walls neatly just yesterday, all gone.

"But who would do such a thing?" I ask. "Who?"

As if in answer to my question, Papa leaves me and runs into the house, snatching his hat from the wall, and jamming it on his head. He puts on his driving gloves and hastens for the barn, where I imagine Dolly and Papa's horse munching their oats, resting from the stress of the previous day. They probably hauled many people away from the inferno that was Falling Waters.

"Papa, what are you doing? Where are you going?"

"I am going to seek justice," Papa says. "I am going to the sheriff to show him what has happened. I am going to find out who stole my things."

He disappears into the barn.

"But Papa, the sheriff won't have time to see you," I call, limping after him. "He will be cleaning up from the fire. This theft, it will seem as nothing to him." *Besides*, I want to scream, *you are a foreigner. You are the last person he is going to wish to protect.*

"Nothing?" Papa bellows. "You call this nothing? How will I pay for this land? How will I feed you girls? How will I keep my promise to your mama?"

He still doesn't understand that my farm has been paying our bills. I don't expect him to.

"I know people who can convince the sheriff...I need money, Annie Laura. I know your secret hiding place. I'm taking it."

I don't have the energy to stop him.

He returns with a pocket full of coins, *my* hard-earned money, money that is meant to buy feed for our critters and food for us until the crops are harvested.

"This will convince the sheriff," he says.

"Papa, what do you mean?" Fear rises in me. Is Papa planning to bring a gang of ruffians in to threaten the sheriff? Even if Papa knew such a gang, it would never work.

But Papa is gone before he can tell me his plan.

This is small fry to the sheriff. Neither mine nor Papa's nor my family's trouble will concern him. Not my assault, not the theft of our baby, not the theft of Papa's livelihood. We are all dirty Germans according to him, and even if he suddenly changes his colors and feels we deserve the same justice as the native born, our problems will all pale in comparison to the utter devastation that is Falling Waters, Florida, on this day after the great fire. For the sheriff, the important things will be the things that happen to the wealthy people who can make sure he gets reelected, not what happens to people like me. Or Papa, or Margaret or John Sebring.

The sheriff will laugh at Papa's threats.

Whoever planned to bring my family down on this date planned carefully and effectively.

But they don't know me very well.

Chapter 23

I put on my bonnet, mount my stubborn mule, and set out to find our baby.

Tom's boys greet me at the door of their surprisingly neat cabin. Someone has planted a lovely vegetable garden across the front of the house. Marigolds surround it, lifting their yellow faces to the sun. On the front row are collards and on the next row dusty tomato plants, the tiny new-growth tomatoes the same green as the leaves. Next is another row of marigolds, planted to keep the bugs off the tomatoes.

"Morning, Miss Annie Laura," says Seth, one of Tom's twin sons, opening the front door and greeting me with a sweet smile. "Is Eva all right?"

It's unusual to find him at home, but the fire kept everyone up for the better part of the night, and most people had gone home to sleep and recuperate. This would not be a normal work day for anyone in Falling Waters.

"Good morning, Seth. Yes, Eva and all of us are fine. What about you? Are you ok?"

"Yes, ma'am. We were the lucky ones. What we saw last night would make a hollow man cry," he says. "Everything was burned clear to the ground. The church, the school, every store. People lost everything they owned. Some lost everyone they loved in less than an hour. It was horrible, Miss Annie Laura. Horrible."

"I'm sorry you had to see it," I say.

"Why is your ankle all wrapped up?"

"I took a fall," I say.

He seems satisfied with my answer.

"Can I get you something to drink?" Seth asks.

"No, thank you." I hesitate. "I need to ask…"

At that moment, Seth's twin brother Isaac bursts through the door, tousled and dirty from his fight with the fire. "The only thing the fire missed was the railroad station and the trains. They are still running right on time," he says. "I've never seen anything like it. It was crazy, people running everywhere, children crying, women screaming, men hoarse from calling 'Water.' We formed a line, all of us—I didn't even know half the people—and we passed buckets down the line all night long, buckets of water from the well. I thought surely the well would go dry, so many buckets we passed, but it never did."

"We finally got the fire under control about dawn," Seth says. "The Lord was good to us. There was no wind, so it didn't spread to the woods around town. That could have been the end for all of us. The woods are dry this time of year, we haven't had nary a drop of rain in three weeks. It wouldn't have taken much."

I knew that as horrible as things were, they could have been worse. I could have lost my sisters, my house, my crops, everything. A very tiny spark of hope flickers inside of me. It *could* have been worse.

"I reckon you are looking for my mama," Isaac says. The twins stand together, arms crossed to contain what tiny bit of dignity their mama has left behind.

"Yes, I am."

"She lit out," Seth says, his voice so quiet a gentle breeze could blow his words away. "She's gone. Packed all of her stuff and everything of value in the house and lit out."

The boys study the boards beneath their feet.

"She took my baby sister," I say.

Seth doesn't even look surprised. "I'm sorry, ma'am," he says. "It's not the first time. I don't reckon it will be the last."

"Daddy's had to take three babies back to their mamas what my mama stole. She ain't right in the head. She takes on moods and when she does, she goes to stealing babies. Her sister said it's on account of how her babies all up and died, that is excepting us two boys and our Emma." The words tumble from Seth's mouth, and his brother reaches out as if to catch them before they all fall to the ground.

I'm less stunned than I might be. Maybe I'm past being surprised by people's actions.

"We tried to be good this time," Isaac says. "I reckon we wasn't good enough." He looks like he might cry.

"You're as good a boy as I've ever seen, the both of you. I couldn't be prouder of you two than I am. You work hard, you are kind, and you are honest. Don't take on so. I'm sorry your mama didn't appreciate all the good in you."

"Daddy went after her, ma'am," Seth says, cutting me off. It seems my compliment is more painful than his mama's leaving. "But he might not be able to find her. She took the early-morning train yesterday. That means she's got a two-day lead. She could be halfway to Californy by now. I don't reckon Daddy'll ever really be able to find her. She's quick as a water moccasin on a fast-moving creek."

"Besides that," Isaac says, "she done took all the money. We ain't got a dime between us."

Nor did I. Papa had taken every bit of cash I had. No more money will come in other than what little we can get by selling our eggs. But even that is doubtful. Given the fire, I doubt anyone can afford eggs.

I will find my baby sister. Even if I don't have a dime to my name. I'm not sure how, but I'll think of something.

Morris. The yearning in my heart swells until it feels like my chest will burn with it. Morris would know what to do. He would know who to hire to find her. I need Morris. I need him here, right now. Tears spill down my cheeks.

"Don't worry," Isaac says, handing me his ever-ready sweat-stained handkerchief. "My daddy, he'll search high and low till he finds her."

I look at the earnest faces of these two young men; I know they will do anything in their power to help me. I also know nothing in their power really can help me. I straighten myself up, brushing away the yearning for Morris to come help us as if it were a pesky fly. I have work to do and things to take care of.

And yet the thought of my baby sister in the hands of the frowsy woman that let Emma play in the poison ivy makes my blood curdle.

"I know what you're thinking, ma'am. She wasn't a good mama to little Emma once she got to be a talking child. But ma'am, she was the best mama I ever seen as long as they were infants. It's just when they took to walking that she didn't have no more use for them. It was like they didn't need her so much, so she was done with them. Like a mama dog when she weans her baby puppies. Just runs off and leaves them to fend for themselves."

And it will be a year before the baby walks. It's not much, but it's the only consolation I'm going to get. I'll have to accept it.

I head back home, looking out on the corn planted in the weeks before the fire. Normally I draw strength from the neat rows. Today I'm not so sure. The land that I believed to be inherently good has betrayed me as surely as the very town I called home. The land lured me with its siren's call, and, heeding it, I neglected the people I love the most.

When I return home, Eva reports that Papa has changed his mind about going to see the sheriff. He has, instead, gone to Cottondale.

I feel hope rise in spite of myself. A few weeks ago, when it was clear the stoves weren't selling, only the pots and pans, Papa had talked about making boot scrapers. He thought he might be able to find a mold in Cottondale, buy it on credit, and start all over again.

I thought the stolen equipment would be the last straw for my Papa. Perhaps not.

Chapter 24

Without my knowing about it, Tabitha sent for Morris. I discover her treachery when I receive a letter announcing what he believes will be the date of his arrival, sometime in July.

"Why?" I ask. "He is halfway across the world. It's not going to do anybody any good for Morris to know."

"He was the only one who could handle Benjamin after his mama died," Tabitha says. "He still is."

I don't want to hear the name spoken aloud. I want to forget that night. I want it washed away like loose dirt after a rain.

And now Morris is coming home. I have two months to prepare.

Meanwhile, Tabitha won't leave me alone. She brings something to the house every day. One day it's a pound cake. Another day, greens from her garden. The next day, three baby chicks.

"I gave Tabitha the mending," Eva announces one day. "She persisted. Every day she has asked what she could do to help us out. I told her nothing, but she spotted the pile of clothes you were working on. She said she would do anything for you. Why? Why is she here every day, Annie Laura? Why is she so worried about you?"

I can't tell Eva. The only person I could tell would be Margaret, but Margaret is gone. I have to settle for long talks with Jesus out in the fields that no longer bring me peace. I need Tom back here to help with everything. The farm has grown beyond my ability to tend it, even with the help of the boys. They need Tom's direction. The crops will surely fail if he stays gone any longer. I don't feel strong anymore.

As if responding to my heart, Tom returns. He's discovered that his wife has gone to Atlanta to be with her people. I can alert the authorities in Atlanta while Tom and the boys manage the farm.

I write to everyone I can think of. The mayor of Atlanta. The police chief.

When I hear nothing back, it seems my letters are being ignored. And I'm certain it has something to do with my German last name.

I pull out the money Papa missed. It's all I have. I pay an Atlanta attorney to get my baby sister back. But it does little good. He writes and explains that there is no chance of finding her. Tom's wife has left her family in Atlanta. She's headed west, and all communication is lost. Her very wealthy father has paid hundreds of dollars to find her, but she's left no trail.

I wad his letter into a little ball and sob. When I have the money, I will find my baby sister. I can only hope that Tom's wife takes care of our little Laura Viola. And that my mama, safe in heaven, will not fault me for what happened.

I spend the final days of May in the fields working alongside Seth and Isaac, planting peanuts and cotton. Tom protests, says they can handle it without me, but I cut him off.

"I'm not out here to help you. I'm out here for me. Let me be." My outburst is harsher than I intended. I throw up in the field in front of him.

Tom never questions me again.

I work hard to ignore the nausea, and I refuse to count back the days since my last monthly. When the peanuts and cotton are taken care of, I set to work on a double-layer henhouse. I saw one over in Marianna and want to copy it. My own henhouse is full.

My work saves me. What once gave me joy now gives me the blessed relief of exhaustion. I work to pass the days, I work because I have to support my family, I work because that's what I do. I feel nothing, not even when my belly grows round.

I focus on the new henhouse where I will be able to double my production of eggs. I might have enough egg money to help pay for a new mold for Papa once he returns. If I'm careful, I might even be able to afford the blower. At least that can get him started.

If he focuses on smaller pieces—the boot scrapers, match holders, and maybe even the fence railings I'd seen cast over in Vernon—Papa might be able to start over again. People are not willing to pay for his artistic renderings when all they're interested in is something to cook on. Besides, now they can get cheap woodstoves out of factories in Cincinnati shipped directly to Falling Waters.

But they will pay for boot scrapers and match holders. This hope for Papa gets me through the final stages of building the henhouse. To save Papa's pride is worth something.

And he will need his pride saved when he realizes I'm with child.

I plan to surprise him with new molds when he returns home. He's been gone for nearly two months. This is not unusual. Papa is by nature a wanderer. He often travels far to sell his goods. I no longer wonder what is taking him so long. The cold spot that has taken the place of my heart leaves me no room for worry.

I finish the henhouse in the middle of July, and I busy myself moving the hens into their new abode. I rescue an egg from a corner of the henhouse floor—some of the hens haven't yet figured out that the nests are for them, and I find stray eggs all over the place. It will take the hens a few weeks to get used to the new house, but when they do, my egg gathering will be ever so much easier.

I'm placing clean straw in the hens' nests when I hear a horse coming down the lane. I try to ignore the thing that happens to me every time I hear this sound. My hands tremble. The straw slips through my fingers and tumbles to the ground in gently arcing circles. The egg splatters. My throat feels full and my eyes tingle. I shut them against the tears. I am not well.

A male voice calls my name. I clutch my apron and panic, but quickly realize that it's Morris. I'm not ready for him yet. He's not supposed to arrive for another week. I don't want to be in the smelly henhouse when I meet him.

I wipe the straw from my hair and brush it off the gentle rise of my pregnant belly. I walk out of the henhouse, still trembling, to face Morris.

He doesn't see me. Will he think less of me? The thought makes it hard for me to breathe. Will he see me as damaged goods? Beyond repair? I swallow twice. I wipe the hair from my face. I plant my feet on hard-packed dirt and wait.

He's running toward me. I tense. When he reaches for me, I flinch. But I can't stop him from engulfing me in his arms. "Oh, Annie Laura," he breathes into my hair.

And just like that, I melt. My tears wet his soft cambric shirt, and I cling to him. I feel like I've come home.

"I need to know," he says quietly.

I wanted to savor this moment.

He pulls away, only slightly, still holding me. He steadies me, running his hands up my arms to my shoulders. "I need to know if Tabitha is telling me the truth."

He waits for me to speak, but the words choke me.

"Speak to me, please, Annie Laura. I know Tabitha wouldn't lie about a thing like this, but I need to hear it from you. Is it true?"

My ears whir, and my legs feel weak. "I have to sit." Morris holds me and helps me to a grassy knoll beside the clay road. There we sit, the harsh late summer sun baking the clay, scalding the leaves, glinting off Morris's watch chain.

Morris breaks my silence. "Is Tabitha telling the truth?"

And though I barely move my head, he reads my answer as accurately as a mother reads her child. He stands, helping me up. He walks me to the front porch, sits me in the rocker, and says, "I'll be back."

His face contorts a split second before he turns. His fury frightens me. He leaps astride his horse and is gone in an angry swirl of dust.

Chapter 25

I've never felt quite as alone as I do when Morris rides away. The heat makes me dizzy and sleepy, and I sit in the porch rocker and doze off, exhausted.

Words come to me like gently falling rain. *Therefore, since we are surrounded by such a great cloud of witnesses, let us throw off everything that hinders...let us run the race marked for us, fixing our eyes on Jesus.*

It's my mama's voice. *"You remember these words, my Annie Laura,"* she said, long ago. *"You never know when you might need them. There are going to come times in your life when you are going to need the strength of all your mothers and grandmothers before you. Let them bathe you in hope. They will urge you to keep your eyes on the one who loves you, who promises peace amidst chaos, who soothes broken hearts and heals wounded souls."*

Can Jesus fix my pain?

I hear Mama's voice answer me, *"No, my child, Jesus doesn't take it away. He just gives you the strength and peace to get through it. And always, always, Jesus takes the messed up, awful things that happen in this world and makes something good come out of them. But you must believe, Annie Laura. You must have faith, and you must look for the miracles. You will see them. I promise you, they will come."*

"You know what I want for my birthday, Annie Laura?" Maisie's voice jolts me fully awake, Emma trailing close behind. They look up at me, their sweaty faces glowing. An afternoon breeze rustles the dry, crackling leaves of the cabbage palms, rising like guardian towers over the young oak trees marking our property line.

Maisie's hopeful eyes draw me in. Perhaps she is today's miracle. "What, sweetie?" I ask.

"I want a doll baby."

"But you have a doll baby." I can see Maisie has something very specific in mind.

"I saw a doll baby once," Maisie says. "It was big like this." She marks the height of the doll at her chest. "And it was skinny," she says. "And it was soft like Mama's petticoat. Can you make it for me? And one for Emma?"

I laugh at the girls' eager faces. I can do this. It will keep my hands busy and my thoughts occupied by something other than myself. "Yes. I believe I can. But only if you help me."

Maisie grins like she's won a prize.

The girls jump up and down with excitement, hugging each other in their delight. "I told you, Emma," Maisie says. "I knew Annie Laura would do it." She turns to me.

"Emma said you would be too busy to make a doll. She said her mama always had things to do and was busy, busy, busy, and never could make her a doll. And she said since you were like our mama, you would be busy, too. All mamas are busy, she said. Too busy to help little girls."

I'm thankful for the diversion. Morris is going to find Benjamin. I don't know what he will do when he finds him.

"If we make a doll as tall as that, what shall we stuff it with? We may have to make smaller dolls."

The little girls grin at one another. "We found something," Emma says.

"We found it under a bush," Maisie says.

"Right over there." Emma points to the railroad tracks.

"Well, what did you find?" I ask, amused by their mysterious giggles.

"Come with us," they say. The girls latch on to my hands and drag me until I'm running with them.

"Slow down," I beg them, laughing but breathless.

Emma slows, but Maisie keeps going. "Slow down, Maisie," Emma says, stomping her foot for emphasis.

Maisie turns. "I'm just so excited. I can't wait for you to see!"

"Don't you know Annie Laura isn't as young as we are? Now slow down!"

I try to contain the giggle that bubbles up inside of me.

Maisie stops. We are surrounded by green. The world is alive. Purple and yellow flowers sway gently in the breeze, dotting the field with color. If I were an artist, this is what I would paint. I breathe in the fresh air, raise my hands up to the sky and dance.

"What are you doing?" Maisie asks.

I laugh and twirl. And the girls twirl with me, turning and turning like dandelions blown in the wind until, dizzy, we all three fall to the ground. We giggle and lie on our backs, gazing up at the puffy clouds dotting the blue sky.

"I see a butterfly," I say, launching into Maisie's favorite game.

"I see a bucket," Maisie says, pointing excitedly. "See it? There are the handles."

"Where?" Emma asks. "I don't see any butterflies or any bucket."

"That's 'cause of you're not using your imagination," Maisie says.

"What's that?" Emma asks.

"That's when you play pretend and fill in the sky with pictures. See, the clouds look like things, and you just kind of squint until you see something."

"Oh," Emma says soberly. "I see it, I see it!" she says, pointing up. "Look! It's a whole castle, a fairy-tale castle like in the book Annie Laura read to us. Do you see it?"

The biggest cloud, the one right above us, has arranged itself into a giant castle with turrets and a drawbridge.

"If only we could find the princess," Maisie says.

"I know where the princess is. And I know where to find her sister!" I say.

"Where?" Emma asks.

"Right here!" I say, and tickle both girls.

They laugh. "You be Princess Mary," Maisie says, "and I'll be Princess Victoria. Only now she's an old queen, right, Annie Laura?"

"You're right. How did you know that?"

"Papa has a picture of her in one of the papers from Germany. Someone drew it, I think. She looks beautiful in the picture, but

Papa says she is too old to be that pretty and that someone was taking liberties."

I laugh.

Maisie sits up, the white down of dandelions feathering her hair and clinging to her skirts. She looks troubled and wipes the down from her skirt. "We almost forgot! We must show Annie Laura our treasure, Emma. Come on, get up before someone else finds it!" She pulls Emma up, and they head to the railroad tracks.

The railroad trestles are built high to avoid river flooding. Alongside the "railroad mountain"—the term Maisie and Emma affectionately call it—there are bushes growing wild, a tangled mess of yellow flowering Virginia willow and poison ivy.

I hope the girls have not gotten into the poison ivy.

But where they point is even farther down the hill, below the tangled bushes. Sitting alone in a clearing is what appears to be a giant brown package. Maisie points. "It's still there!" She runs toward it.

When I draw near, I recognize it to be a bale of burlap-wrapped cotton. It must have fallen off a train sometime back in October when the bales were taken north for ginning. Why had no one seen it before? Or maybe they had and ignored it. The bale is the height of a tall man, and the width of our porch steps. It's dried out from the long drought, but I warn the girls to stay away from it.

"There's no telling what kind of animals are living in that thing," I say. The girls are right, though. There is enough cotton here for many, many dolls, and just about anything else they would like to make. It's on my land, but so well hidden by the trees and bushes that no one has seen it. From our vantage point, the woods and fields are a hundred shades of green, and the burlap stands out like a speck of dirt on a white shirtwaist.

I grab a stick and walk over to the bale. I prod it cautiously all around. No woodland creatures emerge.

It's like finding gold—white gold. My old henhouse is nearly the perfect size for storing the bale. The tough part will be getting the bale to the henhouse.

"Maisie, you and Emma run and find Emma's daddy and the boys. Tell them to drop what they are doing. I need their help!"

The girls hold hands. Grinning, they run towards the field where Tom and his sons are pulling weeds and lugging water to the peanut and cotton plants that are threatening to dry up beneath the unremitting sun.

My head is full of all the things I can do with this bale of cotton. I had to sell all of my bales last fall, leaving my family with precious little for our own clothing. I know well how to clean the cotton, spin it into thick thread, and then weave it into homespun cloth. And Eva will be in heaven. She can spin to her heart's delight and crochet the lovely bedspread and tablecloth she's dreamed of for her hope chest. I can hardly believe our good fortune. We can stuff every mattress in the house, fluff up pillows, make whatever dolls Annie and Emma can dream up, and still have enough cotton to last a few years. The cotton is a treasure, a sign of hope.

Chapter 26

Once Tom and the boys have the cotton safely stored, the girls and I get to work on the dolls. Morris has not yet returned.

I hum away my worry and make a pattern from Papa's newspapers. The girls giggle when I ask them to lie down so I can trace their bodies for patterns. Then, we draw and redraw until Emma and Maisie are pleased with the size and shape. I lay out an old petticoat of Mama's, double it, lay the patterns on top, and begin cutting. I'm not good at fine clothing work. Eva is best at that. But I can make a doll. The girls sit wide-eyed and silent. It's as if they are afraid to speak lest I mar their new dolls.

"I like it when you sing like that," Emma says shyly. I look up at her, my mouth full of pins, and smile.

"That's not singing," Maisie corrects. "That's humming. You can't sing with a mouth full of pins."

I laugh and the pins fly all over the floor. Maisie and Emma scamper to pick them up.

I secure the doll front to the doll back with a few pins, and the girls do the rest, pinning to their heart's content. Too many pins will be fine. They pin until they run out of pins, and then I pull out Mama's hand crank Singer.

"Where's Eva?" I ask. She's better at handling the sewing machine than I am.

"She went to give something to Tabitha," Maisie says.

My body stiffens. I don't want Eva anywhere near Tabitha, because she might run into Morris or Benjamin. She doesn't need to know what happened to me. But I can't leave the girls alone. I have to trust that Tabitha will keep Eva safe and away from any trouble.

I focus on helping the girls turn the hand crank and try not to worry. I let Emma sit at the sewing machine and guide the fabric through while Maisie cranks. Their delight makes up for the extra time it takes. When the girls finally grow tired of the project, I send them outside, draw the doll's faces, and try not to think about what might be going on at Tabitha's house.

Papa, who is truly an artist, could make these doll faces look real. When will he return? He is completely unpredictable. Sometimes Papa stays gone a day, sometimes a month. He never seems to know how long he'll be gone. And since he's working on starting his business afresh, maybe it will take longer than normal.

But somehow, Papa's absence seems different this time.

Of course, everything seems different now.

I choose a skein of blue and green embroidery thread for the eyes, red for the lips, and black for everything else and begin embroidering the dolls' faces.

I want the faces to look happy, peaceful. I close my eyes and think of Mama's face. I work hard to match her peaceful countenance.

The work is surprisingly soothing, and my thoughts wander to Morris. Wouldn't it be nice if he could send Benjamin as far away from Falling Waters, Florida, as the moon? Or the Transvaal? And suddenly it seems a sick joke of the universe that it's Morris who is now living on the other side of the world, and not Benjamin.

I'm no longer worried about my land, and that's a comfort. The lawyer Papa consulted made it clear that if Papa is living, the land is safe. When I turn twenty-one, the land will be mine with no more worries. That will happen soon. Besides, Papa's health is good, and if he gets his business going again, it will all work out for the best.

I decide to cross the hurdle of telling him about this baby only when I have to.

Morris. He was so angry when he left. I hope he set out to scare Benjamin and not kill him.

I focus on the doll's eyes, where Mama said you could see a person's soul. The thread is a soft blue, the color of the sky and Mama's eyes. Mama would love that I'm making the dolls for Maisie and Emma. I'm nearly finished. Mama didn't have much time to sew for Maisie before she passed. She had been hard pressed to get enough baby dresses made. She'd given away all of Maisie's baby dresses since she'd thought of Maisie as her last baby. *I need to give these to those who need them. We don't need them anymore,* she had said.

And Maisie should have been her last baby. I'm surprised at the sudden anger against Papa that burns in me.

Tears drop onto the white muslin, spots appearing where the eyes will soon be. I miss Mama so much. I had no idea the pain could be so big, and I need Mama now more than ever.

I focus hard on putting final touches on the dolls' faces. When I finish, I examine my handiwork. Not bad. The girls can dress them in some of their old too-small clothes. With Mama gone, they've not yet been given away to *someone who needs them more than we do*—Mama's words. I smile and think of all the many clothes Mama had given away.

The front door flies open. "Annie Laura!" Maisie says. "Annie Laura, come quick. It's Eva. She's come home and she's a hollering for you.

I lay the dolls on Maisie's bed as though they are holding hands and turn to greet Eva.

She stumbles in red faced and exhausted.

"Whatever is the matter?" I ask, fighting to keep my voice steady. I'm afraid I already know.

"It's Morris," she says. "He shot Benjamin."

I sit down hard on the kitchen chair, making it groan across the wooden floor.

"Shot him dead?" I ask, hoping, praying it isn't true.

"I don't know," Eva says. "Soon as the shooting started, I ran. I was scared, Annie Laura. Real scared. I met the sheriff on the road. I reckon he heard the shooting and came running. He lives real close to the Blakelys, you know, practically in their backyard. I imagine he was eating his dinner. And next thing you know a shot is fired and Benjamin goes down. And that's what happened, sure enough."

"Who else was there?" My heart thrums in my ears. I fear the worst for Morris.

"It was just Tabitha, Morris, and Benjamin," Eva says.

"What exactly did you see?" I asked.

"Well," Eva says, eyes shining with excitement, "I was walking down the road headed to see Tabitha. In a whoosh, Morris comes hurtling down the road. Benjamin meets him at the property line, a shotgun in his hands, blocking the way."

"Benjamin was blocking the way so Morris couldn't go home?" I ask.

"Yes," Eva says. "He hollered out at him, 'This ain't your property so you might as well turn that fancy horse around and head back to Cairo where you belong.'"

"What did Morris say?"

"He didn't say anything. He stayed on his horse and looked at Benjamin for a while, just stared him down, cold like. Mary Scarlet came running up from the yard.

"'What is it, Morris?' Mary Scarlet said.

"'I've got something Benjamin needs to read,' Morris said.

"He handed a rolled-up piece of paper to Mary Scarlet. She unrolled it and started to read it, but Morris stopped her. 'I said Benjamin needs to read it.'

"Then Tabitha stepped in. 'He can't read, Morris. Didn't you know that? Mary Scarlet has been reading for him since he first started school.'

"Mary Scarlet shot Tabitha a look like she wanted to kill her.

"Morris nodded his head, but he didn't look any too happy letting Mary Scarlet read it.

"When Mary Scarlet finished, she crumpled it up and threw it on the ground. 'Lies,' she said. 'It's all lies.'

"'What does it say?' Tabitha asked.

"'It says my daddy is not my daddy. It says John Calvin Blakely's only surviving child is Tabitha Blakely. It says my mother's children were not his.'

"'What do you mean?' Benjamin said, 'Not his?'

"'The document is clear, Benjamin,' Morris said. 'Get off Tabitha's land.'

"Then, Benjamin lifted his shotgun to Morris, but Morris was quick and shot his leg before he could fire. The sheriff showed up about that time. I mean it, Annie Laura, you need to come now," Eva says.

I pick up my shawl. Where did Morris get such a document? Is it true? Eva runs ahead of me, but I pull her back. "The girls," I say. "They don't need to see any of this."

"I'll stay back, I reckon." It's clear Eva wants to go with me. "He needs you, not me," she says in a rare moment of insight.

Maisie and Emma cling to me. I lean down and say, "I'll be right back!" a bit more brightly than I feel. "You two take care of Eva, ok?"

They nod solemnly. "You'll finish our dolls when you get back?" Emma wants to know.

"There's a surprise on your bed. Maybe Eva can help you with some clothes." The girls jump up and down and run to the bedroom. I hear their squeals of glee as I clasp my shawl around me and walk out of the house. And then I run, holding tight to my flapping shawl—though the day is warm, I need the security of that shawl. It was Mama's and makes me feel safe.

The trees part for the Blakely property. I hide behind a palmetto thicket.

I see the sheriff first. He towers above Tabitha and Mary Scarlet. Benjamin is on the ground, blood seeping through a cloth wrapped around his leg.

Morris stands over him, his arms crossed defiantly.

"I reckon you got yourself into fine mess here, Mr. Blakely," the Sheriff says.

Is he talking to Benjamin or Morris?

"I reckon you both need to clear out of town until this little spat between the two of you is settled."

I can see the sheriff trying to piece together why Morris, normally a calm, law-abiding doctor, has shot his brother. He waits in the way lawmen often do, hoping someone will talk to fill the silence. But no one does. The sheriff shakes his head.

"Morris, I'm not going to arrest you for the shooting of your brother. But that's only if you disappear. I don't want to see your face in this town as long as I am sheriff here. Otherwise, you'll go to jail, and I'll see to it personally that you stay there."

Morris is silent.

"Benjamin, son, you got to get out of here for a while, just until the excitement dies down. I hear there's work in Marianna. Maybe you ought to head over there."

"He can't walk," Mary Scarlet says, indignant at the suggestion. "Morris shot him and he can't walk."

"Well," says the sheriff, examining the wound and then scratching his head, "it ain't much more than flesh wound. I reckon he'll be all right come morning. Morris here wasn't aiming to hurt him for real it don't look like. He's a right smart man and a doctor to boot. I reckon he was just aiming to teach him a lesson. I don't know what happened, but that's the way it is with brothers sometime. I know. I been around long enough to know not to meddle in family matters."

He turns to walk away, and then looks back at Morris. "The older brother never likes it when the younger brother starts showing him up. What did you do, Benjy, steal his girl?" The sheriff guffaws and strides off. He mounts his horse and pounds away.

"You might say that," Benjamin says once the sheriff is gone, a shameless grin snaking its way across his face.

I feel sick. I want to leave, go back home to the sweet girls and the innocence of sewing a baby doll.

Morris springs forward. He rests his large hands casually on Benjamin's neck. When Benjamin tries to wrestle him off, Morris bears down. He bends close to Benjamin's ear, but his whispered words carry in the stillness.

"You go away and stay away, little brother. If you come near Annie Laura, this land, or this town again, you are a dead man. I've got eyes all over these woods now. You've got enough enemies to populate a small town, and don't you think for a minute they wouldn't all give their right arm to see you dead and buried. Get your sorry ass up and go. Now!"

184

"Stop it," Mary Scarlet says. "You're hurting him." And she dives in to rescue her beloved Benjamin. But Tabitha grasps her, fingers clutching like steel.

"Leave him be, Mary Scarlet. Leave him be."

Mary Scarlet spins around and faces Tabitha. "You are always protecting Morris. Benjy is the one who is shot."

"You don't get it, little girl. Benjamin raped Annie Laura." Tabitha delivers the words like the first stones of an avalanche.

I feel my legs give way. I hit the ground, but no one sees or hears.

Mary Scarlet steps back and gasps. "No! That's a lie. Tell her she's a liar, Benjy."

"I didn't give her nothin' she didn't want."

I hold my hand over my mouth and gag. I can't throw up here. I can't. I fight it with everything I have.

Morris springs forward. Tabitha stops him.

"Why? Benjy? Why?" Mary Scarlet pummels Benjamin in the face with her fists. He covers his head and rolls up into a ball. Mary Scarlet kicks his shot leg, and he screams.

"He has a list," Tabitha says.

"What do you mean, a list?" Morris asks.

"He threatened to kill you or Mary Scarlet if I told. I've helped the girls as best I could. There was a baby with that sweet Isabelle. I did all I could, but that baby died."

"Isabelle?" Morris says, his voice stone cold. "You are responsible for that, too?"

Morris moves with grim determination to Benjamin's horse, tied loosely to the hitching post. He unties the horse and leads it so close to Benjamin that he shrinks away. "Get up," Morris says.

When Benjamin doesn't move, Morris hooks his boot under Benjamin's shoulder and lifts him as if he's a piece of dung that needs kicking. The horse shies and rears, its hooves coming down inches from Benjamin's good foot. He screams.

"Get on your horse. And leave. Now," Morris says through clenched teeth as if the effort to keep from killing Benjamin here and now takes all his strength.

"I'll go away," Benjamin says, scrambling up and into his saddle, groaning with the effort. "But what I took from your girl there, you can never have." Benjamin slaps his horse, and flying hooves scatter red dust all over Mary Scarlet's white apron.

Benjamin pulls the horse up short. "And if she's carrying a brat, it's mine!"

Morris springs forward and yanks Benjamin to the ground. Benjamin laughs, and Morris wipes all the laughter from his face with his fists.

Benjamin's nose spews blood, and Morris pummels him with blind fury. Benjamin goes down with a thud.

But Morris isn't finished. Benjamin lies still in the clay, and Morris bends down to finish him off.

I run to stop him from murder.

"Stop it!" Tabitha says, and she, Mary Scarlet, and I pull Morris off Benjamin.

Morris takes a shaky step back and the three of us drag Benjamin to his horse. We struggle to heft his unconscious body onto the horse. He slides off twice before I grasp his blood-soaked hair in both hands and yank him so hard that pieces of dark brown hair come out in my hands, but his body is now balanced enough for Tabitha to tie him to the horse.

She secures the knots so efficiently that I wonder if she's done this before. Tabitha slaps the horse's rump with all her might. "Git," she says.

The horse rears up and Benjamin flaps precariously, but as soon as the horse starts running, Benjamin is jostled back to his secure seat, facedown, belly first over the saddle.

"I'll shoot him if he tries to come back," Tabitha says, brushing the clay dust from her hands and wiping them on her apron.

Chapter 27

In late fall, we get word that Benjamin has married a girl over in Marianna. Someone says it was a shotgun wedding. His new wife of three months is seven months pregnant. According to Tabitha, who has kin in Marianna, when Benjamin heard that I was pregnant, he bragged that it was his. Benjamin's new father-in-law got wind of it and told Benjamin that if he ever came back to Falling Waters, he would kill him.

So we're rid of Benjamin Blakely. But Morris is gone, too, and he can't come back or he'll be arrested.

I return from our newly rebuilt post office, clutching his letter in my hand. He's back in the Transvaal to work his gold mine. My heart aches. He might as well be in another universe. I take a deep breath and look around me as Dolly pulls my wagon home.

In my universe, it looks like snow has come to northwest Florida in the heat of late fall. But it isn't snow. It's another season of cotton. My white gold.

My yield of corn and cotton this season is more than I dreamed. We are rich with it, and I can pay off my land, free and clear. The old-timers said a fire could do that to crops, a reminder of how God makes good come out of bad.

I can't wait until I reach home to read the letter. I open it, even as Dolly plods toward home.

My Dear Annie Laura:

I've thought of you every day I've been here. I think you will be pleased with the house I've built for us. It's white wood with a wide front porch and big kitchen windows. The back bedroom looks out over a vegetable and flower garden tended by Schmidt. He works for me, keeping the place up. I've hired his wife as well. She does my cooking and housekeeping. Liesel can't wait to meet you. She's worked hard on the nursery and hopes to hear by the next post that once the baby is born, the two of you will be coming home here.

187

I know I'm assuming much to believe that you will leave your be-
loved land and come and live with me. Here our land stretches as far as
the eye can see—land that has no complications, no tie to anyone but us.
When your papa comes home, he can care for Eva and little Emma
and Maisie. I don't think he would give me permission to take all of you.
I hope to hear from you soon. I'm enclosing money for passage for
you and the baby. I love you, my dear Annie Laura.
      Yours,
      Morris

I rest my hand on my swollen belly. His words fill me with
hope. Morris understands me. Morris wants me. *We are so loved,* I
whisper to my baby.

Dolly turns an ear as if I've whispered to her.

Something tugs at my heart, and it isn't about the baby. I've
long ago dismissed my fear that this baby will be like Benjamin. I've
carried this little one long enough to consider it mine.

What tugs at my heart is the land. Despite Morris's assurance
that he has plenty of land in that faraway country, how can I leave
my precious acres? I've put my lifeblood into tending them. How
can I trust that Papa will be able to support Maisie and Eva and
Emma—and our Laura Viola, if she is ever found? Though I know
he can as long as Tom and the boys remain. They will work the land,
keeping all of them safe and fed. Probably even prosperous.

What's wrong with me, then? I look around me, breathe in the
clean air, the beauty of the massive oaks, the pines reaching for the
stars. I love Morris. I unhook Dolly, brush her, and lead her to the
barn.

"Yes, sir," I hear Tabitha say through the open window, "I'm
going to get you young'uns married off, and then who am I going to
take care of?"

Married? Who's getting married?

Tabitha meets me at my front door, a big smile on her face.
"Welcome home!" she says. The smell of fresh fried chicken wafts
out the door, along with baked bread and an apple pie sitting on the

woodstove. Tabitha has taken to coming over and cooking since my pregnancy has reached the final months.

"You can take care of me!" Maisie says. "But you can't take care of Eva. She's going to marry Tom."

All eyes turn to me, and a silence falls over the room. "Tom?" I ask. "But he's married. I know his wife left him, but he's still married. You can't think about marrying Tom, Eva." I hold my belly, breathing hard.

But Eva is laughing. "No, not Tom!" she says. "Maisie calls all three of them Tom. She can't keep the father and twins separated. They all look alike, and so she calls them all the same name!"

There is relieved laughter in the room.

"And how in the world did you know anything about us? Little big ears!" Eva says to Maisie. Eva tries to look angry, but her joy seeps over the edges of her scolding.

"We heard you talking 'bout getting married, didn't we, Emma?" Maisie says.

Emma nods her agreement.

"Why, you little snoops!" Eva says, but the grin on her face reaches clear to her hairline.

"So, is it true?" I ask.

"Seth does seem to be interested," Eva says, her face glowing, her cheeks pink.

I envelop Eva in a clumsy, loving hug. "I am so happy for you, Eva! Seth is such a good man!"

Eva just laughs and sets the fried chicken on the table.

Seth chooses this moment to knock on the front door. When he walks in, taking off his hat and hanging it on the hook beside the front door, we all clap. He looks at the hat as if it contains a clue as to why we're clapping. Eva rushes to him, hugs him, and pulls him to the table to sit beside her.

Tabitha says, "So I have to cook enough food for a wedding? You must be kidding! I don't think I can do it!"

"We'll help," Emma volunteers.

"I'm sure you will." Tabitha smiles at the eager girls.

"I say we do a Christmas wedding. What do you say?" Seth asks.

"Don't you think you need to get down on a knee?" I tease.

Seth kneels by the table, knocking the chair over behind him in his eagerness. We all laugh. He bends down on his knee in front of Eva, whose face burns red. But her shining eyes make her feelings clear.

"Yes!" she says.

"I haven't asked yet!" Seth responds.

Eva pulls him, up, and they hug until Seth reaches in for an audacious kiss.

"Why, Seth, what the devil are you doing?" Eva asks. Her blush deepens, and she laughs heartily. "I really want to get married in the church," she adds.

"You are a sweet girl. Let's eat!" Tabitha says.

We all sit down and dig into Tabitha's golden fried chicken.

Maisie is beside me and notices the letter I still clutch in one hand. "What's in your letter?" she asks.

I read the letter aloud and am met by dead silence.

Maisie's eyes fill with tears. "You can't leave us, Annie Laura. You just can't."

Of course, Maisie is right. I can't possibly leave them, at least not until Papa returns.

But is it the girls I can't leave behind, or is it the land?

"I know what you are thinking, Annie Laura," Tabitha says, cutting right into my thoughts. "I know how much the land means to you. But I fear that until your father returns, there is no real owner of this land."

I've forgotten that the land is legally Papa's until I'm twenty-one years old, even though I've sweated my blood in its soil. I've taken it for granted that Papa will be back.

But what if he doesn't come back? What if Papa is hurt somewhere?

"I have a cousin who is an attorney in Marianna," Tabitha says. "He says that according to Florida law, if your papa doesn't show back up again, the land is going to go to probate. It can stay there for years, and at the end of those years, you might owe so much in fees and taxes that the land will never be yours again."

I feel as though someone has slapped me. We need to send someone out looking for Papa. But who? We are all needed here; there is too much to be done on the farm to spare hands. The cotton needs picking. I look at the faces around me. Just a moment before, they were glowing with happiness. And now a pall has fallen.

"The land has supported all of us for these many years. Papa will come home eventually," I say brightly. "He always does. For now, there is a wedding to celebrate."

"Yay!" Maisie says, and she and Emma clap excitedly. "Can we be flower girls?" Maisie asks Eva.

And Eva smiles.

Chapter 28

I breathe in the cool December air. The fields are brown now, but I know that come spring, green will dot the field and then fill it with lush abundance. The land is a sure thing.

I no longer go to town on any errands. Aside from Morris, only my family, John Sebring, Tabitha, Tom, and the boys know about the baby. If the town discovers that I'm an unwed mother, they'll no longer buy my cotton or eggs. Nor, probably, would they sell to us. It's a truth I've accepted. It doesn't matter how this baby came to be. Our plan is to pretend we've found Mama's baby, Laura Viola. No one can argue that. We'll deal with the age difference when we must.

Maisie and Emma come running. They're racing, and Tom follows them. I've never seen him run with such exuberance, and I wonder why.

"What are you up to? Emma, you are going to run your daddy to death!" I say when the girls stop in front of me. They usually jump up into my waiting arms when they run at me like this, but my pregnant belly is a hindrance. So instead they rub my belly and talk to the baby.

"Good morning, baby," Maisie says.

"I want to talk to her, too," Emma says, pushing Maisie away from what she considers her side of my belly. "Don't hog."

"I'm quite certain there is plenty of room for both of you!" I say.

Tom breathes hard and wipes the sweat from his face when he catches up with the girls. "I feel like an old man!"

"These two run like lightning," I say. "I stopped trying to keep up with them a long time ago."

"I guess you all have heard?" Tom says. "My boy, Seth, wants to marry Eva."

"That's the best news I've heard in a long time. What's he waiting on?" I tease.

"Well, he's waiting for your daddy to come back home so he can ask him proper."

"My papa isn't coming home," Maisie says, taking Emma's hand. "Let's go find some treasures," she says to Emma. The two of them head away.

"Wait," I say, trying to keep my voice calm. The certainty with which Maisie uttered her words is unsettling. "Why do you say that, Maisie?"

"I saw him go away on a train. A long time ago. I was playing down by the track with Emma. It was the day we found the cotton. I forgot to tell you about it, Annie Laura. Now come on, Emma, let's go play."

Emma looks down, and I know she's hiding something. Cold fear grips me.

"Tell her that other thing," Emma urges, her eyes wide. "Go on ahead and say it."

"No," Maisie says. "It's not true."

"What, Emma?" Tom asks, kneeling beside his daughter. "What other thing do you need to tell Daddy?"

"Well, one day, a man rode his horse up to the house, but he didn't go in," Emma says. "Come on, Maisie, we've got to tell. You go."

"Hush, Emma." Tears well in Maisie's eyes. "You're going to get me in trouble."

"But we need to tell," Emma says.

Tom looks at me. "Don't worry, Maisie," I say. I take her hand and walk over to a fallen tree. I sit down heavily. "Tell me what you need to say. You won't get in trouble."

"You promise?" Maisie asks.

"I promise," I say.

Maisie twirls a curl around her finger and studies it like it's the most interesting thing in the world. She looks up at me, as if measuring my face to see if she can trust me. My insides quiver, and it has nothing to do with my baby.

"What is it, sweetie?" I fight to keep my voice calm.

"Well. The man, or maybe he wasn't a man. You know, he's the one who delivers telegrams."

I know him well. It's the Johnson boy, and he has a tendency to read the telegrams and say the news contained therein before anyone has time to read it for themselves.

I nod so she will continue her story.

"Well," Maisie says, "he came up to me and Emma one day. We were playing at the foot of the drive, you know right where the yard starts, the part we sweep?"

"Yes," I say, "I know the place you are talking about. It's where you and Emma play almost every morning."

"Yes, that one," Maisie says. "He had on funny clothes and he said my daddy was dead. He said the letter said so." Maisie's face reddens, her lip quivers, and she puts her head down in my lap.

"What letter?" I ask, squeezing Maisie's hand more tightly than I intend.

"Ouch," Maisie says, and jerks her hand away.

"The letter he had," Emma says, walking over to where we're sitting. "But Maisie and I talked about it. We said if the letter said he was dead, we could burn the letter and make him undead."

"We were just five back then. Now we're six," Maisie says as if that explains everything.

"And so you burned the letter?"

"I'm sorry, Annie Laura. I didn't mean to do it." Maisie clutches my cheeks. "You were already so sad. I didn't want to make you more sad." She bursts into tears and cries as if her heart is breaking.

Meanwhile, Emma has crawled up into Tom's arms, and he's holding her. She's sucking her thumb, something she hasn't done since she first moved in with us.

"Well, girls," I say, my voice a whispery thing, "I'm glad you told us. And it's ok. We won't hold it against you. You thought you were doing the right thing."

No one moves. No one knows exactly what to do.

I peer out to the edge of the land. A cabin on the outskirts sends up a thin spiral of smoke. A north wind blows. The sky turns suddenly cloudy, and the temperature drops. Maisie shivers.

"We had better get to a warmer place," I say. "Come on."

We walk slowly toward our house.

Upon confirmation of my father's death, the land goes into probate. Just as Tabitha had warned.

Chapter 29

I will never know exactly what happened to Papa. The little girls have said all they know. Perhaps one day, I'll come across someone who remembers what happened to the German woodstove maker. Until then, I have my memories and a matchstick holder he made for Mama. It's the last thing he crafted, and I treasure it.

We decide to hold Papa's funeral in our backyard. It's a small ceremony with John Sebring's friend, the Methodist preacher, officiating. Since there is no body, we bury his beloved volume of Shakespeare beside Mama. It seems fitting.

Christmas comes, and Eva and Seth are happily married in the Methodist church as Eva had wished.

The New Year, and with it the new century, 1900, comes in cold and rainy. The woodstove chugs merrily in the kitchen, but it's hard to heat the bedrooms. The temperature has fallen well below freezing for three nights in a row. Rain comes during the day. The dampness will not go away. It exacerbates the cold. Clothes won't dry. Florida houses are not equipped for ongoing cold weather, and for the next two weeks I feel every draft in my body and in my heart. Even though Tabitha stays with us, and will be with me when the baby is born next month, the house seems empty without Eva.

I write Morris. It's the hardest thing I've ever done, but I have to tell him that I can't join him in his new country, not right now. The property situation is a mess, and I pour out my heart. I share with him my dreams and my fears, and I pray he will understand.

He doesn't write me back. John tells me it's because of the war. The English have gotten greedy for the Boer diamonds and gold. But my heart tells me it isn't just the war. Has Morris moved on to another woman? Have his letters gotten lost? He usually writes once a week. Have I scared him away? Is it the pregnancy?

Tabitha is busy chinking draft holes in my cabin walls with moss she pulled from the towering oaks. She boils the moss, killing the bugs. Next, she mixes clay and lime and sets it in a bucket close to the wall most in need of chinking. When Tabitha finishes filling the holes with moss, she wets the clay and lime mixture with a little water, stirs, and then coats around the moss. Tabitha won't let me help her fill in the holes. She says it's too much reaching and bending. Eventually, the bedroom will be airtight, and the new baby will be safe from the winter wind.

I must make myself useful. I can't just sit around all day twiddling my thumbs and waiting for this baby to announce its arrival. I stand in the back garden, surveying the old brown sweet potato, squash, and watermelon vines, the fallen beans, the shrunken tomatoes. Only the collards brave the winter cold. They're tough plants, their leaves spreading in defiance of the harsh winter with its unremitting cold and rain. The collards' courage makes me smile. If they can survive their conditions, then surely I can survive mine.

I force my rake through the stubborn, tangled and yellowed watermelon vines. They run amuck all over the garden. I bend down to wrestle them from the ground.

The pain starts in my back. Surprised, I place a hand there, trying to push it away. Have I pulled a muscle trying to coax the stubborn watermelon vines from their stronghold in the ground? The pain travels to my belly and squeezes me.

The baby can't come today. I'm not ready. I haven't sorted out the property; I haven't found a lawyer I can afford. If my property is in probate, what will happen to us?

I worry that Tabitha will see me grasping my back through the bedroom window. I try to mask my pain with a smile. It isn't easy. I hope she's so busy at her task of chinking and daubing that she won't notice me.

When my water breaks, running in rivulets over my black laceup boots and spilling into the already damp soil beneath, I know the baby is coming today.

I think about Mama.

It was only a year ago that I helped Mama give birth. Mama's labors went fast. I try to think about what she told me about her first labor. Was it as fast as her fourth?

197

What does it matter? Tabitha is here, and everything is ready. But Morris is not. And I need Morris. Tears bubble in my eyes, burning my throat and reminding me how very much I miss him. I ignore my wet garments and shoes and return to my raking. In the gentle rhythm of preparing my garden for new growth, my labor progresses, but my heart aches.

"Annie Laura?" Eva calls me from the front yard. I grasp my back, waiting for the latest pain to abate, then hurry around to the front, surprised to see a wagon full of people. Tom, Eva, and Seth sit on the front seat of the wagon, and Emma and Maisie sit in the back. Isaac walks alongside the wagon. How long have I been out in this garden? I've been so focused on trying to get through my pains that I missed the girls getting up and dressed, ready for their trip.

The entire family, except for Isaac, is heading to Atlanta to spend a few weeks with Tom's parents. They all decided that this is the best possible time for them to go. The harvest is in, and there is really nothing that needs doing for the next three weeks. Seth's twin, Isaac, will stay behind to do the small daily chores. He has a girl over in Cottondale he's sweet on. And I'm glad they're going. I'll need a quiet house when the baby is born and time to sort through my feelings. Tabitha will be with me, and Isaac and John Sebring are close by.

But in the midst of my labor pains, I've forgotten today is their departure day. I'll have to mask my pain completely, or Eva will insist on staying. I pray the pains will slow so I can bid them farewell with a calm face.

Tabitha comes out of the house, diverting their attention just long enough for me to press my back, hard. Tabitha comes down the steps and hands them a basket filled with fried chicken, biscuits, and apples.

Of course, Tabitha has been packing the basket full of food between the chinking and daubing. That's why she's not noticed my labor. I force a smile. Blessedly the pain passes, and I can hug them all goodbye. Maisie and Emma hug me longest, and I finally have to unclasp their arms and push them away.

"You need to get on the road so that you have a nice place to stay before dark. Be sweet and mind Eva," I say.

Emma is bringing Maisie to meet her granny. "Maisie's my new sister. That makes Granny her granny too, right, Daddy?" Tom agrees.

I know that Tom misses his folks but has been ashamed to visit them since his wife left him. Having a new daughter-in-law gives him an excuse to visit and takes the focus off his shame.

Another pain grabs me. I'm able to mask it by standing still and gripping the edge of the wagon while Isaac loads a final bag. But I can feel Tabitha's eyes boring into the back of my head. I pray she will keep silent.

Tom and the rest deserve a break and a nice visit with family. They don't need to stay back and babysit me. Tabitha and I can handle the baby.

Tom waves and says, "Giddy up," and the wagon lurches forward. The little girls wave until they're out of sight down the road.

Isaac chases them down the lane for a bit, waving as hard as he can.

As soon as they've rounded the bend and Isaac heads for Cottondale, Tabitha says, "How long have the pains been coming?"

She is so close that I jump. Another pain clutches me, and this one brings me to my knees. Tabitha leans down with me. "It's ok," she says. "Breathe. Don't hold your breath, it makes the pain worse."

When the pain ebbs, I say, "They are getting closer together. I probably need to go inside."

Tabitha helps me up the porch steps. I grip the slippery wet wood rail and squeeze. The sharp pierce of the pain bends me in two. It passes, and I walk inside, stopping this time to clutch the back of Mama's rocking chair.

"The baby's coming soon from the looks of you," Tabitha says and bustles about boiling water, stacking clean sheets, and fluffing the baby's new mattress, stuffed with the cotton Maisie and Emma found.

I try to help, but the pains clutch me with each step, and getting to my bed takes every ounce of strength I have. I'm thankful for the cold house now. I'm dripping sweat; my shirtwaist is soaked with it.

Tabitha helps me out of my clothes, and in the sea of pain I think I hear someone beating on the door. "What's that?"

"I don't know. It sounds like someone is nailing something to our front door, but they'll just have to wait."

I clutch the feather bed and squeeze so hard that the feathers poking through the ticking stab my palms.

"It's coming," Tabitha says.

I'm now flat on my back in the bed. The pounding continues, and I feel the overwhelming need to push, push, push with everything I have.

I scream.

"It's the head," she says, and reaches down to help my baby into the world. I feel a pain like I've never felt in my life. I want to die, and I push with all my might.

"One more," Tabitha says. "There's a girl, one more."

The incessant pounding stops, and with it the pain.

"Your new baby girl," Tabitha says, tears streaming down her face.

She places my daughter in my waiting arms. I gaze into her beautiful eyes, touch her cheeks, her perfect hands, her belly, her legs, and her tiny toes. Our new Laura Viola—for she must have the same name as my lost sister—is perfectly formed. A plump little thing, she fits snugly in my arms while Tabitha cuts the cord. She takes her from my arms for a moment, rubs her clean, wraps her in a soft cotton blanket, and places her at my breast.

The baby nurses for a moment and then falls into a deep, newborn sleep. I sleep with her.

Tabitha must have eased the baby away while I slept because when I awake, she's sleeping soundly right beside me in the cradle Papa made for our first Laura Viola. I lean over and wonder at her perfect beauty. Have I really given birth to this lovely angel?

I can't help myself. I have to pick her up and hold her close, even though she is sleeping so soundly. She sleeps on even as I touch a finger to her soft cheeks, then feel her tiny, perfect hands and all ten fingers. I unwrap the blanket and caress the tiny toes and soft feet. I've never seen such a beautiful baby. She's perfect.

When the baby wakes, she looks up at me with soft blue eyes for a few moments. Tabitha urges me to nurse her again. I do, and she falls asleep almost immediately.

For three beautiful days, this is the rhythm of things. Sleeping and waking. Nursing and caressing. Tabitha is here every few hours to change the baby's diaper, to help me from the bed to the bath, empty the chamber pot, wash the diapers, and refill the washbowl. The wind howls outside the window, but inside the snug room with the woodstove fire dancing merrily, enveloping us in warmth, I feel we're in a cocoon, safe from the rest of the world.

I want to stay here forever.

Chapter 30

I awaken the third day to Laura Viola making little grunting sounds in her cradle. I pick her up and hold her close. She's nursing frequently, and it's lovely. I make my escape from the bed to Mama's rocking chair while Tabitha burps the baby. It's the first time Tabitha has allowed me to move out of the bed for anything other than the necessary. She's old-fashioned that way.

But I'm ready to get up now, ready to start working. The soft lull of the days directly following the baby's birth has melted into a firm resolve to get busy with the land.

John Sebring and Mary Scarlet have visited a few times. They come together, which feels quite odd. Tabitha allowed Mary Scarlet to remain living in Tabitha's house, as long as Benjamin never stepped foot on her property. And Mary Scarlet seems to finally have had enough of Benjamin.

Mary Scarlet holds Laura Viola while John Sebring and I talk of the future. He asks if Morris's attorney has visited me yet. I say no, and that I expect he never will what with Morris so far away.

John Sebring surprises me by saying he plans to move to the little fishing village on the coast, Anderson, where a big wood-mill is being built. He figures it will be a great place for a man to start over. Falling Waters is too hard for him with Margaret and the baby gone.

"Will you go to Morris?" John Sebring asks.

"As soon as I get this land in shape. As soon as I can guarantee that it is going to support Eva and Seth, Tom and Isaac, and Maisie and Emma. I can't leave them yet. They need me."

John Sebring looks troubled. "I'm not sure you can do all of that."

"What do you mean? No one is better than me at keeping this farm profitable."

"That's not what I mean. You have an illegitimate child. And you know as well as I do that it doesn't matter that none of it is your fault. The town already judges you as a foreigner. And now they have fuel for their fire."

"I don't need them, and besides, they'll never know."

"Don't be a fool, Annie Laura. There are plenty of small-minded people in this town who can make your life miserable. And most are friends with Benjamin. They know. Benjamin made no secret of the fact. Told people you wanted him."

"I don't care." But I have to hide my face in Laura Viola's sweet-smelling belly. It can't be true. We have such a good plan.

"You will when it affects Maisie, Emma, and Eva. They won't be able to go to school or church."

"They did nothing!" My rage at the world startles Laura Viola. She cries, and I cover myself with a shawl and nurse her. She relaxes, and so must I.

"Nor did you, but that's just the way things work. The town sees you as a fallen woman, and because of that, all the women related to you are considered tainted."

I know he's right, but I rail against the unfairness of it all.

"What should I do?"

"You have to leave. Go on to Morris. Between all of us, we'll make sure that Emma and Maisie are cared for."

I look at the sweet, innocent baby in my arms. It isn't fair. "I have to stay long enough for the spring planting. And then I'll go."

My heart hurts.

"Please listen to me," John Sebring says. "Every day you stay will bring more damage on the girls. Please, go to Morris. We can get you on your way tomorrow."

John Sebring and Mary Scarlet say their goodbyes to me. Why are they together? Since when are they a unit? Will she be joining him in Anderson?

"He's right. You can't stay," Tabitha says after they're gone. She's holding a paper in her hands. It looks thick and has holes in it. "I wanted to wait a few days to show you this, but I reckon now is as good a time as any."

My heart pounds. What can it be? I take the paper Tabitha hands me. Her finger marks the hole at the top. A nail hole. And then I remember the pounding the day Laura Viola was born.

I read the paper.

"How can this be?" Anger boils in my gut. "It says notice was posted after Papa's death, and that we had sixty days to show up and claim the land, but no one showed. What notice? Where?"

"That sheriff," Tabitha says. "He was after this land from the beginning, once he saw how rich you made it with the hard work you, Tom, and the boys put into it. Your papa's funeral gave him all the permission he needed."

"I am not going to leave this land. Not unless I'm in a pine box. I've worked like a dog to survive, and I am not going to have some arrogant, greedy, self-important sheriff steal it from me."

"And Laura Viola? And Maisie? And Emma? Are you willing to risk them?"

"Maisie and Emma are gone, for another month at least. That's what Tom wrote and said. And I can take care of my baby, don't you worry about that."

But there is a rip right down the center of my soul. I look down at my innocent baby, lean down to kiss her, and Laura Viola's sweet, milky breath caresses my cheek. Would I really put my sweet child in danger over land? How can I protect her when I couldn't even protect my baby sister?

I shake with the unfairness of it all. Why? Why is this happening? Haven't I paid my dues? How much pain is one person allowed to have? *Enough, God! I've had all I can stand.*

I take Laura Viola back to her cradle and lay her down. I lie in the bed beside her. I don't have the energy to fight. I'm worn out, beaten down, exhausted. My land has betrayed me.

Someone knocks on the door.

"I'll get it," Tabitha says.

The knocking turns savage. Someone pushes against the latch and bursts through the door. Tabitha screams. Heavy boots stomp towards me.

I snatch Laura Viola from her cradle and clutch her to my breast, covering her with my bed blanket.

The bedroom door slams open.

Benjamin Blakely.

My gorge rises at the sight of him.

"How dare you burst into this house acting like you own it! What do you want?" Tabitha yells, yanking at Benjamin's coat and pulling him back and out of the room.

Benjamin swings around and strikes Tabitha. She falls against the open bedroom door.

He snatches the covers away from my Laura Viola. He makes to grab for the baby, but I leap across the bed, clutching her in my arms.

"Feisty little thing," he says. "Not to worry. I just wanted to see what was mine. The sheriff is coming right behind me. Illegitimate babies must be taken care of, you know. You have no means of support, having lost your land and all. The baby is now a ward of the state. He's coming to give her a proper home. I just wanted to see what the bastard looked like before handing it over."

Benjamin laughs, but he doesn't see what I have hidden under Laura Viola's cradle.

"Are you satisfied?" I ask, putting her down, pretending to fuss over her blankets while I reach under the cradle.

He guffaws. Until he sees me.

I stand in front of the cradle and cock my rifle. I don't have time to aim good, and when the gun goes off, I think I've killed him.

"Damn you, woman," he says, clutching his shoulder.

He's not dead. I wish he was.

"Get out of my house. If you come back in, I'll shoot to kill." I cock the rifle and point it at his chest.

His face goes white. Laura Viola wails.

Chapter 31

"You should have killed him," Tabitha says. "Now, it's his word against yours."

The Swiss cuckoo clock ticks on the wall, and despair washes over me.

When the cuckoo emerges, chirping the hour, Tabitha shudders. "You don't have much time."

The baby turns fractious. "Let me calm her down before we figure out what to do next," I say.

I try feeding her, but she refuses my breast, turning her little mouth away. She cries like she's in pain. I hold her close and pat her tiny back. I walk up and down the wooden floors to quiet her, back and forth from kitchen to bedroom and back to kitchen again. If the weather would allow, I would take her outside. Don't babies need sunlight?

But the sun hasn't shone a single day since Laura Viola's birth.

"Let me take her," Tabitha says after I walk the baby for a solid hour, pausing only to change her diaper. I try again to feed her. The baby will not be soothed.

"It's your milk, I'm afraid," Tabitha says. "You have to stay calm so your milk will sweeten up."

"How can I?" I ask, doubly panicked. "I'm scared, Tabitha. I'm afraid of what Benjamin said about the sheriff taking my baby. I'm afraid it can happen. She is a bastard child. She could be a ward of the state. They could take her anywhere. Why didn't I marry Morris when he wanted me to?"

"I don't know about any of that," Tabitha says. "What I do know is that you have to calm down or your baby won't live long enough to be a ward of the state."

Tabitha is right, and I think of Mama. I can almost hear her. *Sing, Annie Laura. It will make everything look better.*

I hum. It's what Mama taught me when I was a girl and Papa was gone on one of his long business trips. I missed him and feared never seeing him again. Mama told me to sing, and if I couldn't sing, to hum.

Music soothes the soul, Annie Laura girl. When your heart feels heavy and you feel despair, sing. It helps. I promise.

And Mama was right. It always worked. Even when I didn't want to, even when every muscle in my body said no, if I could force myself to sing, I always felt better.

The baby has to be soothed. Her shrieks are piercing. I hum softly. It's all I can muster.

I hum until I find the courage to sing. I feel my heartbeat slow and my tense muscles relax. When I finally feel peaceful, Laura Viola calms herself enough to nurse, suckling greedily, then falls into a restful sleep.

"I think you can put her in the cradle, Annie Laura. She will be fine while we pack your stuff."

"Pack my stuff?"

"You have to get out of here. Before the sheriff comes, throws you in jail, and snatches Laura Viola. We don't have much time."

I stare at Tabitha.

"You pack up the baby's things," she says. "I'll pack yours."

And I do as she says. Mechanically. Slowly. I don't want to leave.

Tabitha works with the energy and efficiency of a squirrel gathering Spanish moss for her nest.

"I've packed your bag. You have to go. Now!"

She wraps Laura Viola securely over my chest in a makeshift baby sling. "Get on the horse and ride as quickly as you can. Hard Labor Creek. No one will find you there. No one will guess you would go that far. Can you get there?"

I can't remember where Hard Labor Creek is. How am I going to find it?

"Your father's friend, Annie Laura. Think. The pastor, the one who helped him stop drinking. She and her sister live alone. I know her. She will take you in. But you must go. Now!"

Tabitha walks me out to the horse where she's strapped two saddlebags filled with my belongings. She gives me clear directions to the sisters' church and farm. She makes a step for my boot with her hands and gives me a leg-up onto the horse. I settle in the saddle. It hurts. I'm too close to the baby's birth. How am I going to make it? But the warm breath of my baby reaches me, and I know exactly how I'm going to make it.

Tabitha slaps the horse's rear, and we take off galloping in the direction of safety. The rhythm of the ride clears my vision. With each jolt of the saddle, the pain forces me to think clearly. I know Tabitha is right. I have to find a place far away from Falling Waters, Florida, where my baby will be safe. I have to use my wiles to outsmart Benjamin. It's my only hope.

Chapter 32

I ride until daylight turns to dusk and then to a black velvet star-filled night. I stop only to feed Laura Viola. A full moon rises, and I navigate my way to Hard Labor Creek. Laura Viola sleeps, lulled by the pounding hooves, but each hoofbeat makes me feel like I'm going to die.

Why is this happening to me? What awful thing have I done in my life to deserve this? Am I being punished because I dishonored my father by not being what he wished me to be? Am I being punished for wishing Benjamin Blakely dead more times than I can count?

I have to make it to the sisters. I can't pass out on this dark road. I imagine wild animals wresting Laura Viola from my arms.

When the pain has nearly claimed me, the glow of lights brings me to the church. I'm fighting to stay conscious. The pain screams louder. I make it up the church stairs and fall down, my child cushioned in my arms.

Laura Viola's cries wake me, along with ladies' voices chattering excitedly over my head. One holds a kerosene lamp close to my face. I feel its warmth and smell the acrid smoke.

"I don't know her, Mary. She's a stranger come for shelter."

"The poor little lamb."

Warm brown hands lift me and carry me into in the church. They heft me onto what feels like a wooden pew. I'm not sure how long I lie there.

"Look here," one of them says, and I feel a gentle finger on my bodice. "She's soaking wet. Why, she's got a baby somewhere."

Laura Viola! Where is she? Have I dropped her? "My baby!" I scream. But the scream is only in my head.

"You don't suppose she lost it on the way here, do you?" one asks.

"Do you reckon we ought to send someone to look?"

209

"Get her some water," another one says. "Maybe we can revive her enough to get her talking."

I hear water sloshing in a pail, and then a cool, damp cloth is placed on my forehead.

"Here, sweetie," a gentle voice says, "try drinking a little of this."

I lean over to the cool water and drink. I drink again and again. The kind woman fills the tin cup four times before my thirst is quenched.

"That's a nursing mother if ever I saw one," the woman says.

"Where's your baby, honey?" asks the woman holding the tin cup of water, caressing my forehead gently as she speaks.

"Oh, Lord," she says. "The child is hemorrhaging! Go get my sister. Get Mary."

A few minutes later, I hear my baby cry and feel the warmth of the women as they cluck and cuddle me. And then blackness swallows me.

When I come to, it's to the comforting murmur of female voices.

"She's gonna be fine," a lady with a husky voice says. "The horse ride just sped up what nature was trying to do. She's not hemorrhaging. She's just expelling lochia, normal bleeding for days after you give birth. Don't any of you remember?"

"We're not *that* old."

"Well, you act like you got the old timers."

"And the baby is fine?"

"Yes, the baby is fine. I heard her crying when I brought my workbag in. I took her out of her mama's arms as she lay on that front step, and I've been holding her since then. I told the little mama that the baby would be fine. And she is."

Thank you, Lord. My baby is fine.

Under the hands of these ministering angels, I feel myself grow strong. They feed me some stew that tastes like heaven, and plenty of water. I nurse Laura Viola again.

I'm surrounded by a sea of expectant faces. They're waiting for an explanation, and they're too polite to ask.

When my story tumbles out of my mouth like water over river rocks, I'm as surprised as anybody.

"Nine months ago, a man took me against my will. That same man tried to take my baby away and make her a ward of the state. His name is Benjamin Blakely." I find it strangely empowering to name my attacker.

A woman gasps.

"I shot him when he came trying to snatch my baby."

"Shot him dead?"

"No, just wounded him in the shoulder. My friend Tabitha knew that they would come after me, arrest me, and take my baby. She sent us here to the lady preacher who helped my daddy back a few years ago."

The little church is silent but for the bugs knocking against the windows trying to get in to the light.

"What did you say your name was?" the lady preacher, Martha, asks.

"Annie Laura Brock," I say.

"Well, Annie Laura Brock, it is nice to meet you." The pastor is dark skinned. Perhaps a mix of Indian and White and Colored. Her face is kind. Her hair is white and pulled up in a loose bun, its tendrils escaping in soft curls around her face. "Your father told me all about how proud he was of you, what a wonderful little farmer you are, and how you will make it in America because you understand the ways of the new world in a way he never would. He was so proud of you, Annie Laura."

How I wish he'd spoken those words to me. They were the very words I'd lived my life hoping for.

A look of concern crosses Martha's face. "Where is your father?"

"He died," I say. "I'm not certain how. He left on a train last spring and never came back. A man brought a telegram saying he was dead."

211

Martha's forehead wrinkles. "He came through here a little over a year ago. He told me about your mother and his excitement about her new baby. He was doing so well. He hadn't touched a drop of drink since he found out she was with child. And your mother," the woman says. "How is she? And the new baby?"

"Mama died in childbirth," I say, "and our neighbor stole the baby." The words sound harsh against the warm pine walls.

A compassionate murmur sweeps through the women like the beating of a thousand moth's wings. It encircles me in its delicate breeze, enveloping me in the love of a room full of women yearning to soothe my pain.

I close my eyes to mark the comfort of this moment. "It's been a troubling year," I say.

"You say so?" one asks, and the women in the room burst with laughter. But it's a laughter I'm surprisingly able to share.

"Well, ladies," the preacher lady breaks in, "I'll take our new friend home and let her have some much-needed rest. You all do what you came to do!"

The women hug me goodbye and move the pulpit out of the way to set up a large quilt stand.

"It's Tuesday night quilting," the preacher tells me. "Tonight, we're making a wedding quilt for Mabel's granddaughter."

"My Oma back in Germany had a quilting circle," I say wistfully. "I remember her taking me. I would sit and thread needles for her friends who had trouble seeing the tiny eye. I haven't thought of that in years!"

And just for a moment, I long to be a little girl again, in the protective care of my grandmamma.

But the thought of having to experience this year all over again makes me shudder.

As we're leaving, I overhear hushed whispers that carry in the empty sanctuary. And they aren't about quilting.

"I reckon she's being punished for some sin she committed. Otherwise, something so awful never would have happened to her."

"Mabel!" one woman cries. "How could you say such a thing?"

212

"Well, I just believe it might be true." But her voice falters like she isn't sure, like she is posing it as a question rather than a strident assurance.

The preacher lady turns around like she's been struck by lightning. "That, my child, is heresy," she says.

"Are you calling me a heretic?" Mabel places her hands on her hips.

"No. I'm calling the idea that bad things only happen to bad people heresy. That line of thinking is the reason Job's friends were idiots, and God told them to ask forgiveness for their wrong thinking."

"I don't follow," Mabel says, and I detect hope in her voice.

The same hope I'm feeling.

"Bad things don't happen to good people because they sin. Bad things happen to good people because this world is a fallen place. God grants us hope in the midst of this fallen world. He promises to be with us through the storm and create streams where we think there is only desert. God is love. Never forget that, Mabel."

I feel like Martha is talking to me. And the tears that flow down my cheeks have nothing to do with my exhaustion or my pain. I'm weeping from sheer relief. God is not punishing me.

This preacher lady, Martha, knows my mama's God.

Martha takes me back to the tiny cabin she shares with her sister Mary. It looks like a fairy-tale cottage with neat, miniature fixings. The table, sitting atop a cheery red and white rag rug circle, is just large enough for two plates. The fireplace looks to be built for elves—even the woodstove is tiny.

"Your father built that for us," Martha says, her smile crinkling the corners of her eyes. "I needed a small one, and he said he could do it. That's how I first met him." She looks away like she's remembering something she had rather not.

"He was drinking hard then," I offer.

"Yes," Martha says.

"Thank you for helping my father quit drinking the alcohol."

"I understood his problem better than most," she says.

Martha moves to the fireplace, signaling the end of the conversation, though I long to know more.

The fireplace fire burns low, and on top of the coals are six sweet potatoes. Martha hangs her wrap on the peg beside the door and turns the sweet potatoes over in the coals.

"We like sweet potatoes. My sister is fixing you a place to sleep over there. Don't mind us. We're a couple of night owls. You just sleep. I know you need it."

There's a tiny cradle beside the bed. When I look surprised, Martha says, "My sister's a midwife. Sometimes she has to bring the mama and baby home here."

I touch my baby girl's cheek and then snuggle into the feather bed, and Mary places a light cotton red and white Irish chain quilt over me. I imagine the women back at the church stitching it lovingly, solving their daily problems, sharing their hopes and dreams.

"We keep it real warm in here, so if you get hot, you just shuck this quilt. My sister can't stand cold. It's why we built the cabin so small," Mary says. "And don't be afeard if a man comes in the morning. Our son, Leonard. He's tall and dark-skinned with brown and gold eyes and coal-black hair. You'll know him if you see him. He comes and takes coffee with us most mornings."

I nod, looking around. The homespun charm of the cabin soothes me, and the warmth makes me drowsy. Laura Viola sleeps, and so do I.

Chapter 33

I'm awakened by a knock on the door. The midmorning sun dapples the white-washed floor and brightens the red-work tea towels and coverlets that dot the cabin. I've slept late. I remember Mary mentioning her son, Leonard. This must be him. I wonder if he always knocks.

But then I recognize Isaac's voice, bolt upright, and wrap the quilt around me. What is he doing here? Laura Viola awakes, and I pick her up to nurse her. The sisters let Isaac in like they know him and offer him some breakfast. I stay in bed with the baby, listening from behind my makeshift door curtain.

"Boy, it's gone cold on us, and you've still worked up a sweat," Martha clucks.

"I got up early, long before the sun rose. Miss Tabitha knocked on our cabin door last night at midnight. She'd heard some bad news. Daddy sent me here."

"Well, sit down, drink a mug of spring water and eat some of these cinnamon rolls. And tell us all about it," Martha says.

"Thank you kindly, ma'am, but trouble is on its way."

"What kind of trouble?"

"Miss Tabitha says they're coming for Annie Laura."

"Who is coming for Annie Laura?" Mary asks.

"Benjamin and the sheriff and a whole posse. They somehow figured out she was here. I don't know how."

"Why are they coming after her?" Martha asks. "What are they hoping to get from Annie Laura?"

"Benjamin wants her in jail. Said she shot him on public property. Looks forward to a jury putting her behind bars for life. Or, he says, the crazy house. Said she was a crazy woman and didn't belong in town with sane people. He's spread his trash talk all over town. He's got everyone believing him. Telling folks things that ain't fit for a lady's ears. I just hate it. I don't know how to stop him."

"You can't stop him, Isaac. Mean people, full of venom, want others to be as miserable as they are. It's a sickness. Benjamin Blakely is bent on hurting folks as bad as he hurts. I don't know why he's picked Annie Laura as his target, but he has," Mary says.

How does Mary know so much about Benjamin Blakely?

Laura Viola finishes nursing. I burp her and change her wet diaper. I hold her in my arms and wonder at her beauty. How blessed I am with this perfect baby. My life has taken on new meaning. I feel a joy like I've never felt before. *Thank you, Lord, for this gift. Thank you for making good out of horror.*

My baby falls into a peaceful sleep. I kiss her soft forehead and settle her into her tiny cradle.

"I wish Leonard weren't off hunting in the woods this morning," Mary says.

"Don't you worry," Martha says. "We're ready. Having Leonard would be a bonus, but we can guard our land."

Mary laughs. "You got that right, sister. We been doin' it for years."

I step out from behind my curtain just in time to see Martha pull a ragged bundle from beneath her bed. It's the size of a small child and wrapped in an old wedding ring quilt whose bright red stitches have not faded with time. She unveils two ancient rifles.

"They were Daddy's," Mary says to me. She uses the quilt to wipe down the rifle Martha hands her. "He got snake bit and died soon after the war of northern aggression. He left us the guns, an iron stew pot, and a Confederate 100-dollar bill."

"That's when I took to preaching," Martha explains.

"She makes a good living," Mary says.

"But Mary and I, we practice."

"Shooting," Mary chimes in.

"Why, we can shoot near about anything." Martha says.

"Martha took down a bear once," Mary says proudly.

"Aww, that wasn't nothing. He was a lazy old black bear. Now, Mary here can shoot a pheasant a whole cornfield away."

216

"I reckon Annie Laura is in good hands," Isaac says, sounding relieved.

I give him a shaky smile.

The sheriff and Benjamin Blakely are coming for me. Will these two little middle-aged women be able to stop them? I hurry to the washbasin to wash my face and rinse my mouth.

"How far does your land reach, Miss Martha?" I ask.

"Right past the church. Why?"

I look into the mirror and know I have to make a decision. I can't wait on others to take care of me. I know Blakely and what he's capable of. I'm not waiting for him. Benjamin Blakely will have to play by my rules.

"We're not going to wait on them to come here. I don't want them messing up your house or your garden. Take your guns. We're going to meet him head-on at the road. Let's go." I pray for the Lord's protection over Laura Viola here in her cradle as we do what we have to do.

I stride out the door.

The sisters follow me down the steps of the cabin and the dirt road. Mary and Martha haul their rifles right behind me, and Isaac takes up the rear. We move past the church, stopping just before the end of their property.

We wait. Birds sing in the stillness.

Isaac clears his throat. I jump.

Martha and Mary cock their guns.

The hoofbeat of a single horse sounds on the road. We listen for a second horse, the sheriff's, and for a clattering posse of horses. None come. Just the single horse and rider.

Mary looks at Martha. The horse is close enough to see. Martha signals once, and the two women, in synchronized motion, steady their rifles against man-thick shoulders, set their sights, and aim. Their trigger fingers twitch.

I can't allow these women to go to jail for murder just for me.

I step out in front of them and motion for them to lower their rifles, out of Benjamin's sight.

Benjamin pulls his horse up short, like an arrogant little Napoleon, so close to me I can feel the horse's breath. I don't back away.

"What a lovely surprise to see you, Annie Laura, on this fine morning," he says, tipping his hat in mock servility. "Where is your little bastard baby?"

The anger starts in my feet and travels to the top of my head.

I step aside and motion Mary and Martha with absolutely no remorse.

When Benjamin registers that I've cleared the way for two rifles to be aimed at his chest, his bravado wilts. He kicks his horse to back away, but all he manages is a tight, foolish little circle.

When Benjamin's horse settles down, Martha speaks in a cheerful voice. "You got business with this man, Mary?"

"Not that I know of. You got business with him, Martha?" Mary asks.

"No. I don't do business with low-down filth, crusted with slime and topped with horse shit." Martha cocks her gun and aims it at Benjamin's forehead. "I've got me a clean shot here, Mary. You think I could splatter his brains on the road?"

"You could, Martha. But I'm afraid that would make a mighty big mess."

"Yeah, and he doesn't really look worth cleaning up after," Martha agrees.

Benjamin trembles and glances back at his gun, strapped behind his saddle. He can't unbuckle it without getting shot. His bum arm is wrapped up from where I shot him in the shoulder.

"Cat got your tongue, mister?" Mary asks.

Benjamin is silent.

"Well, now, sir, my sister and I don't usually pull our guns out on strangers, but you're special. Did you have some business here you wanted to attend to?"

Benjamin points to Annie Laura and says in a shaky voice, trying to regain some dignity, "She's got my baby."

218

"Really?" Mary says. "You're a married man, aren't you? Does your wife know that this woman took your baby and that you're over here looking for it?"

"I know a better question," Martha says, scratching her nose with the back of her hand, the barrel still pointed at Benjamin. "Does her daddy know you're over here in Hard Labor Creek trying to track down some other woman?"

"He will soon," Mary says, chuckling.

"How's that?" Benjamin asks, trying to sound tough but betrayed by the little-boy blush traveling across his face and covering his ears.

"I just sent Ida Mae's boy after him. Your daddy-in-law's sister—that would be your aunt by marriage—is in my quilting circle. Your aunt said she thought your daddy-in-law would be interested to know you were visiting this girl here."

"That's crazy," he says, huffing his chest out defiantly. His horse chooses this moment to let loose a stream of urine, significantly reducing the impact of Benjamin's huffed chest.

Martha raises an eyebrow, closes one eye, and holds her finger to the trigger.

"You ready, Mary?" she asks.

"Yes, ma'am, I am," Mary says. "I'm hungry for a hand," she says and chuckles.

"I'm wanting me some head cheese," Martha says.

Benjamin's eyes widen, and fear makes him tremble. "Y'all are crazy women," he says, yanking on his horse's bit and kicking him savagely. The surprised horse responds by rearing so high that Benjamin slides down his back. The horse bolts down the clay road, and Benjamin lands in an undignified heap in a puddle of horse urine. He looks at the guns aimed at him and bounces up as quickly as he had fallen. He turns and scrambles off in pursuit of his runaway horse.

"Whoa," he yells. The horse pays him no mind and pounds down the road, Benjamin falling farther and farther behind.

We stand listening until Benjamin's voice disappears, covered over by the rustling of pine, and he is a dot in the distance.

The sisters explode in laughter and discharge their guns. Isaac hoots and throws his hat up in the air.

"I don't reckon he'll cross the Jackson County line again until his daddy-in-law is cold in his grave," Mary says.

"How did you find out all that about his wife's daddy?" Martha asks Mary.

"Well," Mary says, smiling, "I got up early this morning and took some homemade cinnamon rolls around to one of the ladies in my circle. When Ida Mae gasped right after Annie Laura named her attacker the other night, I had a feeling that she knew Benjamin Blakely. I just wanted to find out how. And when I did, I knew Annie Laura's problem with Benjamin Blakely might be over. For good. Ida Mae made it clear that the only man alive meaner than Benjamin Blakely is Benjamin Blakely's daddy-in-law. He is very protective of his daughter. Ida Mae assured me his daddy-in-law will shoot to kill if Benjamin Blakely ever threatens to leave Jackson County again."

Chapter 34

Fog laces the Spanish moss-coated century oaks. Although my hands are cold, unprotected against the early morning haze, I feel strangely comforted by the damp closeness. The fog shrouds me as safely as the two women sleeping peacefully in the snug cabin. Like the fog, my shelter with them is temporary, but soothing in the stillness of morning.

Benjamin Blakely will never come back. And if he does? I have only to shout for the sisters and they will appear, shotguns cocked and aimed.

Squirrels scamper across branches, busy gathering food for their morning meal. My baby girl, satisfied from her own early morning feeding, sleeps snug against my chest in a wool shawl that I have tied into a baby sling. I take my time walking down the narrow path to the well, my footsteps softened by strewn pine straw and dense air. I want this peaceful feeling to last forever.

Over the past few days, I've grown accustomed to Mary and Martha's ways, how they mull over their thoughts for hours sometimes before speaking, how they seemed pleased as punch to have me here.

In this safe place, I've once again buried myself in the enchantment of mothering my precious newborn—an enchantment that robs me of all logical thought. I can hardly believe that this miracle of life came from me. Her perfect little hands, her soft, tiny feet, her eyes searching for me, and the satisfying rush when she latches on to my breast. I'm in a blissful, beautiful motherhood delirium. In this cabin, I'm not afraid of Benjamin Blakely's nonsense. The curse he believed himself to have lain upon me has, in truth, saved me. It's people, not land, that save a person.

A spirit beyond my understanding gave Tabitha the good sense to send me to these two sisters, women who knew what it was to be unmarried and with child, having been in their youth exactly where I am now. The two of them raised a baby, one the world deemed an illegitimate child. And look at them now. They filed for and were given their own land grant, land they own free and clear. And they raised their boy Leonard, now a grown man, on this land. They urged the land to produce, and it did.

If they could do it, surely so can I. The land will make me strong. I am ready to begin again.

The thought fills me with bright hope.

Slowly, carefully, like a bear emerging from winter's sleep, cautious and hungry, I'm surfacing into this new world, a world that I understand a little better. It is true that people are capable of inflicting hurt I could never have imagined. But I prefer to believe that the world is populated with only a few Benjamin Blakelys. With the preacher lady, Martha, and her midwife sister, Mary, I'm making progress.

When the squirrels scamper, chattering away to a distant oak grove, I guess it to be because the food is more plentiful elsewhere.

I steady the tin bucket and hoist it to the ridge of the well before hooking the handle, lowering, and immersing the vessel in fresh, cool water. It's only when I raise the filled bucket and set it on the ground beside me to secure Laura Viola's wool sling that I notice the silence. The squirrels are no longer chattering.

The metallic taste of fear fills my mouth. A fear I thought had been erased during my days with the sisters.

A horse whinnies, and I clasp Laura Viola. She startles. And in no longer than it takes a flash of lightning to terrorize a farmer in the middle of a newly sown field, I'm yanked back in time to that horrible day. All the progress I've made towards forgetting is obliterated. I slip behind the well and kneel, cradling my baby. My legs tremble, my head feels light, and I fight the darkness that threatens to take me down.

Breathe, I tell myself. *Deeply*. I close my eyes, holding my precious child, and fight for breath.

I hear footsteps and the muted clop of horse hooves padding through the pine straw-strewn pathway.

I gather enough courage to leave the bucket and run for the house, Laura Viola clutched safely against me.

When I return to the cabin, it's as if I've never left. The sisters are piddling about, doing their morning chores. Martha looks up at me standing at the door.

"Girl, you look like you seen a ghost!"

"No, ma'am, it wasn't a ghost. But someone is headed our way."

"Look at this poor child," Mary says. "Shaking like she's got the fevers."

"Now, don't you worry none," Martha says. "Why, that wasn't nothin' but our Leonard heading home from getting us sugar and coffee from the Vernon store."

I sit in the rocking chair by the fire and allow myself to be soothed by their gnarled hands and kind ways.

"Missy," Martha says when the evening has turned to night and a cold chill settles on the little cabin. We've gathered around the fire, and she turns the sweet potatoes slowly, meditatively.

"Missy," Martha says again, "it ain't the same."

I wait for Martha to finish her words, the fire crackling, the embers dancing and sparkling, flakes of ash flying up the chimney like winged creatures. Laura Viola sleeps snuggled in my arms, and the dark cabin, the warm fire, and the silence make my eyes heavy. Though I fight valiantly against the robber, sleep, I succumb.

Martha's voice startles me out of my brief slumber. "I know what you're a thinkin," she says. The baby startles with me, though she doesn't wake. I blink my eyes, try to think clearly. Since Laura Viola's birth, sleep—even brief sleep—robs me of all reason, and I have to fight my way to understanding.

"It ain't the same. Sister and me didn't have no man trackin' us down trying to snuff out the life of our baby. No sir. Our baby's daddy…"

I try to remember which of the sisters actually gave birth to the baby Leonard, who lives next door in the cabin he built with his own hands.

"…he forgot about us soon as we conceived."

"Yes, ma'am," Mary chimes in. "We had our fun, and then we left."

The sisters giggle, and I feel heat climb up my cheeks, unrelated to the warmth of the fire. I've never been around anyone who talked so freely about enjoying the relations between man and woman as these sisters do. They do give me some hope that the horrible thing I experienced is not what keeps men and women together in the marriage bed.

"We didn't know which would take, but once it did, we was off to our land grant. Had to have somebody to pass this land down to, don't you know."

I have to laugh. The sisters are completely, outrageously wonderful.

They exchange glances and smile.

"Sister here knew a thing or two about birthing babies and was able to pick up the extra cash we needed for things like sugar and coffee, and all."

"I still do," Mary pipes up. "I still do."

I remember her able hands, helping me with my afterbirth pains. Those hands were certain and sure, and I trusted her like dozens of other women must have over the years.

"But didn't nobody need to hold a gun to his chest, neither."

The tone of the conversation shifts with the suddenness of a rifle shot. A chill descends over the room.

Martha is speaking of the daddy of Benjamin's wife, away over in Marianna. I know what she means.

"We found out a little more of the story of Benjamin Blakely's father-in-law. That man held Benjamin at gunpoint. He made him promise two things. One, that Benjamin was going to marry his daughter." Martha stops like she can't go on.

Mary picks up for her. "But before he would allow the marriage to take place, given the amount of property his daughter—and Benjamin—stood to inherit, he made Benjamin promise that he had left no other illegitimate brats lying around. And if he had, he'd best get rid of them soon."

Chapter 35

In the darkest hours of the night, the Florida weather shifts like it often does in late January. One minute the camellias are showing their pink faces, the new green grass is reaching up to the sun, and the next minute there's a storm tearing down the trees and flattening the grass with all the ferocity of a wild boar. This particular storm blows down a century oak beside the well, narrowly missing the opening. And today it's cold, bitterly cold. There's an icy ring around the top of the well. It matches the icy feeling in my soul.

Had Benjamin come here before to "get rid of" Viola Lee? Will he be back to try again?

When John Sebring rides up in the early hours of the morning, the sisters aren't the least bit surprised. They battle the chilly morning with coffee warming on the woodstove and fresh sweet potato bread baking in the oven. The pleasant aroma fills the room.

I can't remember the last time I was so happy to see anyone. John Sebring meets me with his big smile and hugs me tight. But when I gaze into his normally sparkling blue eyes, he looks away. Something is not right.

I pull him in out of the cold, take his coat, and lead him to my sleeping baby.

He touches Laura Viola's face with a gentle finger and asks to hold her. He gathers her in his arms like she's a delicate hot-house flower. He cups her head gingerly in his broad hand and holds her up to the weak sunlight coming through the window. In answer to the chilled room, he bundles her more tightly so that only her face is revealed, the perfect peace of a sleeping newborn.

I love her fiercely.

"Where can we talk?" He delivers the words like a verdict.

My heart pounds and the blood rushes to my face, making me hot in spite of the chilly day. We pull up stools close to the warm fire, and now the acrid aroma of roasting sweet potatoes drowns out the friendly scent of baked bread and fresh coffee and makes me nauseous. Laura Viola wakes up, hungry, and I'm glad to have the excuse to get away from John Sebring and whatever it is he needs to tell me. I don't like this unaccustomed shuttering of his normally open countenance.

I walk to the back of the house into the tiny, curtain-enclosed space the sisters have given me as my own. I sit on the little bed where I've found safety and peace with my child. I close my eyes to the world around me and allow myself to be soothed by my baby's gentle suckling.

"I'll protect you," I whisper. "My sweet angel baby. I'll protect you." But even as I whisper the words, I know they aren't true. I know that I can never do enough to keep her safe, that Benjamin Blakely will never give up, not as long as his life and livelihood are threatened by Laura Viola's existence.

Because now there is this. A father holding a gun to Benjamin's chest, forcing him to marry his daughter, knowing that in marriage her land is now Blakely's. But forcing him to swear there are no more brats of his blood that might split the inheritance away from the farmer's direct bloodline. And Benjamin had, according to Martha, promised he'd sired no other brats, though this is a lie.

Now Benjamin is hunting his wild game. He's determined to gather the children he's fathered and make them all disappear. He can kill and then pretend it was yellow fever or any of a dozen childhood maladies. The area is too rural, too far removed from any city for the threat of a sheriff to come hopping down the bunny trail after the truth.

And I know in my heart of hearts that the only way I can keep my baby safe is to go far, far away and start over again.

Like the sisters? No. They were lucky when they were caring for their own baby. No one was chasing them.

And what if I can get away? What skills will I use to make a living? I'm uneducated, without money, and presently without land. Laura Viola and I are destined for the poorhouse, and that's if we're lucky enough to find one.

What kind of life can I offer this precious child?

I wrack my brain to think of what I can do, where we can go. But there is nowhere. There is no one. Papa and Mama are dead. I have no living relatives in Germany, and even if I did, how would I pay my way to get there? And who would take me in, an unwed mother with an illegitimate child?

No one.

My only hope is Morris. But no one has heard from him in months.

I burp Laura Viola, busying myself with the normal tasks of motherhood, seeking in the mechanics of living an answer to my soul's dilemma. I change her wet diaper and kiss the tiny feet and hands, lay my cheek on her soft, warm belly, and let my tears tickle my baby's sides.

Finally, I dress Laura Viola, wrap the warm flannel blanket around her, and cradle her against my chest. I sing to her, crooning the gentle lullaby Mama sang to all of us.

John Sebring walks across the cabin and stands behind the curtain that hides my world from his view.

"May I sit with you?" he asks.

I swallow. I pull the curtain aside. I pat the washed-out quilt on the bed for John Sebring to sit beside me.

He wipes a tear from my cheek and shakes his head, his face creased in sorrowful sympathy.

"Sadness has rained down on us, Annie girl."

He hands me a letter. It bears a strange stamp.

When I open it, the language is one that I can't read. It's Dutch. If only Mama were here.

"You've read it?" I asked.

"I had it translated," John Sebring said. And his soft blue eyes fill with tears. "It's about Morris. He's missing in action, presumed dead."

"Oh, Morris." It's all I can say. John Sebring allows me to cry, brings me a dipper of cool spring water, and takes Laura Viola from my arms so that I can drink it.

The possibility of any life for Laura Viola and myself is gone, just like that. Because even if Morris is not actually dead, it could be months before we hear from him. Laura Viola will be a ward of the state or dead by then.

"I'm so sorry, Annie Laura. He wouldn't have left if he had known there was to be a war and that he might get caught in the middle."

I nod. There is no one in the world who knows the pain in my heart so well as John Sebring Corley.

"There is more," he says, kissing Laura Viola's cheek. He raises his head and tries to look directly into my eyes, but can't. "I married Mary Scarlet."

I shake my head and smile. "Now is not the time for one of your jokes, John Sebring, though I do appreciate the attempt to bring some humor into this otherwise dreadful moment." And I do laugh, because if anyone can make me laugh at a time like this, it's John Sebring. Only those in the same depths of despair can rise with you to laugh at the pain and absurdity of life. I wait for him to laugh a little and apologize for a bad attempt at humor.

But he doesn't. Instead, the silence separates us. Laura Viola gives a contented infant sigh in John Sebring's arms. I don't know what to think. Is it true? Is Mary Scarlet really his wife?

"You said there was more. What is it?" I ask.

"Mary Scarlet has talked Benjamin into letting us take Laura Viola and raise her as our own."

My quick intake of breath and the jolt of my entire body pushes John Sebring away from me. And I turn on my friend, hissing like a mother cat attacking one who has ventured too close to her newborn kittens.

If Laura Viola were not been sleeping so soundly, I would snatch her from his arms.

"I wouldn't let Mary Scarlet Blakely take my baby if she were the last person on this earth."

John Sebring sighs, unperturbed by my outburst. "I know that, Annie Laura. But will you let *me* take your baby?"

"If I die, you are probably the only person I will let take my baby." I breathe deeply to regain my composure. "There are plenty of sweet girls in Falling Waters who would be honored to be your wife. Pick one. Pick a sweet one, like our Maggie."

We don't even have any tears left to cry over that loss. The pain is so deep that only emptiness remains.

For me, there's the fear of a new, searing pain. The pain of a cow whose calf has been taken to the slaughter; she hears her baby's bleat and then smells blood.

I already feel it. I know my baby is going to be taken from me.

But not to Mary Scarlet. Never, ever to Mary Scarlet. She loves Benjamin way too much. Why, she might even suffocate or drown my precious baby girl if it promises to keep her beloved brother out of trouble.

"Look," John Sebring says and pulls a rumpled paper from his coat pocket. "He's signed something. Signed this. Promises never to come near Laura Viola until she turns fifteen and becomes a woman in her own right."

My Laura Viola a woman? This tiny thing in my arms? I can't see past her next feeding, much less to the day when she becomes a woman. What is he saying? That Benjamin Blakely will somehow be allowed to visit Laura Viola when she turns fifteen?

"The day that happens, it will be over my dead body. Do you really think that I would ever in my wildest dreams leave this innocent babe vulnerable to Benjamin Blakely? Evil. Pure, unadulterated evil."

"Evil?" John Sebring asks.

"He is *EVIL*," I shout. "And don't give me that 'he had an awful childhood.' His entire family had an awful childhood! But I don't see Morris or Mary Scarlet…"

I cover my mouth with my own hand.

Mary Scarlet. Morris. I've put them in the same sentence. As if they are similar in any way.

I reach for the paper in John Sebring's hand, but he pulls it back. He studies me as if he fears I intend to tear the paper into shreds, his face a shield of protection.

"I only want to read it."

He acquiesces and hands it to me.

I read.

I fold it neatly.

I hand it back to him.

Is this my only choice?

If I can have a hand in raising my baby, I might consider it. Even Moses's mother could nurse her child.

"I trust you," I say. "You are probably the only one I trust. And, as difficult as it would be for me, I would trust you to raise Laura Viola. But I can come too, right? I can live right next door to you and...whomever you marry." The words come with great difficulty, like there is a big ball of something in my chest expanding, robbing me of breath.

John Sebring looks away and through the tiny window at the cloud closing the sun's feeble attempt at light. The darkness travels over the carefully swept floor.

When he doesn't answer, I push down the ball in my chest and continue, breathless in my desire. "I can be there to nurse her until she is weaned, and watch her grow up, and help out with her when...your wife...needs to run errands or entertain friends?"

I close my eyes and force in the picture of a brighter, happier future, the possible answer to this horrible dilemma. Hope rises in me, a glimmer of light.

I look up at John Sebring, but he will not meet my eyes.

"It's not possible."

"But it's your name. It's right here, I see it."

I look up into his pain-filled eyes, and I understand. I understand the unbelievable sacrifice he has made to protect me, to protect Laura Viola. He was not joking. He has married Mary Scarlet so that he can protect Laura Viola.

"It's what Maggie would have wanted me to do," he says, and tears fill his eyes. "You were her dearest friend."

"Oh, John." I put my hand on his kind face and know he believes he will never love another woman anyway, so what difference does it make whom he marries? The depth of his sacrifice is unfathomable.

"Well," he says. His mouth opens, and he tries to quip something that might have been funny in a different place, a different time.

I hug him, silencing his attempt. We can work out the details later. Right now, my friend needs comforting.

The baby between us makes snuffling sounds, grunting, making us both laugh with the antics of her facial expressions, first a smile, then a frown, and then a look of worried concern as if her facial muscles are practicing all the expressions of adulthood.

After a moment, John Sebring breaks away and stands as if to leave.

"What I do, I do for you and Laura Viola. And Maggie. Never forget that. No matter how things look."

Is that a warning?

Chapter 36

By the end of the week, it's clear that my only choice is to give my baby to John Sebring for safekeeping. He will meet me today at the county courthouse in Vernon so that I can sign papers giving over custody. We can't sign in Falling Waters. I'm wanted there for shooting Benjamin.

Besides, I don't really want to face the townspeople in Falling Waters. According to the ladies at Martha's church, as soon as the townspeople discovered I'd given birth, the gossip was rampant, twining its way down dirt roads and into sandy front yards. They were far less concerned about me shooting Benjamin than they were about me having a baby. *What do you expect from her kind? Penniless. Landless. Friendless. German whore.*

In order to convince myself to go, I must believe that I'm only offering John Sebring temporary custody. I can't think of Mary Scarlet. If I see only John Sebring's face, if I erase Mary Scarlet's, then I can live with myself. But barely.

I leave my baby girl, bundled in the soft muslin blankets Maggie embroidered for her Bonnie, etched with such love that I know any baby enveloped in those blankets will be forever cherished. I also know that, holding Laura Viola in his own daughter's wrappings, John Sebring will love and protect her as his own.

When I close the door behind me, a door that opened its heart to me, a cabin that gave me sanctuary, I close it on my baby girl cradled by Mary and looked over by Martha. It's this picture that I'll cherish. I'm leaving her in the care of two angels of mercy, angels who will pass her into her new life, whose seer-like wisdom I trust to discern good from evil. They will meet Mary Scarlet. They will task her with the responsibility of raising my child. And they will know in a heartbeat if this decision is the correct one.

I mount Dolly, my faithful mare, and set out on the long road to Vernon.

Can I do it? I don't know. I might get there, walk in, pick up the pen, and refuse to sign. Some inner knowledge, something that will alert me to danger, to my baby's life being something other than the life of love I can provide. And, yes, only I can do it properly. Only I can love her as she deserves to be loved.

But by some massive fissure in universal justice, I am unable to do so.

The sunny morning with its singing birds and blooming flowers taunts me. Dolly plods forward, taking me out of the enchanted forest where I've been allowed to be a mother and into the cold hearth of Vernon, Florida, where a mother is not allowed to keep her own flesh and blood.

If Laura Viola stays with me, eventually Benjamin Blakely will come for her.

In order to save her life, I have to give up my heart, for she is my treasure. Indeed, after signing a piece of inconsequential parchment, I will not be allowed to see her again until she turns fifteen.

I plod on, the morning turning to high noon, the birds growing quiet. In that silence, I hear a baby cry deep in the woods. My milk lets down, my body ready for the noon feeding. I drop the reins and clasp my breasts. Dolly stops. Milk seeps through my cloth breast bindings, wrapped ever so carefully by the sisters before dawn this morning. The milk soaks through to my shirtwaist, and when it seeps through my cloak, I pick up the reins and turn the horse sharply around.

Back to my baby girl.

When I arrive, breathless and spent, I can hear her plaintive wails, the desperate cry of hunger, the frustrated wail of a child, robbed of its mother's breast.

I leap from the horse, throw the reins over the hitching post, and burst into the cabin. Mary holds the baby, pacing back and forth, jostling her to soothe her while Martha warms a bottle nestled in her sweet potatoes.

I throw off my bonnet and snatch Laura Viola from Mary's arms, lift my shirtwaist, rip off the cloth binding, and nurse my baby girl.

A spray of milk showers her face. She gasps and gurgles, snuffling until she is able to latch on and soothe her hunger, and my soul.

I close my eyes and hum into the bliss of motherhood.

When she is satisfied and my breasts are empty, I wrap her gingerly and hand her back to Mary. My fingers cling to the very edge of her blanket, and I can't let go. Mary waits, the baby in her arms. She summons silence against the war raging inside me.

"I can't do it," I say with calm certainty. "They will have to kill me first. I cannot, on my own, leave my baby girl. I don't care if it is to my dear friend John Sebring. Nothing can induce me to do so."

"At any moment, Benjamin Blakely can change his mind." Martha uses an old rag to remove the bottle from amongst the sweet potatoes. "He can come after Laura Viola and finish her off. The only protection you can offer her is Mary Scarlet and John Sebring. He won't hurt her if they claim her as their own, and his father-in-law will be none the wiser."

"But you'll protect us," I say.

"Yes, we will protect you as far as we can. But Blakely…"

I know what she means. I've lived it. Benjamin Blakely is like a panther. Patient, stealthy, conniving. He will wait until our defenses are down. He will pounce, his claws raking my precious child.

"It's not forever," Martha says.

She is right. It isn't forever. Nothing is forever. I will get my baby back, my precious gift to the world.

"Change your clothes, and I'll take you on in to Vernon." The masculine voice startles me. I'd not seen him when I rushed in. Tall, dark-skinned Leonard with Mary's brown and gold eyes and Martha's coal-black hair sits whittling a plow handle by the light of the fire. Leonard is a quiet man, not yet eighteen, and more like Mary than Martha. He works hard and helps his mother and his aunt manage the farm they've created out of their long-ago land grant.

He's kept himself scarce since I've been here. Mary says it's because he's shy.

"I'll hitch the wagon," he says. "We best be getting on." The door closes behind him.

Perhaps it's his calm reason. Perhaps there is a wisdom in my soul that defies my heart's longing. Whatever it is, I listen to him.

But though I listen, and I hear, I can't let go of the blanket.

Mary's gentle hand massages my fingers, her loving caress easing my grip on what I cannot have. My hand drops to my side, a leaden weight.

"You ain't in any fit condition to travel all that ways by yourself. I don't know what we were thinking." Martha places a bottle, filled with her special recipe for newborn formula, on the warm hearth.

"Leonard knows the way. He'll hold you steady." Mary and Martha exchange glances. "And besides, there's some things we're needing from the town."

I feel unsteady on my feet. Martha sees and pushes a kitchen chair beneath me. I sit, gazing at the fire. My body is no longer my own. I can't seem to move from the chair.

"Mary'll make you a potion to calm your nerves and help you get over the worst of it." Martha takes Laura Viola from Mary's arms and settles her in her cradle.

Mary busies herself amongst her herbs. Soon, she has a steaming drink in her hands and bids me drink.

I take the potion as proffered. Leonard carries me to the wagon. I don't remember the trip to Vernon.

Chapter 37

March 1900

Leonard. What would I do without him in these dark days, days when I can barely see the ground in front of me, days when to rise from my bed takes an effort so Herculean that I don't think I can even make it to the outhouse?

Even as my hair falls out, strand by strand, until it's as thin as an old woman's, Leonard looks at me with a delight in his eyes that is difficult for me to ignore. And, in spite of myself, I yearn for someone to understand my pain, to see through it to the woman I still am.

Though Morris has abandoned me, Leonard is here.

The paper I signed, giving up all rights to my child, including visitation rights, is a dark mark on my soul. How is it that Benjamin Blakely has all the power? How is it that this accursed man can choose the way of my baby girl? But I've signed a legal document that can't be revoked.

I resign myself to living for the day, my child—my gift to the world—is of an age where she can choose to see me. I pray that John Sebring will not let her forget.

One morning, I hear Leonard open the front door of the tiny cabin. I doze through the murmur of voices but awaken when I realize they're hatching a plan that involves me leaving them. Have I been a burden to these kind women for too long? Where am I to go?

"Annie Laura?" Mary's kind voice breaks through my ongoing lament, the one that circles itself over and again in my mind, winding itself in a twisting, choking hold until all I want is sleep, sleep that will rescue me from the reality of what is. I lay flat on my stomach, my breasts, dry and flaccid, no longer a hindrance.

"Take that pillow off your head, child."

I sit up, pull my thin hair back, wind it around my finger, and knot it at the nape of my neck.

"Your fortunes have turned."

I shoot a look up at her and something courses through me that feels like life itself. "My baby?"

She looks away out past the window. I follow her gaze, hoping to see a wagon pulling up bearing John Sebring and Laura Viola.

But the road is empty, and there is no comforting sound of horse hooves or John Sebring's cheerful voice. It's quiet outside but for the singing of the birds.

How dare they sing? I lay back down in the bed and push the pillow over my head. Childish, I know, but what do I have left to live for?

As if reading my thoughts, Mary says, "You have to live for yourself. For the possibility of a future that is brighter than it looks right now. And for your sisters. They need you. You need to visit them, let them remember the sort of strong women they come from."

I look into her eyes. Is that it? Is she here to give me a resounding reminder that my sisters need me? That's a lie. With no land to support them, they've been parceled out to work for families in town like property. I can't bear to visit them. The one time I let myself go to them, I did nothing more than crush their hopes of my ever coming home. I had nothing for them. Nothing but the worn-out, washed-out me, unable to lift myself against the world anymore.

"There's talk in town that the sheriff is in deep trouble. There's a man here, a Mr. Liddon. He wants to talk to you."

I drag myself out of the bed, splash water on my face, and put on the newly washed and ironed dress Mary holds up for me.

"Thank you," I say.

Her smile is filled with hope.

Mr. Liddon appears to be in his mid-fifties. He's a tall man with a bald head, bright blue eyes, and a cheerful smile. He shakes my hand, his rolled-up sleeves revealing a heavily muscled forearm, and offers me a seat at the kitchen table. He's already spread legal paperwork across the polished pine tabletop.

"My friend, Morris Blakely, hired me to take your case. He paid me in advance. I've been working on it ever since. When I worked on it enough to realize we could win, I searched for you. You aren't easy to find! But I discovered two important things in my search for you. First, you're now of legal age."

He's right. I completely missed my own twenty-first birthday.

"And second, you signed paperwork that reinstated your land to you and your family."

What is he talking about? "No, sir, I didn't. The only paperwork I've ever signed is to give my baby up to John Sebring."

He studies me as if he wants to tell me something but thinks better of it.

"Will you go into Falling Waters with me and see if we can get everything cleared up?" he asks.

"I don't mean any disrespect, but, sir, if I go into Falling Waters, I'm very likely to be arrested for shooting Benjamin Blakely."

"You need not fear being arrested upon coming home to Falling Waters," he says. He points out the sentence he wants me to read. "According to the law, you were within your rights to shoot the intruder on your property. The property had not yet been legally transferred to probate. The sheriff would be remiss were he to attempt to incarcerate you." He rests a hand on the holster peeking beneath his frock coat.

I feel relief like butterflies in my belly. Whatever he thinks I signed can be straightened out later. This is wonderful news. "I can go home? I can get my land back?"

"You can," he says.

"And my baby?"

A shadow crosses the attorney's face. "That is another matter. The law is a bit more complicated about illegitimate children."

I feel my face grow hot. Will I carry this shame for the rest of my life?

"It seems that new legislation has been created, making it necessary for the child to be taken care of by a married couple."

Tears burn my eyes.

"But I do have some more good news. It seems that there is a possibility that some of your father's property—equipment and such—might have been reclaimed."

It's a small consolation. But a consolation all the same.

Mr. Liddon offers to accompany me to Falling Waters, where he says we both have some business with the sheriff.

Chapter 38

Nothing really matters to me but the hope of regaining my daughter. If this journey to Falling Waters with Mr. Liddon will bring me any cash, anything that might be considered viable property that will help me reclaim my land and build a life for Laura Viola, my sisters, and me, the trip is worth it to me.

The sheriff's office smells of old sweat and rancid tobacco. The sheriff doesn't rise when we walk in. Instead, he leans back in his chair, props his legs up on his desktop, and takes a puff of his cigar.

"Expensive taste," Mr. Liddon says, sniffing the smoke from the cigar and pointing to the fat stub dangling from the sheriff's yellowed teeth.

The sheriff grins. "Something I can do for you and the little German whore?" he asks, his tone dangerously cheerful.

I feel the hair stand up on the back of my neck.

"Yes, thank you so much for asking," Mr. Liddon says, his gracious tone belying the muscle that twitches in his cheek.

I fear his power.

He pulls a chair out for me, and when I'm seated he pulls one out for himself. The sheriff watches. Mr. Liddon folds his six-foot-four frame into the rickety wooden chair. His sleeves are rolled up so that the muscles in his forearms bulge. He packs a Colt in each holster.

"I see you come prepared," the sheriff says, eyeing him up and down.

"You can never be too safe," Mr. Liddon says playfully.

The sheriff coughs, and an armed deputy comes from the jail cell holding up a double-barreled shotgun. He aims it squarely at my chest.

"Really, gentlemen," Mr. Liddon says, as calmly as if he were greeting visitors at church, "you aren't interested in playing fair?"

"We don't play fair in Falling Waters, Florida," the sheriff says, his grin revealing the blackened and missing teeth on either side of the yellowed front ones.

"Yeah," the deputy says, "we play to win." He cocks his gun.

"And what, exactly, is it that you plan to win?" Mr. Liddon asks, calm as you please.

Tiny droplets of sweat drip down the center of my shirtwaist. This is not how I had envisioned the scene playing out. I grip the edges of the oak chair.

Mr. Liddon continues talking in a calm monotone as if the raised gun is a picture postcard. "I see you have the most up-to-date weapons in your arsenal. Good choice. That is a very nice Lefever SxS double-barrel 12-gauge shotgun. Mind if I hold it?"

"Are you crazy?" the deputy asks. "Do you think I would fall for that? Why, that's the oldest trick in the book." He shakes his head and spits on the floor.

"You ever shot anything with it?" Mr. Liddon asks.

The deputy reddens. "That's none of your business."

"Speaking of business," the sheriff says, "I believe your business here is finished. So if you'll excuse me, I have work to do." He plants his feet on the floor and stands to usher us out.

"Don't let us get in your way," Mr. Liddon says. He settles back into his chair. "But if you don't mind, we'd like to sit here and rest for a few minutes. We both took a long ride to get here. You got anything wet we might drink?"

"I don't give a damn about your long ride here," the sheriff says, fists clenched.

"You weak blooded or something?" the deputy asks, holding his aim. "And we got some wet horse piss if you'd like some of that." He guffaws, and his shoulders are shaking so hard as he laughs at his own humor that I fear he'll set off the gun.

The sheriff shoots the deputy a look that shuts him up.

The deputy adjusts his aim. Now, his gun is pointed at my head.

"There's a water spigot down the street. Now go."

I stand, and Mr. Liddon motions me to sit back down. "I was just getting comfortable," he says.

"If you don't leave, I'll shoot," the deputy says, somewhat rattled.

"Are you threatening me in a public building?" Mr. Liddon asks.

"That's not a threat," the sheriff says. "That's a promise. This ain't no public building. This is my building, and I don't need some smartass Tallahassee lawyer trying to act like it ain't. Now get the hell out of here before we both shoot." He stands and pulls out his own Colt 45.

"Looks like an m1892," Liddon says. "Ever have any problems with that cylinder getting stuck?"

The sheriff's eyes widen. Liddon has hit his mark.

"I had one of those myself. Near about killed myself with it. Accidentally, of course," Liddon says, smooth as silk.

I am close enough to Liddon to see that sweat is beginning to form at the edges of his hairline. Something is not going as planned. My stomach clenches.

Suddenly, a shadow outside the window catches the attention of all four of us at once. The sheriff strolls over to look out. When he turns, his face is white and his eyes are wide with fear.

"Put down your weapon," he orders his deputy.

The door bursts open and a tall man in uniform appears. Behind him are several other men similarly dressed with their guns raised.

"It's about damn time," Liddon says. "Where have you all been?"

The U.S. Marshal standing in the doorway tips his hat. "Ma'am," he says.

And I smile.

"My men were having some trouble seeing inside the back window," he says. "It appears that back jail cell is slam full of I don't know what all."

The sheriff reddens.

243

"Mind if I have a look at all the stuff you go back there?" the marshal asks. "My boys won't be but a minute. I'm sure the paperwork is in order for all the property you purport to hold in 'guardianship.'" The marshal glances at the sheriff's hand, resting on his Colt. "Boys, I think we are going to have to take these two in for pulling a gun on civilians in a public place."

"Now wait just a minute," the sheriff says. "This is my building."

"Really?" the marshal says. "Not according to the U.S. government. This is a federal building built on federal property with federal dollars. Your job is to uphold the law and protect the citizens. When you start plundering the citizens and pulling guns on unarmed females, your job is over."

"If you had to work a day in your life rather than wandering around in that fancy-ass uniform," the sheriff says, "you'd be doin' the same thing."

"Somehow, I don't think so," the marshal replies. "Cuff him."

The sheriff shuffles by and spits his cigar on Mr. Liddon. Spittle dots my shirtwaist.

Mr. Liddon uncoils like a rattlesnake. "Easy, brother," the marshal says. "Remember, you gave up this job to root out the bad guys. It's our job to take them in. Rest easy."

Mr. Liddon burns red and puts his Colt back in its holster.

When the sheriff and deputy are gone, Mr. Liddon leads me to the jail cell where the sheriff keeps his plunder. The federal agents have already begun sorting the jumbled mess into neat piles.

At the very rear, beneath mattresses and tables, lamps and quilts, is a large black woodstove surrounded by matchstick holders and beautifully wrought iron hot pads. It's a treasure trove of goods. It includes my father's equipment, stolen by the sheriff in that fire so many months ago.

When I look more closely, I find potholders embroidered with Bible verses as well as dish towels, hand towels, and quilts, all handcrafted by my mama. My chest feels tight. The sheriff took all the belongings from my home and stuffed them in this room.

I reach for a quilt in blues and pinks and bury my face in it. It still smells of Mama.

"I don't think getting your land back is going to be a problem," Mr. Liddon says. "Is any of this other stuff yours?"

I can't speak through the swelling in my throat. Warm tears trickle down my cheeks. Mr. Liddon nods. "All right, then."

I rub my hand over the stove, across the blue tiles, the illustrations from *Winter's Tale* coming to life beneath my fingertips. I grab the potholders, the dishtowels, the quilts, and everything else I can hold, pile them into Mr. Liddon's waiting arms, and say, "I can't thank you enough."

Chapter 39

"And that's not all," Mr. Liddon says, gesturing to all of Mama and Papa's belongings, stuffed haphazardly in the Falling Waters jail. "According to the federal marshals, all the land the sheriff has stood 'guardian' for is to be handed back to the owners."

My heart leaps with delight. I'll get my land back. I can bring my sisters home, and Tom and Seth and Isaac and I can work the land. We can all be together again on the land we've worked so hard to conquer.

But in the very next moment, I remember the sideways glances of the women and men in Falling Waters. I am a fallen woman, and my child will never be anything other than a bastard.

"The thing is," Mr. Liddon continues, looking slightly embarrassed, "you need a friend to stand with you so you can get your land back. The friend has to be land owning himself, and out of debt. The law protects any ruses of folks in debt taking advantage of the weak for their inheritance."

"So you can stand with me as my friend?" I ask.

"I'm so sorry," he says, loading my papa's equipment and my mama's handicrafts onto the wagon he's borrowed for the purpose. "Your lawyer doesn't count."

I think of who I know that owns land. Tabitha is my first thought. "Tabitha it will be," I say.

"I'm so sorry, again," he says. He looks ashamed. "It has to be a man."

Of course. Women can't vote. Women can't sit on juries. And, apparently, women can't stand as friends. The irony is almost too much.

When I return, I present my problem to Martha and Mary. They have an answer so quickly I wonder if Mr. Liddon has told them of this problem beforehand.

"Mr. Isaiah Alsobrook would be willing to stand as your friend," they say, like some sort of Greek chorus in one of Papa's books.

"What does he want from me?" I ask. I know better than to think some strange man is doing this out of the kindness of his heart.

"He wants you to sell him your land in Falling Waters and buy his land, which is right here, adjacent to ours. We would be neighbors!"

"It might solve a few problems," Martha says.

I ponder her words.

What do I feel for my land—the land over which I've sweated and bled and which finally betrayed me? Living on my land in Falling Waters means when I get my daughter back, she'll be subject to shaming. Forever the illegitimate child of the fallen German whore. And for my sisters, it will be the same.

That plot of land on which I have sweated and Mama is buried, what is it to me? I think of the joys we have shared on that land— Papa's hope in making a new life in America. Mama rattling away on her Singer sewing machine, hemming black dresses so that Papa could maintain his dignity. My dear little Emma and Maisie for whom that land is like the Garden of Eden, a place where they can romp and play freely, discover abandoned cotton bales that turn into dolls, discover woodland hideaways for elaborate doll tea parties with palmetto frond plates and wild blackberry delights.

And for me, the land has been a place where dreams are made. And, for a brief moment, where dreams had lived. I remember my first snowy cotton crop, the mystery of seeds that became tall stalks of corn, tiny vines that shot forth magnificent melons. I believed the land to be imbued with magic. It saved my family from starvation.

But it couldn't save me.

And now, looking into the faces of the kind women before me, I know that it isn't the land that is responsible for any of it.

It's the people. The people whose lives are either filled with the spirit of the creator or not. Those filled with the spirit of the creator give freely, work the land diligently, and love fully. Like Mary and

Martha, my mama, Tabitha, Morris, Margaret, John Sebring, Tom, Isaac; the list of those surrounding me who are filled with that spirit of love is long. I am so blessed.

The land is not responsible for such a one as Benjamin Blakely. Benjamin Blakely is responsible for himself.

But what about the healing spirit I feel when I work my land? Do I have to give that up? My heart hurts at the thought. I can't count the number of days during which working the land has filled me with hope, making me believe that I'm here for a reason.

But what if that healing spirit is not limited to a specific piece of land?

What if land is land, one piece of rich farmland as good as the next? More importantly, what if land is not ours to own? What if we are but caretakers, charged with the responsibility of protecting its regenerative power?

I guarded my parcel of land in Falling Waters for many years. I poured into it love and care, was thankful when it produced. And now, perhaps it's time to pass that particular plot to someone else. Perhaps it's time for me to take up this new piece of land and care for it as I seem called to do.

"I will agree to Mr. Alsobrook's deal. And besides, I really like the idea of living next door to y'all."

"Well, wash up," Martha says matter-of-factly. "I'll fetch Leonard to see when would be a good time for Mr. Alsobrook to go to town so y'all can work out your deal."

Martha winks at Mary.

Chapter 40

A new beginning. I'm dizzy with the possibility. While I will never be able to rid myself of the shame and pain of losing my daughter, at least I can make a living for myself. Once I'm successful, I'll fight with everything I have to get her back. Meanwhile, I can give my sisters a home. The thought brings me joy.

After Mr. Alsobrook and I sign the papers officially swapping our land, I decide to visit the post office. The possibility of a letter from Morris outweighs my fear of the gossip surrounding my appearance in Falling Waters. Though I know Morris is still missing—John Sebring brought me that sad news—I yearn for one final message.

I'm holding on to the unlikely possibility that maybe he isn't really dead.

Maybe. At this point, hope is the only thing that keeps my heart beating. Hope that I can make my new land produce. Hope that I can find my lost baby sister make all my sisters happy again. Hope that Morris is alive. And more than anything, hope that one day I will get my Laura Viola back.

Though the red bricks of the Falling Waters Post Office were milled and baked under the hot Georgia sun and sent down by train to Falling Waters, Florida, the building inside is icy cold. The high ceilings so welcome in the merciless heat of summer now hold all warm air captive high above in the rafters. The people in line below shiver and huddle close together.

The scent of camphor emanating from the woman in front of me assails my nose. I back away and stumble over the booted foot of the woman behind me.

"I'm so sorry," I say.

I'm met with silence. Perhaps she didn't hear me. I turn to apologize again and find myself face to face with Mary Scarlet.

Her arms are empty. Where is my Laura Viola? Has she left her in the arms of someone I don't know, some nursemaid who might forget her and leave her to smother in her blankets? Or who might drop off to sleep while she is nursing my baby so that she falls from her lap and sprawls on the floor, her head cracked open?

"Where is she?" I ask, tempering the desperation in my heart, trying to speak calmly and not to shake Mary Scarlet by the shoulders, though that is exactly what I wish to do.

"Don't you know? John Sebring has her, will barely let me touch her." She spits the words like she has a mouth full of bitters.

She glances behind her and across the street. I follow her gaze and see a clutch of men gathered around John Sebring. He towers over them, and the smallest bit of white flows between the men. It's Laura Viola's blanket.

I rush out of the post office, step off the wooden sidewalk, and sink into a pothole left by the spring rains. I slip down into the sticky, slick clay, push myself up, and run for the street. My baby girl is almost in my arms.

Before I can cross, hundreds of hooves pound the clay and the ground trembles beneath my feet. It's a cattle drive headed for the docks in St. Andrews. The cattle come in waves, stretched as far as I can see. The brutal thundering noise feels like an assault. I search for a hole to dart through, a moment when there is enough spread of cattle that I can squeeze in between. Because over the heads of the baying bleating skinny Florida cattle, I can see the men across the street drifting apart and John Sebring walking down the wood sidewalk, Laura Viola cradled in his arms. He looks angry.

"JohnSebring!" I call, but I might as well be whispering. The words are lost in that wave of pounding hooves, the cries of the cowboys roping the cattle in. I can see John Sebring carrying Laura Viola to his wagon. She is nearly out of my line of vision, and still the cattle keep coming. I search for the end of the drive, and my heart falls. John Sebring and my baby girl will be far away, down the road by the time the drive ends, and I've been warned not to follow him home.

Suddenly, I see my chance. I spring off the wooden sidewalk and fly through the patch of daylight I've spotted between this and

250

the next wave of cattle. I run as quickly as I can, but I've misjudged the speed of the cattle. Before I can think clearly enough to retreat, a strong arm encircles my waist and yanks me away from pounding hooves and sharp horns. I fight against my rescuer; I kick and scream to get to my baby, just as she completely disappears behind the buildings where John Sebring has parked his wagon.

I am not thankful to Leonard for rescuing me from being trampled by the feet of a thousand cattle.

When the dust clears, John Sebring and his wagon are gone.

"There she is. The German whore."

The words travel from Mary Scarlet's Sewing Notions storefront where Mary Scarlet is unlocking the door. The women waiting for the shop to open keep talking, as if they want all ears to hear their gossip.

"I told you all those foreign women are the same. They only want one thing: to tie a full-blooded American down with a baby on the way. But this time, she didn't get her way, did she?"

"I heard she traded that baby for a piece of land. But what about that bastard?"

"She did. She traded that baby for land, and everybody in town knows it. Well, if that's what they want to do, I reckon they have a right. But mark my words: that baby won't be welcome in any decent home in this town, that's for sure. Her blood's tainted."

I watch Mary Scarlet turn and approach the two well-dressed women with cold-blooded fury in her eyes. Her store, filled with the finest notions and fabrics, caters to the wealthiest Falling Waters ladies.

"Store's closed," she says through tight lips.

"Why, don't be silly! You've just unlocked it!"

"I said the store is closed." Mary Scarlet stands at the door, arms crossed, daring the women to walk past her. When it's clear she's quite serious, the younger of the two women touches Mary Scarlet's arm. Mary Scarlet jerks it away as if she's been burned.

"Oh, now you mustn't take on so, Mary Scarlet. You know we don't mean a thing by our prattle."

251

"You call those lies prattle? The only whores I see are the two standing in front of me in the fine garments paid for by husbands about whom they don't give a damn."

The women's mouths fall open, and their cheeks are flushed.

"And furthermore, even when this store is open, it's no longer open to the likes of you."

"You don't mean that!" one of them says.

"That's *my* child you are talking about," Mary Scarlet says, her voice a guttural growl. "I'll not see her maligned in her own hometown. In fact, from now on, you'll have to travel over to Tallahassee for your finery. John Sebring and I, we're moving out of this sad little town. We're going to a place where my child will be loved for who she is, and folks won't waste their time gossiping about the whens and wheres of things that aren't a bit of their business. I'm sick of you penny-pinching bitches anyway. Get on out of here. I'm going to pack up my store."

The women back away in stunned silence. They brush their backs against Leonard's wagon, and when they look up to see this German whore's face peering down at them, they snatch their skirts away so quickly that they collide with one another. I bubble over with laughter. I can't help myself. The spectacle I've just witnessed is completely unexpected. Completely wonderful. The women bustle away down the sidewalk.

I had no idea how much Laura Viola is loved—and fiercely—by that little spitfire of a woman.

My eyes meet Mary Scarlet's, and it occurs to me that my loss is matched by hers. We've both been robbed of our innocence and our girlish vision of who we are.

But I've witnessed a fierce determination rise in Mary Scarlet—the same vicious intensity shared by women from the beginning of time, the gritty resolve that has guaranteed the survival of humankind.

Orphans, Mary Scarlet and I had each put our faith in people who ultimately deserted us. Each of us has taken a place in spaces reserved for men. And we've both been brutalized by the same man.

Benjamin Blakely has robbed us of our innocence, of our belief that the world is a safe and trustworthy place.

And just as Mary Scarlet seeks relief in her needle, creating beautiful quilts, a living exhibition of her soul, so I will seek relief in the land that sustains me. I will plant new fields, and from those tiny seeds my faith will grow.

Because despite everything, we have survived. While some might have given up, allowed themselves to be defeated, we have steadfastly refused. We have fought hard and still hope and believe that ultimate victory will be ours, against all odds.

And it is that iron will, that belief that no matter what happens, we must be strong, we must be courageous. We must fight until there is nothing left of us to fight. This is the legacy that I know Mary Scarlet will pass to my baby girl.

And because of this, I will give this gift, this child, Laura Viola, to Mary Scarlet for safe keeping.

For now.

As for me, I must start over again, build a life my daughter will be proud of when we are reunited.

There are crops to be planted.

Book Club Discussion Questions*

1. In *Annie Laura's Gift*, community is an overarching theme. How do you define community? In what ways are community built? Would you say that your definition of community is different than how the people in Falling Waters, Florida, define it, or is it the same?

2. In chapter 2, Annie Laura asserts that her land "makes her American." To what degree do you think land ownership helps in building one's ties to their homeland or adopted country?

3. In reference to question #2, do you feel that one can be tied to their country without a relationship to the land? If not, what do you think makes a person who is not a landowner or who live nomadic lives connected to their homeland?

4. There are so many rich depictions of womanhood in this novel, is there any female character you feel specifically drawn to? Why?

5. Do you have sympathy for Tom's wife? Based on what is said about the way she distances herself from her children after infancy and how she sometimes "snatches" children from other women, do you think that in modern times that this woman may have been diagnosed with suffering from post-partum depression?

6. Annie Laura's character is set in direct juxtaposition to Mary Scarlet and Eva in this novel. How does each of these women

work within the parameters of "traditional womanhood" during this era? How do the characters circumvent tradition and the laws at the time to establish themselves as their own person?

7. Are the men in *Annie Laura's Gift* shown to be traditional figures of the working class and sharecroppers in the 19th Century? Who is your favorite amongst the cast of men?

8. Another resounding theme in this novel is one of culture. On page 51, Otto, Annie Laura's father, has a very specific definition of "culture," which he finds acceptable as a Prussian. For him, culture involves taking in and creating art as opposed to getting your hands dirty. How do you define culture? Do you agree with Otto on his definition?

9. Otto's definition of culture and success vastly differ from his daughter's definition. This causes major tension and anger on both characters' side. Do you think that the animosity Annie Laura feels for her father is warranted? Keeping these two character's relationship in mind, at what age/point in your life did you come to realize that your parents were "only human" and learn to offer them grace?

10. Even though Annie Laura is continuously at odds with her father, she and he share many of the same traits (e.g., stubborn, headstrong, etc.). Which of your parents are you most like?

11. Along with having different ideas of success and culture, Otto and Annie Laura also have different relationships to the land they live on based on the time in their lives that they immigrated to America. As an adult immigrant, Otto finds it hard to

make the connections that Annie Laura does to the land and its people once they move to Falling Waters, Florida. How do you think age places a role in the connection that a person who is building a new life abroad may feel as they work to become immersed in this "new world?"

12. There are several types of "foreigners" or "Others" in this book (e.g., Papa as a German, Annie Laura as a female farmer, Tabitha as a spinster, Mary, and Martha as women who cohabitate, etc.). What do you think causes someone into this role based on what you observed in Falling Water, Florida? Do you find "othering" to be a warranted practice when building your community?

13. Land ownership is another central thematic point in *Annie Laura's Gift*. Throughout American history, the ability to acquire land has been seen as a means of becoming "upwardly mobile" in society for immigrants and different ethnicities. To what extent do you feel that Annie Laura's attempts to make her land profitable is her way of assimilating into her new home? How does land ownership play a role in the Clayton family and the breakdown of family ties over time?

14. Papa tells Annie Laura, "you never know what goes on inside a family unless you live there." In what ways does this quote ring true for each family in the novel?

15. Both Morris and his dad ask their love interest "to wait." Is there an "expiration date" on waiting when it comes to love?

16. While reading *Annie Laura's Gift*, it is clear that the titular character is the rock of community. This can be seen in the fact

that even when Annie Laura is processing her pain, grief, or trauma, she is still forced to think of other people. Can you think of a time when you had to put yourself last to support your family, community, or others in general? Do you think that Annie Laura does the right thing in these scenarios?

17. Benjamin is a character that is continuously aggressive, manipulative, and outright violent to everyone in the novel. Yet, he garners sympathy time and again. Why do you think other characters allow him to get away with the shenanigans he does? Are these feelings of sympathy warranted?

18. Ultimately, in chapter 34, Laura realizes, "it's people and not land, that saves a person." When thinking of your own definition of community, who sticks out as a person that you cherish? Is this person tied to any particular geographical spot or location for you?

19. As a woman, there's something distinctly familiar about Annie Laura's frustration in chapter 39 that "women can't vote, women can't sit on juries. And, apparently, women can't stand as friends," when she is attempting to get her land back legally. As you were reading *Annie Laura's Gift* and hearing about her constant uphill battle to fight for her right to own and work her land as a woman, what emotions came to mind? Did you find her inability to be her own "legal guardian" odd as a modern reader looking back on that time period?

20. Were you satisfied with each character's ending in the book? Whose story would you like to hear more about?

*These questions are by Adira-Danique Philyaw.